Copyright

All rights reserved

The characters and events portrayed in this book are fictitious. Any similarity to real persons, living or dead, is coincidental and not intended by the author.

No part of this book may be reproduced, or stored in a retrieval system, or transmitted in any form or by any means, electronic, mechanical, photocopying, recording, or otherwise, without express written permission of the publisher.

ISBN-13: 9781735804927

Cover design by: Robert P. Arsenault
Library of Congress Control Number: 2018675309
Printed in the United States of America

CONTENTS

Copyright	1
I. CARS AND PHONES ARE LUXURIES	5
II. CHEMICALS EVERYWHERE	9
III. UP IN THE AIR	13
IV. MILK – AT LEAST IN PART	21
V. WHITE LIES	27
VI. WORKING FOR A LIVING	37
VII. GOING UNDER THE CANOPY	50
VIII. SCRATCHING THE SURFACE	59
IX. NOT GOING NATIVE	79
X. GOING DOWN THE WRONG PATH	89
XI. THE WEBS ONE WEAVES	95
XII. GETTING INTO THE ROUTINE	107
XIII. SMALL DETAILS	129
XIV. CONCESSIONS	135
XV. THE DANGER ZONE	150
XVI. LOCAL WONDER	161
XVII. LOOKS CAN BE DECEIVING	171
XVIII. DINNER AND A DIAGNOSIS	184
XIX. KINDNESS GIVEN IS RETURNED	202
XX. TIME TO GO	211

I. CARS AND PHONES ARE LUXURIES

"I don't want to buy a car. It's an unnecessary expense."

"But we can't go anywhere except where we can walk or you can ride your bike."

"I thought that's why we moved down here, so we wouldn't be tied to unnecessary possessions or costs."

"That's maybe why you moved here. I came here thinking we could start all over and have a lot of fun. We've been together off and on almost two years, after all. We need a car so we can get around more easily and do things."

Elias looked at the floor in the apartment and not at his girlfriend, Beth, as he formulated a reply.

"Things like cars tie us down. Then we have debt and the responsibility to pay for them and insure them and maintain them. We can pay our rent easily and we have food to eat every day. Cars are a recent invention of man. We survived tens of thousands of years without them. I do not see why we can't. I agree, we can walk or even bike to anything that we need to do."

"Do you hear what you are saying?" her blue eyes fixated intently on him, scrutinizing his mannerisms. "Sometimes I wonder if you are still taking your medication, Elias. You say you are, but you act like you're not. You don't even have a fully functioning cell phone. All you can do is call in or out locally and you have no data plan. You should upgrade to an international plan so you can call your parents. The way you are set up now they always have to call you. We both have a lot of money saved and that we've inherited from our families, more than most people see in a lifetime, and we live like we're in dire need. We can pay for any car we get in cash. Are you sure you're taking your medication every day?"

"Of course I am." The truth was that he had stopped a few weeks prior and now flushed the symbycerol pills down the toilet or into the sink drain daily. That way, the rats and underground dwelling animals in the sewers of San Jose, Costa Rica, could suffer their cursed effects that included dimmed awareness, clumsiness and diminished capacity to think.

"You know those drugs could kill me, don't you? I could possibly lose all my white blood cells and die from septicemia."

In her heart, but not her mind, Beth knew he hadn't been taking the drugs. She did not mind asking if he had stopped, but was not at a point where she wanted to risk making a straight up accusation.

"Neither you nor your parents told me why you take these medications, but that is one of the side effects you said that the doctors told you about. You also said they also told you that as long as you obtained regular monthly complete blood count tests they could adjust the medication accordingly. For some reason, you wanted to move to Costa Rica where we've found it takes days just to get an appointment and then you forget to go on the day we can get one. We could have moved to any Spanish speaking country, including ones that have very modern medical services. You wanted to come to Costa Rica, so here we are."

"Are you sure you are taking the medicine? The doctor and your on-line therapist said it's absolutely critical to your health and, by extension, our relationship, that you take the medicine. You do not act like you are."

"I am taking it," he lied again. "You keep upsetting me with all this talk about possessions and things that we just don't need. I still don't understand the need for the therapist you want me to see. I'm fine."

Stopping the medication did not occur as an intentional act in the first instance. He took the medication as prescribed at the same time every day. A few weeks prior, he put the tablets on the vanity as he always did. Beth called him from the apartment door that they would be late for a tour of the city they had scheduled if they didn't get going, and he absentmindedly left without taking them. When he got home, he felt so good that he decided to forego that day. His focus improved even more overnight and he simply decided he didn't need the meds anymore. With each passing day, he realized how much they held him back from his true abilities and resented his parents and the doctors who forced the drug on him to begin with.

"You think you don't need possessions or the therapist. I do. The therapist was not my idea and you know it. You keep skipping the counseling sessions I have set up on-line on my computer. That has to stop. Your parents set those up and pay the bills and you know they find out if you haven't gone. I know you don't have a computer or like them, but I do. Why on earth did you major in computer science if you dislike them so much? We've been here for a month or two and I know we each have plenty of money, but don't you think it's time for you to get a job if you want to stay here for a while? Living here trapped in self isolation in the apartment is basically like not living here at all. You have so many qualifications with your college degree, pilot's license and you're even a licensed massage therapist. You speak French, Spanish, English, Hebrew and Aramaic. You have so many skills!"

"You're right. That's the next step for me. I'll go see what I can find." He knew that since he spoke fluent Spanish, he'd find a job within a day of two of looking. "Have you looked yet?"

"You know I already have an offer from the US consulate to be a local liaison. I took care of all of that back in the US when I applied through the Foreign Service at the Department of State. My language test and background check for a security clearance came in yesterday afternoon and I start on Monday."

"I forgot," he said. "You've waited so long for those results it frankly slipped my mind. I'll go to the local in-country airlines and see if any of them need a pilot. They always have ads out for certified pilots and I've kept current."

"Sounds good, Elias. Just make sure that you are taking your medications every day. You probably can't fly without those. Remember, you will need to tell them what you are taking so they can make an informed decision. You may not be able to fly if they think the drug can affect your motor skills."

"I know," he replied, without any intention of telling them about the prescription. It wasn't that he couldn't fly without them. He knew he couldn't fly with them because they wouldn't hire him. "I'll make sure they know."

"And about the car, if you do not agree I'll end up buying one with my own money. I guarantee I'll need it for work in any event."

"I wish you wouldn't. I thought we came here for a simpler life."

"Simple does not mean Spartan or destitute, Elias. One way or another I'm getting a car – and a cell phone plan for you that works here so I can reach you if I need you in an emergency."

"I do not agree, but I certainly couldn't – or wouldn't – try to stop you. Please don't expect me to drive the car or ride much in it unless there is no other option. We're in the heart of the city and everything I need is within walking or biking distance. Speaking of which, I need to go food shopping."

"OK," she sighed. "Please take my list from the counter."

II. CHEMICALS EVERYWHERE

"It's beyond belief that I can't find milk without chemical treatments in it," Elias said to no one in particular in the dairy aisle. He spent 30 minutes checking the label of every brand of milk in the store and not one just said "milk," or "from a cow."

"Did our ancestors homogenize and pasteurize and add chemical stabilizers to their milk?" he mumbled to the yogurt display. "The answer is unequivocally "no." Someone got brave enough to squeeze the udder under a cow and drink whatever came out and that somehow led to this chemical bath and processing abomination. Is there really any milk left at the end of the day?"

"Do you carry any milk that isn't processed?" he asked the stock person in the aisle.

"What do you mean?"

"I mean purely organic milk without chemical and heat processing."

"Of course not," came the reply. "People used to die from the diseases in unprocessed milk."

"We lived for thousands of years without those things," Elias said, believing it to be a strong rebuttal.

"And people died at the average age of 28. Now, people live to 82," the clerk deftly countered.

"Yeah, but after sixty – and usually after 50 given how most people live and treat themselves - the quality of life for most people sucks. Who wants to live lingering in a motorized recliner until your body shuts down from boredom and inactivity? So, you don't have any purely organic milk?"

"We do, but if you mean unprocessed, then no, we do not. By the way, everything is organic. Everything we eat, wear or use is made from organic things. I defy you to think of something that isn't."

"Agreed," Elias said. "It's the mixing of the organics that I don't want to happen in the things I eat. They occurred separately in nature and should stay that way until they are mixed in my gut when I eat them. Who are we to think we can improve on what the earth gave us?"

"Look, I just fill the milk and dairy shelves here. I'm not a philosopher or a chemist. We don't have what you're looking for so I'm just going to keep working because I need my job to pay bills. Maybe you should go to a farm and see if you can buy raw milk directly. They'll likely make you sign a liability waiver."

"I may do just that rather than drink these products pretending to be dairy," Elias said, and walked toward the next aisle after getting Beth her fake milk and fake flavored coffee creamer.

"Is there any corn in this can?" he asked rhetorically to himself. The first ingredient on the can said so and then it went on for a paragraph or so of preservatives, dyes and other items he couldn't even identify. "If Beth were here and had her cell phone with the internet," he thought, "she could look up the ingredients and tell me what they were." He dismissed that thought as quickly as he had it. "If I have to use technology to decide if something is edible, then it isn't really food," though he dutifully got everything on Beth's list before entering the produce department.

"What's the difference between organic lettuce and regular lettuce?" he asked the produce man.

"Well, not much, but organic lettuce isn't treated with pesticides and generally doesn't have much of a shelf life. You basically pick it and have to eat it within a day or two. The regular lettuce is grown from a hybrid seed, is treated with pesticides so you don't have as much chance of eating insects or their eggs or dung and generally is better tasting to most of the customers. It also has a longer shelf life. That said, the organic lettuce costs almost twice as much because it is so much harder to grow and has to be thrown out so quickly if it doesn't sell."

Elias perused the bunches of arugula, iceberg and romaine lettuce with a befuddled visage. "Are any of these natural growing lettuces? Can you even find lettuce growing in the jungle or wherever it is that lettuce grows?"

"I doubt it," the man said. "Even the organic lettuce was likely grown from a hybrid seed. Almost all of the vegetables we eat are from genetically engineered hybrid seeds these days. Even places that sell so-called "heirloom" vegetables like tomatoes got their start somewhere in a lab or by a farmer cross pollenating among strains to make a better, more hardy product. The only difference is that heirloom vegetables are naturally pollinated by wind or insects."

"So none of these are naturally occurring?"

"I'd have to say no."

"And yet you still eat these products? Is what you said true about everything in these bins that say "fresh organic produce?""

"Of course. What else would you eat? Is there an alternative? Everything here in the store has been genetically engineered or crossbred or hybridized to maximize speed in growing, nutrition and taste. It's the best of everything with very few of the weaknesses. How else could you feed everybody? There's too many people for conventional growing methods."

Elias' stomach churned uneasily and a bit too loudly. "I think I've kind of lost my appetite. Thank you for the explanation." He turned and began systematically working his way back through the store looking for all natural foods man had not been altered in any way.

"Didn't you get anything for yourself at the store?" Beth asked upon his return as she unloaded the bags.

"Yes. I got some honey, oatmeal, and quinoa. Nothing else looked good to me today."

"Well, that's not much. You know you can have some of what you got for me. If you're not eating well you should get a multivitamin supplement. You know, you might be showing some signs of orthorexia like the doctor said. You know, where you get fixated on clean, healthy eating and just stop eating groups of food. It certainly looks like you're headed in that direction."

The thought of ingesting even more chemicals in a supplement made him fleetingly nauseous. If Beth ate those foods, chemicals would emanate from her skin. He didn't even know how he'd sleep with her tonight, but he would to make sure she didn't think something was amiss.

"I'm really starting to worry about you, Elias. I'll ask one last time. Are you taking your medication?"

"Yes."

"You know I check the bottle to count the pills like the doctor asked me to so you don't forget, but I can't know if you really took the pills or not. I can only take your word for it, so I hope it's true."

III. UP IN THE AIR

"I'll see you tonight after work," Beth said as she left the apartment Monday morning for her first day at the embassy. She gave him a kiss as she left.

"I hope you like the job," Elias said.

"Good luck at the airport!"

"Thank you," Elias said, retreating back into the apartment. He had a 9:30 interview and was trying to decide what to wear. He put on one of his suits at 0745 and immediately started scratching at his arms.

"Why is everything so itchy?" he said, speaking to his reflection in the mirror. He took the jacket and pants off and looked for signs of redness or irritation on his legs, which seemed to burn. He looked at the label of the jacket and saw that the material was a polyester blend.

"That's the problem. Polyester is not a real fabric. It's a bunch of chemicals put together to imitate fabric. Cotton and wool are fabrics." He went to the closet and looked to see what else he had for options. He found a lightweight wool suit, some cotton shirts and a few nice cotton pullovers that he could wear with khakis. "The suit is blue so it probably has a lot of chemical dyes in it and God knows what would be in those colorings. I'll wear the white cotton pull over with the khakis." He put his ensemble on and decided that it was more than adequate for the task at hand.

After a breakfast of oatmeal sweetened with honey he walked the two miles to the local airport rather than ride his bicycle.

"How are you today, Mr. Ross?" the company owner said as he greeted him. "You're a bit early. I like that." Elias shook his hand and gave him a folder with all of his flight certifications inside it.

"Good to meet you, too. I'm well, Mr. Sanchez. Please call me Elias. I'm hoping you are still looking for pilots. I'm certified and licensed in the US on all small prop driven planes including the Caravan, which appears to be the aircraft of choice here."

"We are always looking for pilots, Elias. The pilot turnover rate here is quite high. That occurs because flights in and out of the San Jose can often be quite rough as you hit the turbulence entering and leaving the valley. We pay well above the going rate, but most pilots don't want to deal with the jostling updrafts and the occasional resulting sick passenger. You need to be instrument savvy as well because the cloud cover and fog make 50-70% of the flights instrument only until you drop out of the clouds to land."

"None of that is a problem, Mr. Sanchez," Elias replied truthfully. I'm instrument certified as well and have flown hundreds, if not thousands, of hours in fog, cloud cover and darkness." He intentionally left out his psychiatric history and the medicines that he was supposed to be taking.

Sanchez finished his review of the credentials.

"Well, your papers are all in order. Are you ready to show me your flight skills? I want you to go through a full pre-flight check, contact airport control to set in your course, and then we'll run out to the Barra Colorado where you can land on one of the jungle strips and then return here. We'll take one of the Caravans up and I'll copilot. I have to tell you, a few times guys forged their paperwork and I ended up taking the controls before we got off the runway."

"That won't happen today," Elias said. "Ready to go when you are."

"Well, then let's roll. I have to say your Spanish is impeccable."

"There's no way I could work with mechanics, air traffic control, or other staff if it weren't," Elias said. "I'm working in your country so I need to speak your language."

"Well said. Speaking of being in Costa Rica, you will need a work visa. If you do a good job today, we will take care of that for you. You're going to find some parts of this hiring process is far easier than the US and other parts a bit more involved. The good thing is that if you are hired you can begin work while we do the processing. Otherwise, you'd be waiting at least three months to get started."

"That's great to hear and very much appreciated. Why don't you give me your preflight checklist and a clipboard and pen so we can get out to the hanger and get started. I want to get up in the air as quickly as possible."

"You just passed the first part of the interview by asking for it," Sanchez said as he slid the clipboard across the desk. "Most interviewees fail right here before we even get to the plane. Let's go."

As they walked, Elias continued to impress his knowledge on Sanchez during the short walk to the hanger.

"I'll need the current weather report from the tower and I assume you have an airworthiness certificate and weight and balance certificate in the cockpit of the plane we're using?"

"Yes, we do."

"Good, so while we wait for the weather report I'll do an exterior check." He went up to the Caravan and walked around it, inspecting the aircraft skin for dirt, corrosion and dents, noting on the plane diagram where he found any. He then checked the flaps and the fuel tanks in the wings before going to the propeller to make sure it was defect free.

"Are we ready to board as yet?" Sanchez asked.

"Not yet," Elias said. "I like to back up 15-20 meters and look at the whole craft just to make sure everything looks right."

"You are particular, Elias. Excellent."

They moved into the cockpit and Elias checked the fuel and oil pressure as well as all gauges, moving item by item systemically, in accordance with the checklist. As Sanchez would serve as the co-pilot on the trial flight, he held the clipboard and checked the items as Elias scrutinized each entry as it was called out.

"OK," he said after checking the fire extinguisher and the ground crew gave him the weather report. "I assume you have the flight plan we'll be using so I need to review and submit that to flight control and then we can get going." After perusing the single sheet, he confirmed the thirty-three minute flight to the tower so they could approve it from the copy they had at their end.

Elias donned Ray Bans Sanchez offered him and taxied the plane out to the runway.

"I've flown so many Caravans this is second nature," he said as he adjusted flaps manually and set up for takeoff. He intrinsically knew all of the instruments.

"You are clear for takeoff," came the call from the control tower.

"Here we go, Mr. Sanchez." Elias revved up the engine and took off down the runway, smoothly taking the plane up. He noted with interest that the airport property sat smack in the middle of a highly congested residential area, but the jungle lapped at the edges of the neighborhoods, an inexorable force that would take over the whole area again, sooner or later, regardless of what humanity tried to do to hold it back.

"Smooth sailing so far," he said to Sanchez. "I'd appreciate it if you could give me a sense of where I can expect the up or down drafts as we leave the valley. They often occur in the same locations, but I am aware that they can take place in an unpredicted manner as well."

"I usually experience them when Mount Arenal is due north of us. You will be able to see the smoke rising from the volcano as we pass. It is about 60 kilometers away to the north."

Sure enough, as they crossed that point the plane precipitously dropped one hundred feet and, at the same time, entered a dense cloud bank, effectively reducing visibility to zero. Elias checked the instruments to make sure altitude stayed constant after he recovered the lost elevation and the plane stayed on course for the Barra Del Colorado.

"I know you said this cloud cover occurs on most flights," Elias said conversationally and without a hint of concern. "Is it usually this dense?"

"Yes, Elias. It's one reason we lose a lot of pilots. Very few pilots, even experienced ones, want to fly blind virtually all the time. I can see that you have no issue working in these conditions."

"None whatsoever. The Caravan is about as close to a flying tank as you can get and it is vastly overpowered given the maximum payload. I learned to fly in an aviation club at the private high school I went to and kept flying right through college. New York has a lot of overcast and cloudy weather, so this is nothing."

With about five minutes left in the flight and the mountains well behind them, Elias dropped suddenly out of the cloud cover as he made his initial approach to the runway.

"I'm just going to fly over it once to get a look at the airstrip and then circle back and land."

"Sound decision, Elias."

He approached the runway at 500 feet and passed over it, noting that it was visibly raised at least a couple meters above the surrounding terrain, that it was military grade and that the area was all jungle except on both sides of the strip, where villagers built their houses. The Colorado river flowed perpendicular to the runway about 300 meters past where it ended. He couldn't have landed on the first pass anyway because a dog was sleeping in the middle of the runway two thirds of the way down. He watched a child run out and chase it from the tarmac as he passed above.

"This village only has a few hundred people. How come this runway could handle a military transport and looks like the US built it?"

"That would be because both of your statements are more than likely true. Rumor has it that it's an old launch point for US forces when they were engaged in Nicaragua, which is only 30 kilometers north of here," Sanchez said. It's all before my time, but we used to hear gossip and hearsay about this being a clandestine US runway. Who knows for sure after all this time? All that happened almost forty years ago. I can say that someone or some government rebuilt this runway about ten years ago and replaced the bumpy old asphalt version with this concrete masterpiece with expansion joints, proper crowning in the middle of the strip and mini channels placed crosswise each couple centimeters so water can run off quickly."

"It's a great runway. Do the villagers make a habit of letting their pets sleep and run around on it?"

"Tragically, you have to check every time. Even though there is a chain link fence around the perimeter, the villagers use the runway as a road to visit each other and a place to socialize that's off the grass, so they made holes in the fence. You'll see people, dogs and horses quite often."

"No problem. The first few times I'll make an extra pass until I develop complete confidence. The runway is clear so I'm going in to land now."

He brought the plane in deftly towards the oasis of the village in the middle of the jungle so that it skimmed slightly above the trees at the south end of the runway and landed the craft without so much as a bounce, coming to a halt parallel to where the Costa Rican police checkpoint stood.

"Excellent," Sanchez said as he unbuckled. "When we get back we'll schedule your physical and you'll be good to go."

"Thank you," Elias said, knowing full well that they would perform their own physical and not ask him for anything other than a check the box form for prior medical issues or medications.

He cut the big single motor and opened his door into and unexpected assault of blazing heat and humidity. San Jose, in the mountain valley, hovered around 75 degrees Fahrenheit, as did the cockpit with the air conditioning running. Here, the temperature stood at 91 degrees Fahrenheit – 33 degrees Celsius

- according to the thermometer on the police shack and the humidity was utterly oppressive.

"Wow," Elias said. "This is hot!"

"Yes, indeed," Sanchez said as he greeted the machine gun armed police and gave them his ID and Elias' passport for scrutiny. "Once you leave the comfort of the valley the temperature rises dramatically. Remember to always bring your ID out here. These guys," he said indicating the police, "are law enforcement but they are basically only drug enforcement and they are very particular. Drugs are a big business out here and they are intolerant to any lapses in identification. The vast majority of your passengers coming out this way are coming to catch tarpon, a big game fish, at the lodges on the river. Otherwise, it's all jungle out here except for Tortugero and Limon where the other strips are located south of us. Even those destinations exist almost exclusively for tourism. When you fly to the west coast of Costa Rica, it's a different world of resorts, casinos, eco-lodges and sport fishing. There's still a lot of pristine jungle, but it's a more of a single man's playground."

"What kind of industry is out here?" Elias said.

"None whatsoever," Sanchez said. "If you aren't guiding at a lodge or commercial fishing for a restaurant, then you are a subsistence farmer and borderline hunter-gatherer."

That peaked Elias' interest. "They grow or catch everything they eat?"

"Well, there is a store in the village near the school but you'd need money to shop there, so, essentially yes because no one here has much money. OK. Let's head back. I need to get some office work done and you clearly know what you're doing. Your physical will be tomorrow and as long as you pass you can start Wednesday as a co-pilot for a week to learn all the routes and then you can be a pilot. We just have to get you a uniform. Any physical or mental issues I need to know about?"

"None. With regard to the uniform, I have a bit of an allergy to artificial fabrics and dyes. Nothing serious but it can cause rashes. Any chance you have cotton shirts and pants."

"We certainly do – and they're cheaper than the polyester ones so that works out for both of us. Happy to have you aboard."

"Much appreciated."

Elias took off and circled the village once more to "get the lay of the land" as he told Sanchez. He saw the gardens and several small herds of cattle living on several significantly sized islands in the middle of the river, which formed a natural fenced in pasture.

"I'll bet the milk they get here isn't pasteurized or homogenized or treated with stabilizers. It's just milk – like it should be," he thought as he began the route back over the jungle, disappearing into the clouds within minutes.

IV. MILK – AT LEAST IN PART

Mr. Sanchez and Elias landed back in San Jose at 11:40 am. The whole meeting, interview and flight had taken less than three hours. Sanchez gave him a slip of paper with an address for the company physician.

"OK, be at the doctor's office tomorrow at 0900 and we'll see you Wednesday at 0700 if everything there goes well. You're the new guy so your shifts will be at odd hours and different days, but you'll get 40-60 hours a week. We pay hourly at $28 and, if you don't need benefits we can pay $35."

"I already have health insurance so I'll take the higher rate," Elias said.

"Perfect. That is easier for us, too. See you Wednesday."

They shook hands and Elias walked back to the apartment. Beth wouldn't be home until after 6pm so he decided to take his bicycle into the countryside. Before he left he compromised his principles and looked up the address of a dairy farm on Beth's personal laptop, noting that the Garmendia Farm was only 15 kilometers away to the west. He decided to follow the suggestion of the dairy clerk at the store and find out about milk processing for himself.

Donning his helmet, a cotton t-shirt and shorts, he ventured into the midday bustle of San Jose, where, unlike the United States, a cyclist had no right of way and every reason to question their odds of a safe return. Elias always traveled by bicycle so, drawing altogether too many angry horn blasts and curses, he adroitly wove in and out of the congestion until he hit the outskirts of the city. Downtown San Jose housed office buildings and expensive single family homes that surrounded the business district. The income level and standard of living dropped precipitously as he approached the periphery of the city. In the last hundred meters before exiting the urban sprawl he went from a veritable shanty town of impoverished one room tin roof shacks with common walls to dense jungle, verdant and green.

Costa Rican infrastructure designers likely never expected the population explosion that hit the city, and so created highways with one lane in each direction and almost no shoulder for emergency stops. Any vehicular break down or accident routinely left travelers stuck for hours while unintentionally blocking the route for emergency responders. Elias rode along with the traffic and within a foot or two of the mountain walls excavated from stone and shaped almost like steps, or tiers, to hold the road bed together. Trucks and other vehicles moving in the same direction passed him on his left side with six inches or less to spare, often blaring their horns. The distance to the roughly hewn rock on his right side varied from three to five inches from the end of his handle bar while the vortex of the vehicles' following wind buffeted him.

On his right, in addition to the rock wall, vines, ferns and other tropical plants with leaves as big as doormats frequently brushed against him. He knew he was taking a chance that there were no nasty insects or poisonous snakes like the bushmaster, eyelash viper or fer de lance resting in the flora waiting to ambush an unlucky lizard or mouse. He was fully cognizant that an accidental bite from any of those – and they were very common throughout Costa Rica – had the potential to paralyze or kill him within a day. Finding about what could be poisoning him in the milk was worth the risk, he felt, so he pressed onward, ignoring the angry horn blasts and cursing directed at him and pushing the pedals up the near precipitous slope in the lowest gear on his mountain bike to get out of the valley.

"Riding home is really going to suck," he said aloud in an

oxygen-deprived voice when he glimpsed over at the other side of the road. "I guess I get to chance getting squashed into the stone on this side of the road or crowded off the cliff on the other side on the way back." Neither one seems like a good option. "Flying is far safer than this." He irrefutably knew why he did not see another pedestrian or cyclist on the entire route to the farm.

"This is how cows should live," he thought as he cycled across the front of the Garmendia Dairy Farm a short time later. "It's about as bucolic a setting as you could imagine." He stopped in front of the corral fence to watch the herd. The cows meandered through the fields, chewing grass and lying in the heat, switching their tails to ward off the flies and biting insects. At the exact second that he decided to go into the driveway, a ten-wheel flatbed, diesel, truck pulled in ahead of him. It carried pallets of chemical bags and barrels. He read the Spanish labels and saw steroids, Vitamin B, chemical buffers, magnesium oxide, niacin, choline, zinc methionine, biotin, digestive enzymes and many others he couldn't decipher.

He watched with unchecked dismay while a few farmers offloaded the pallets on the truck with a tractor equipped with a fork lift. Before they put the pallets in the barn, they removed the top few inches of shrink wrap and took several bags of each product and stacked them onto a cart hitched to an ATV. The ATV operator then brought them to the outdoor feeding troughs in the corral, using a utility knife to cut them open and dump them into the feeding station. Clouds of chemical dust rose around them as they poured the contents of the bags out. The farmhands then used a shovel to mix the additives into the feed so the cows would unknowingly chomp it all down.

Horrified that there appeared to be more chemicals than oats or other grain in the trough, Elias spun his bike around and began churning the pedals as fast as he could to get away from this place. He saw no need to talk to these institutionalized farmers who clearly believed that maximizing production and profit eclipsed any notion of keeping artificial, and potentially dangerous, compounds out of what nature provided.

"It can't be," he thought, reviewing the travesty in his mind. "I can't even get a glass of milk that isn't rife with man-made, mind-numbing additives." He knew that his mental keenness had improved dramatically yet again with only a day of just eating oatmeal and organic honey and ruling out anything processed. It would only further improve if he stayed away from the drugs and food stuffs manipulated by man for financial gain.

"How did your interview go, Elias?" Beth asked when he came through the door at 6:30pm.

"Great. They said I could start Wednesday after I pass my physical tomorrow. How about you? How was day one at the Embassy?

"It's an awesome job with a lot of young people our age working first jobs. The senior staff appears very receptive to training us for future assignments and Costa Rica is a stable country and a prime location to learn the ropes in the Foreign Service. Like everyone else, I'll be rotating through the various departments so that I can fill in wherever needed. It's going to be a lot of long days, though."

"If you like it that's fine because I'm going to be working very odd shifts with long hours as well. The low man on the totem pole gets the weekends, nights and holidays along with regular time."

"Well, that's certainly a drawback because I want to see this country with you. If it only lasts a couple of months I guess that'll be OK as long as you're happy flying again."

"I am," Elias said. "The country out of the valley is almost pristine, like something out of the garden of Eden. It's wonderful to look at when the cloud cover dissipates. The cover is really dense and the ground simply emerges almost instantaneously, verdant and green."

"Well, let's celebrate tonight," Beth said. "We should go out to eat."

Not wanting her to know that he was on to the systematic

poisoning of the food chain, he agreed.

"Sounds like a great idea. Let's go to one of those farm to table places on the edge of town."

"Perfect. I'll look one up on the computer." She found a listing of restaurants and showed it to Elias. "Which one would you like to go to?"

The real answer was none. The oatmeal and honey were the safest option and more than sufficient to satisfy his nutritional needs.

"Let's try the Tree Frog Inn. That looks interesting – as long as they don't serve poison dart frogs that live in trees here! I mean, for some unknown reason the Japanese risk death eating puffer fish sushi. I hope there are no local traditions equivalent to that here with tree frogs. Did you know the native tribes just rub their arrows against the skin of a living tree frog and it'll kill anything on contact? It makes a near miss as good as a direct hit!"

"Leave it to you to think of such a thing! I'm sure we'll be safe. Let's get going." They went out and she hailed a cab.

"Is the tilapia farm raised or wild caught," Elias asked after Beth ordered the sea bass dinner. To get to their table they walked through the ecologically themed interior and sat outside on an earthen veranda under a large umbrella to ward off the ever threatening rain. Strategically hidden speakers played a jungle noise soundtrack dominated by bird calls and howler monkeys with an occasional roar from a jaguar thrown in for good measure.

"It's wild caught this morning," said the waiter. "The same with the lobster and all of our other seafood entrees."

"Wonderful, I'll have the lobster and tilapia with the vegetable medley on the side. Can you prepare the seafood grilled with a bit of pepper and salt? Just grill the vegetables as well. I like them sprinkled with just a bit of pepper."

"Of course."

"Then that's what I'll have."

"I love the way they built the inside of this place with

bamboo walls," Beth said. "I know you can't drink because of the medications, but do you mind if I get some white wine with my fish?"

"It's pretty cool," Elias said. "And absolutely not. My medications make alcohol off-limits but please get whatever you would like."

Fortunately, the kitchen prepared everything exactly as he had asked. As the waiter placed his food in front of him, his self-described keen sense of smell detected no odor of cooking oil or other foreign substances.

"Good to see you eating everything," Beth said as she took a sip of her wine and he plowed through his meal. "You look like you've lost some weight over the last couple weeks."

"I have to say that everything here is delicious," Elias replied. "I should eat more slowly. I'm down just a little bit because I'm not sitting as the house snacking on the couch anymore. You can't eat plantain chips by the hand full when you're flying a plane."

"Absolutely not! Well, this is certainly a fine way to celebrate my first day and your new job."

"No doubt about that. This was really a nice evening. We need to make this a regular event."

With Tuesday being a work day for Beth, they took a taxi back to the apartment and she went directly to bed. Elias waited for her to go to sleep and then used her computer to research dairy product additives.

V. WHITE LIES

"So, no history or psychological or other mental disorders?"

"None," Elias replied. As far as he was concerned, he now operated at a level well beyond these so-called medical professionals. The symbycerol had markedly reduced his once higher mental capacity, which only now approached operating as it once did and always should have. It had been a few weeks since that morning he truly forgot to take it. Each day, the cumulative effect of having it purged from his system increased his perceptivity.

After the rest of the routine physical, which he passed easily, he headed off to the airport to get his uniforms issued.

"Mr. Sanchez said this package is for you," the woman at the counter said. "He said you wanted some of the old cotton uniforms, so I pulled them out and wrapped them for you. The pants are all adjustable from 32-36 inch waist."

"That'll be fine," Elias said. "Thank you. See you tomorrow at 0630."

He put the uniforms in his backpack and decided to go for a ride. As he cycled along the outskirts of town, he passed what he thought was a herd of dairy or meat cattle. He then realized these were not the Jersey or angus cows he originally surmised. Drawing nearer, he saw that these animals definitely weren't cows or cattle of any type he was familiar with. Remembering an old nature channel show, he recognized them from their horns and size. They were water buffalo.

"What is an African or Indian species of cattle doing in the jungle of Central America?" he thought. He stopped his bicycle and looked around and noted that the animals had no barn, no feeding troughs, and no visible shelter from the weather in any way. He pedaled over to the fence where a farmhand worked industriously to repair a four inch square fence post that was sheared off six inches above the ground. The broken ends were still white with no coloring from aging. Elias guessed a car recently hit it.

"How did these animals get to Costa Rica?" he asked.

"You mean the water buffalo? They were imported here fifty or more years ago by president Pepe Figueres," the hand said as he used a post hole digger to excavate the broken post. He methodically dug down next to it on one side only so he could easily reuse the same hole he dislodged and pulled the broken piece out of. "Great animals to work with. Originally, they brought them here to work on the banana plantations because one buffalo can haul and move more weight than two yoked oxen and it's easier for the handler to maneuver with one animal than two. They don't need hormones or supplements of any kind, they produce milk in greater volume and for a longer part of their lives than Jersey cows and you can even ride them like horses if you train them. They are also utterly fearless. They stomp the snakes and crocodiles if they are forced to and drive off any unwanted predators. I think a jaguar tried to get a calf and they broke this post chasing it away."

"You're kidding."

"Nope. God made these beasts as close to perfect as they can be. They can adapt to any terrain from swamp to mountain. They are basically impervious to the elements in the tropics. You can see I have no barn or shelter for them. There is a lean-to over the hill but they refuse to use it. I put it up because I felt bad but I really didn't need to. They are also extremely prolific. A female can have a calf every year for up to 25 years in a row after she reaches breeding age. I don't even have to maintain the fields. They graze right into the jungle and keep pushing the boundaries back as they eat the foliage, making their pasture bigger on their own so it can support more animals. The only drawback, if you want to call it that, is that they always need copious amounts of water. That's why my ranch is right on the river."

"Did you say you could even ride them?"

"Absolutely. How do you think I got out here?" He pointed to a huge riding saddle sitting in a two wheeled cart up the road. "The big guy out there is my ride home and my diesel motor for the cart." He pointed at a big bull. "He weighs the better part of 1400 kilos, maybe more. You can even ride him in the water if you wanted to. He's a barge propelled by hooves. You know, in some parts of the world, police officers ride water buffalo like horses."

"Wouldn't the crocodiles come after them at the river's edge, though??"

"Not here. A great big male Nile crocodile in Africa or a saltwater crocodile in India or Australia might, out of desperation or mistake, take the chance because they can get bigger and stronger than our crocodilian species. Even they wouldn't have a substantial chance of success and likely would get hurt badly even if they succeeded. Our crocodiles are very big and powerful, but they wouldn't throw caution to the wind and risk injury from an animal three to seven times heavier than them with horns, hooves, infinitely more strength and borderline insane survival and protective mean streaks. That's not likely to happen at all unless they were starving. Even then, they might just starve a little longer and wait for an easier meal rather than take the chance and be crippled."

"Do you sell their milk?"

"We do."

"Is it processed?"

"Not unless you consider refrigeration processing. That's all we do with it before it goes to market."

"Where can I buy it?

"We have a few distributors locally, but for today just ride up to the farmhouse a mile or so up the road and tell Miguel that Leonardo said he could sell you a couple liters. If you want, you can get some cheese as well. Buffalo cheese is extraordinary. By the way, my name is Leonardo," he said as he extended his hand.

Elias shook his hand. "Thank you very much, Leonardo."

"De nada. You can also look at some of the leather products we make when an older animal dies or is harvested for meat. These animals can withstand attacks from lions and tigers in their natural habitats, so their hides are practically bulletproof. The leather is very thick and strong but extremely supple and durable. We sell all kinds of purses and belts and saddles and harnesses made from it. I'm never going back to Jersey cattle. I can tell you that."

"Based on what you're saying, everyone should switch to buffalo."

"The market drives what we farm and the demand for regular milk will always exist. Beyond which, you need a huge supply of water for these animals, so not everyone could successfully raise buffalo. I happen to be situated right on the river by good fortune. If everyone switched it would drive the price for water buffalo products down and I'd make no money, so I like things the way they are. On a personal level, I wish I had transitioned to them many years before I finally did. It seemed too good to be true, but it worked out well for me."

Elias rode home as quickly as he could from the farm with the buffalo milk and a couple small blocks of cheese wrapped tightly in his knapsack. He pulled the two one liter bottles out as soon as he entered the apartment and poured a little into a glass to try it. The milk was slightly thicker and richer than cow milk and stronger in taste. It had a hint of grass flavor to it, probably because the buffalo grazed for all of their sustenance and never ate grain. He thought it tasted like mead did for the gods, and the cheese – mozzarella - was like manna from heaven. They only ate what they could forage, Leonardo had said. Even the grass grew without fertilizer except for what the buffalo produced.

He spent the afternoon on Beth's laptop, researching the history and taxonomy of the Water Buffalo, the Bubalus bubalis in Latin, he noted, and other livestock species in Costa Rica. He shut the machine down well before Beth's arrival home from work.

"This certainly does taste different than cow milk and cheese," Beth said over dinner. An adventurous eater who had traveled extensively, she genuinely enjoyed sampling new foods. "It's really close to the yak milk and cheese I tried in Tibet. In fact, in a blind taste test, I think I'd be hard pressed to tell the difference. There's a real earthiness to this. You should keep these in the refrigerator as I think I'd use them now and again as well."

"I plan to," Elias replied. "How was day two?"

"It's still new so everything is interesting and challenging at the same time. My first training cycle is on the support desk for US citizens traveling abroad. The calls are constant from people losing passports, asking about visas and trying to determine where it's safe to travel."

"That actually sounds kind of fun."

"It is, and it's challenging as well. The people I work with are a great group, too. We're all going out downtown Friday night so let me know what your schedule at the airport looks like. Hopefully, you can go."

"I'll know tomorrow or Thursday. I suspect they'll be giving me some overnights and extended duty because I'm new and they've been down a few pilots for a while, so it's likely I'll get some crappy itineraries."

"Well, let's hope for the best."

"I certainly will," Elias said.

The next morning, he rose before Beth even roused to get to the airport at 0630.

Sanchez met him at the counter.

"Good to see you Elias. Meet Alejandro. You will be his co-pilot this week as he will be visiting pretty much all of our satellite airports."

He shook hands with Alejandro.

"Happy to meet you. Thank you for taking me on."

"No problem. Mr. Sanchez says you know these planes

back and forth so you'll likely be in the pilot seat after this week."

"We'll see, but I certainly hope so."

Given Costa Rica's small size and San Jose's central location, they flew out to the Pacific coast to Liberia, then Guanacaste, Arenal and Playa Tambor and Playa Tamarindo. They departed San Jose International at 0715 with a full complement of 12 passengers with a western course plotted.

"These are all resort areas, Elias." The vast majority of our trips will be out this way as most tourists come out to the Pacific for the eco-tours, zip lining, surfing, the casinos and the resorts. You'll see lots of high end marinas with yachts and a fair number of fishing resorts, some of whom have a fleet of 50 and 60 foot cruisers that travel out to the marlin grounds 100 miles off shore for three and four day trips."

"Sounds pretty easy to deal with," Elias said.

"The vast majority of the time it is," Alejandro said. "We have to keep the tourists happy as they pay the bills. We serve as our own ground crew at the satellite locations and we have to make sure everyone takes their bags out of the cabin. You have no idea how often some of the older guests forget their medicine or their computer bags or some other essential piece of luggage."

"Sounds like we're babysitting," Elias said lightly after he made sure the main cabin speakers were turned off.

"In many cases, that's exactly what it is. A passenger forgets his CPAP machine and we end up flying back for it because the guy will maybe suffer a sleep apnea attack in the night and die. Dead tourists are bad for business and the bottom line," he joked.

Elias studied the ground terrain as they approached Liberia, which was also an international sized airport. The area turned right back into jungle only a few hundred meters from the edges of the airport. Only a single road served the airport, snaking through the hillsides with one lane in each direction.

"It's pretty clear you know these planes at least as well as me. You want to take control and land?" Alejandro asked.

"Sure," Elias said.

He assumed control and landed as smooth as glass even through the light cross wind that Alejandro told him was ever present. Without the drugs he noted his attention to detail and reaction time improved markedly, so he made minor adjustments far more easily than he would have under the haze of a supposed anti-psychotic drug.

"Excellent," Alejandro said as they taxied up to the terminal, really more of a good sized garage than a terminal. "I'm just going to tell Mr. Sanchez to move you up to the two and four seat Cessnas that we pilot alone. No need for you to spend more time with me, except on the twelve passenger Caravans, after this Friday, because you will have seen all the routes."

"Thank you," Elias said. "Much appreciated."

They exited the aircraft and Alejandro opened the passenger door while Elias unlocked the baggage compartment below the passenger seats. He offloaded everything in the compartment and then went to assist the passengers, some of whom were simply too overweight or old to move around the aircraft interior. Five of the twelve passengers needed belt extending straps to encircle their guts merely to get secured into their seats.

"You need help getting down the steps?" Elias asked one of the passengers.

"I do," came the reply. "I can't even see the steps."

"Of course not," Elias thought to himself. "You haven't seen your own feet in 30 years."

He had the passenger sit at the top of the five steps and showed him how to come down them on his butt like a child. Though a bit embarrassing, it was the best and safest way to disembark for physically challenged individuals. Passengers who needed to exit this way surely lost some self-esteem, but it precluded any chance of a fall. Given the lack of hospitals and medical staff in these semi remote areas, discretion was always the better part of valor.

"I couldn't get my fishing rods," another overweight passenger asked. Could you help me?"

"Of course," Elias said. With the cargo space below the cabin limited in length, hardcore fishing guests paid extra to slide their hard plastic rod tubes under the rows of seats or place them in the aisle between the rows of seats. The Caravan had two connected seats in four rows on the right side of the plane as it flew forward and one seat on the left opposing the connected seats for a total of twelve. The heaviest people sat on the left to even out the load, their mass offsetting the two passengers on the opposite side of the aisle.

"Here you go," Elias said, handing the man what had to be a $1500 carbon fiber fishing rod with ceramic guides and tips. Really wealthy, hard core, fishermen used the ceramic guides because they allowed the line to pass through them with less friction, allowing for more accurate and further casting. The downside of ceramic was that if a big fish took the new braid lines against the drag on the reel, it could notch the guide from friction and cause the line to part. If this rod was any indicator, he could only imagine the cost of the reel he said he had in his carry on.

"What are you hoping to catch?" Elias asked, pretending to be interested and actually sounding genuine about it.

"Well, the guys and I are headed to Los Suenos and we'll start off inshore looking for some rooster fish and then we have a charter for sailfish and marlin for three days. Are you hearing any good fishing reports from guests?"

"I just started, sir, so not yet. But everything I've read says Costa Rica is the place to come if you want to land those species."

"This is our eighth annual trip and we haven't had a bad one yet," the man said.

"Then why ask me?" Elias thought. "Well, let's hope this one is as successful as the last seven," he replied cheerfully. They picked up some passengers to replace those who disembarked and headed further south to Guanacaste, Arenal and, finally, Playa Tamarindo, before completing the circuit and heading back to San Jose.

"It's good work," Alejandro said. "It can get a bit tedious, but it's consistent."

"This country is magnificent," Elias said as he watched the terrain with binoculars. "I'll bet over 90% of the country is undeveloped, pristine, land. Back in the US most everything is developed except in the north and a fair bit of the west, where all the national parks are." As he spoke, he spotted a herd of what he initially thought were cows, but as they neared he saw they were buffalo, wading in a river and eating fresh water weeds. Giant crocodiles sunned on the opposite bank of the river and seemed either oblivious or reluctant to enter the water. After all, Elias remembered, a giant crocodile is less than one third the size of the buffalo, and the buffalo has discretion, but no fear.

"In Costa Rica, over a third of the country is made up of ecologically protected national parks. If you think this is undeveloped, wait until tomorrow when we go out to the Barra Colorado. The people there have to chop back the jungle day after day so it doesn't overrun the village, the runway and the fishing lodge. When anything is abandoned for a month or two, the jungle takes it back. That is utter desolation!"

"Actually, I can't wait to see it," Elias replied, privately rooting for the jungle to win that battle.

He clocked out at the airport terminal in San Jose at 630 pm and biked in the dark to the apartment, where he found a note on the kitchen table.

"Out with some of the embassy staff, Elias. They're taking the new people out for a few drinks. I waited until six and assumed you got a late shift. You can meet us at the Green Iguana if you get in early enough. Either way, see you later tonight. Beth."

He decided he'd rather do more research on the buffalo on her computer than go to a place where there would be little to nothing he could eat or drink safely. To confirm that, he checked the menu on line as he ate his oatmeal with honey and buffalo milk with a few slices of cheese. The Green Iguana was a bar with conventional appetizers and he decided he'd be a distraction to the other folks, more than a participant in such a setting. Moreover, his heightened awareness without the medication made him feel too attuned to the world around him to be caught up in a barroom's buffoonery and social scene.

After finding more articles on the buffalos' taxonomy and distribution, he also spent a fair bit of time further researching the side effects of the drugs, particularly symbycerol, he'd been taking until recently. He found that these effects included central nervous system reactions such as sedation, dizziness/vertigo, headache, and tremor, cardiovascular reactions including tachycardia, hypotension, and syncope and autonomic nervous system reactions such as hyper-salivation, weight gain, drooling, and sweating. Ostensibly, when the doctors put him on the medication after his junior year in college, they failed, or intentionally didn't, let him know about these repercussions. His parents said they told him repeatedly about the side effects at his appointments, but he steadfastly denied that. If he took that medication now he'd never be able to fly at all, never mind commercially. A pilot who appeared sedated and also drooled, sweated, shook uncontrollably and had vertigo would have limited job opportunities and not inspire confidence even in a third world country.

Around 10 pm he shut down the machine and went to sleep. Beth quietly came in to the bed around 11:30 pm and he pretended that he was sound asleep. She had work in the morning as well so fortunately she went dropped right off to sleep with her back against his. Elias was thankful she did not want to have sex as he could smell the alcohol on her breath and the cigarette smoke from the bar that permeated the laundry she tossed in the hamper.

VI. WORKING FOR A LIVING

He rose at 0500 before Beth woke and quietly left the house on his bicycle without showering so as not to rouse her. He figured he could get that done at the terminal in the pilots' locker room. Once washed and dressed he sat in the terminal waiting room until Alejandro arrived.

"Today we're heading into the jungle," he said to Elias. "We'll start out at Limon, then go to Tortugero and finally to the Barra Colorado. Limon is a port so there's civilization and industry. Tortugero is a tourist destination for people who want to see the sea turtles and other indigenous wildlife and there are some restaurants and eco-lodges. The vast majority of our passengers flying to the east coast will be coming or going from there. Then, we head to the Barra to pick up some sport fishermen. That is the last stop before our return and there is nothing there but the runway and a small village. Mr. Sanchez said he took you out there on Monday."

"Yes, he did. I loved it out there. In fact, down the road I want to spend a few nights out there and see how the people live. Supposedly, everything there is from a couple generations ago."

"That's how they sell it, but even though there is no running water or indoor plumbing in the village, they do have internet, satellite tv, computers and cell phones. Those villagers are far more savvy than people give them credit for. Many of them speak two or more languages fluently because they work with sport fishermen from all over the world. Keep an eye on your wallet. Most people leave a little lighter than when they arrived. The majority of the locals are the nicest and most honest people you'll ever meet, but some of them can talk a dog off a meat wagon. Never underestimate them or their acuity."

"Well, I still look forward to getting out there."

"Your relatively new in-country so that doesn't surprise me. Why don't you pilot today, Elias? Mr. Sanchez said it would be fine after my report yesterday."

"Happy to. Thank you, Alejandro."

After dropping two of the twelve passengers in Limon and picking up two tourists heading north, Elias brought the Caravan into the Tortugero strip. Elias saw that the runway was bounded by the ocean to the east and the Parismina River to the north and west. The peninsula it sat on was less than four hundred meters wide. Planes landed at the south end and rolled north. As they made a final descent, he saw that the river side of the land from where the runway commenced was peppered with dozens of eco-lodges, the names of which all seemed to have the word "turtle," "frog," "monkey," or "crocodile" in them. Small groups of people walked on the beach side along the ocean.

"Who are those people?"

"They are tour groups out to see the sea turtles and their nests. Sea turtle tourism and the associated bars, hotels and restaurants supports the income of eighty percent or more of the population of this town. The remaining twenty percent comes from eco-tours on the river."

"Then we better hope that the turtle population doesn't decline any more than it already has." Turning his attention back to the airstrip, he looked around for a building. "Where is the terminal?" he said to Alejandro as they rolled to a stop at the end of the runway.

He pointed at a lone figure in a knee length skirt standing slightly off the far end of the runway. "You see the woman in uniform standing next to the cable spool on its side under the palm tree?" he asked Elias, who nodded. "Well, the overturned wooden cable spool is the terminal. You can see her clipboard on it. The woman – Maria - in uniform is the gate agent and security officer. When it's raining – and we get the better part of four meters of rain per year in the jungle out here – she sets up a big umbrella that sits in the hole in the middle of the spool. I always joke a bit with her about her fashion sense because she wears the airline dress uniform with nylons and crappy old beach sandals in case she has to stand in a puddle."

"You're kidding?"

"Nope. All of her boarding passes are reusable and laminated in plastic."

"That's pretty much about as bare bones as it gets."

"Indeed. We'll drop all these tourists here and then go get some fishermen at the Tarpon King Lodge in Barra Colorado. That lodge is the only reason we fly there at all and we only go there if they have six or more passengers coming in or going out. Otherwise, it's an operating loss for the airline. Sometimes they'll pay for one or two empty seats to make a four or five-person group get a flight. When they purchase an empty seat to get a direct flight it's pure profit as empty seats don't require extra fuel to get the plane in the air. If they do not have enough people on the plane and don't buy extra empty seats or pay for a direct charter, they take an hour boat ride from the lodge through the canals and drop their guests off here in Tortugero and then we fly them back to San Jose from here."

After disembarking the passengers and exchanging brief pleasantries with Maria, Elias took the empty plane up and started north. Unlike the previous two stops there were no houses or buildings or other man-made structures below him. They flew along the coast and the jungle ended a hundred or so meters from the ocean, separated by beach littered with washed up tree trunks and other debris. With the plane devoid of passengers, he spoke freely with Alejandro.

"How did the villagers ever settle there?" he asked.

"Most of them came down from Nicaragua during the

war back in the 1970s and 1980s. It was really bad up there. Tens of thousands of people were killed and the Contras and the Sandanistas supposedly had no qualms about hitting civilian targets. The Colorado river is only a few kilometers away from the border so several hundred folks moved into the Barra to be safer."

"The Costa Rican government let them in and treats them as citizens. They get full national healthcare and benefits, so it's a good deal for them. These people have the best deal in the country in one way. The entire Barra is government land. It's all an environmental preserve. The villagers and the fishing lodges are there at the whim of the government, but there's no way the government would displace them or the lodges, which are the only employers out here. Basically, they staked out their land around the runway and on the direct opposite side of the river and here they are."

"You mind if I circle the area once before we come down? I did that with Mr. Sanchez and I want to do it a few more times so I know the area."

"Go ahead. We're way early and the people we're picking up are still out on the water fishing. We can do that and then, after we land, we can eat in the village while we wait for them to come in."

"Looks like everyone has a garden or some animals here," Elias said as he made a relatively tight circle over the village.

"Yes, everyone who doesn't work at the lodge is either a commercial fisherman or a subsistence farmer growing their own food. They are not supposed to hunt because the Barra is a nature preserve, but many of them take deer or any other animal they can get a clean shot at. They'll even shoot the incidental crocodile, which is very tasty I must say. If the police catch them eating crocodile, they'll say they found the animal already dead and that it must have died from some form of lead poisoning. The only lead around here is in fishing weights and bullets, so it's almost an unspoken code for saying they shot it. Sometimes they'll catch a few tarpon, a very large game fish that is also protected except for locals, and divide them up among a bunch of families. If there is enough meat, they'll even give the police and the coast guard staff some of it to eat as well. It's not like the police live like kings out here."

Elias finished his loop and brought the plane in. After their credentials were diligently validated by the drug police, they walked to a restaurant – really just a back room on someone's house – and sat down at a table. The oppressive humidity weighed Elias down and the only relief, meager as it was, came from an old metal overhead fan.

"Watch your feet when you walk out here," Alejandro said as they stepped through the well shorn grass separating the restaurant from the runway. "There are lots of snakes everywhere and the vast majority of them are both hidden and poisonous. If you should see one, assume it's poisonous and keep your eyes on it and walk away. That's why all the people you see off the pavement here are wearing those fireman style rubber boots. They have a wire mesh in them that will stop most of the snakes' bites. The bushmaster snake, which is the deadliest, will bite right through those boots like they are made of cheesecloth. They have the longest fangs in the snake world after some African viper – I think it's the Gaboon viper – and they can weigh up to 20 or more pounds. Stay alert wherever you walk."

Elias looked around himself carefully.

"Believe me, I will."

"To give you an idea how invasive the snakes are, a few years ago the lodge manager, an American with no understanding of the wildlife here, bought a bunch of parakeets and hung them in a big cage suspended over one of the raised decks at the lodge. A few days later a guest came into the dining room screaming about a snake eating the birds. When the lodge mechanic, Luis, went to check, a fer de lance had swallowed two of the birds and had a third in its mouth. It went in between the bars and couldn't get out because of the added girth from the birds it ate. He killed it with his machete and reminded the manager that he had warned her that putting the cage of birds there was basically ringing a dinner bell for snakes. He told me later the parakeets were the equivalent of filet mignon for snakes."

"That sounds too surreal to be true."

"Coming from another American that's quite the endorsement. It is true, though. You can't make that kind of shit up. Another guy found a baby snake on the bar. It was so still and bright red he thought it was fake and someone in his group was playing a joke on him with a plastic or rubber reptile. Thankfully, he took his ball cap off and poked at it with the visor and the snake bit into the hat. The staff member who killed it, Waldo, told me you could see stains on the hat visor from the venom pooling in the visor brim around the fang bites. He said it was an eyelash viper, yet another really nasty creature. At least that guest showed some degree of caution. Usually, clueless people fortuitously blessed with money always think they know everything and can act with disregard for any adverse repercussions." After a pause he spoke again. "You should also stay away from the river banks. The crocodiles here take people several times a year and they are not shy or discerning in what they eat. Some of them are over six meters long. If they grab you, or anything else for that matter, it's all over."

"I guess the beauty of the place belies the reality if you aren't extremely careful," Elias said.

"You couldn't say it any better than that," Alejandro replied as they walked into the restaurant.

"This place has some pretty unusual ambiance," Elias said as he watched the cattle grazing just a few yards from where he sat in the dining area of the restaurant. The room had no back wall so the animals could graze right up to where the grass ended and the tile started. "Those animals look unusual. They're kind of scrawny compared to Jersey cows. What's with the hump on their backs?"

"Those are Brahman cattle, Elias," Alejandro said through a mouthful of rice and beans that the owner always gave him when he came out to the Barra. "Those are a Hindu or Indian breed, believe it or not. That hump on their back serves the same purpose as a camel's hump. It's a storage place for fat and water. Given the nature of the dry and wet seasons in Costa Rica, that hump makes the Brahman a sensible beast to have out here. Farm animals tend grow smaller in the Barra because they don't get any man made feed or hormones or antibiotics or anything else. What you see is what God made. I have to say that God could have made their steaks a bit more tender. Eating a Brahman steak is basically the same thing as chewing a Brahman leather shoe. That's why I always order the coconut milk chicken out here. You'd be wise to do the same. Either that or get a local fruit plate and be prepared to live in the can for the next three days."

"Where do they get their chicken and coconut milk?" Elias asked slightly guardedly, thinking he'd be dealing with Montezuma's revenge for the next 72 hours in order to be polite.

"The coconuts come from the trees in the yard we're in and they are killing the chicken right now. You see that wire pen across the runway – that's where it lived until about 30 seconds ago," Alejandro said.

"Then I'm having what you're having," Elias replied. Even as he spoke a boy came running across the runway with a freshly dispatched bird. He ate the lunch but thought he detected the hint of cooking oils and seasonings that weren't purely organic. It might have just been some residue on another pan. He wasn't sure but he'd be more careful going forward. As they paid their tab, one of the Brahman dropped a cow pie a couple meters from the dining area.

"Now that's ambiance. Can we go take a look at the river?" Elias said once they were done settling up the tab.

"As long as one of the locals goes with us, sure," Alejandro said. "Hey, Alvaro, you want to show the new guy the river bank and the crocodile show?"

"With all pleasure," Alvaro replied. He lived in the house next to the restaurant and was tending his garden. He had also been the guy to clean and prepare the chicken for cooking. He carried the offal and the legs and head of the chicken in a small bucket with him.

They walked down to the edge of the river with Alvaro leading the way through the grass.

"Always walk single file behind me," he said as he walked in his boots. "A serpente could be lying in the grass on either side or in front of us and you wouldn't see it until it bit you."

Elias could not tell if this was an act for the new, American, pilot or if it was a genuine display of concern. He did notice that everyone wore boots and seemed to walk on the paved runway or on raised decks whenever they could.

"Is the river always this dirty? he asked in Spanish, looking down the short slope to the café au lait colored water. The river stretched much wider than it appeared to from the air. It spanned at least a kilometer from side to side at this point in its flow, only three kilometers from the ocean. Two three-meter dugout canoes, innately highly unstable craft, went by upstream with a single paddler kneeling roughly in the middle of each one. Hugging the bank kept them out of the fast moving water in the middle of the river that they'd never be able to fight upstream against. They plied the water with hand-made, solid, hard wood paddles that probably weighed a minimum of ten pounds each.

"There is some pollution," Alvaro said, replying in Spanish now that he knew Elias spoke it. "But this water color is caused mostly by silt runoff back in the mountains around the valley where San Jose is. The top half meter of the water is almost always this color and underneath it is clear. For a short period in the dry season the silt layer is less, but it's always there to one degree or another."

Elias tried to walk around Alejandro and past Alvaro to get to the river's edge, but Alvaro put his arm up and blocked him from passing.

"Not safe," he said. "Stay here and I'll show you."

He grabbed the handle of the bucket in his left hand and the base of it in his right and flung its gory contents into the river a few feet from shore. Almost instantly, a five-meter crocodile rose up a foot from the bank and snapped everything up with frightening efficiency. Its jaws closed with snaps as audible as someone smacking two pieces of 2X4 lumber together.

"That's downright terrifying," Elias said. "Why are those guys out there in those canoes. The crocodile we just saw must be one and a half times the length of the canoes. That must be just asking for it."

"You bet it's terrifying," Alvaro said. "This is how I show people so they don't go near the water. Huge crocodiles, sometimes even bigger than this, hide here in thirty centimeters of water. The silt makes them completely undetectable. You'd have to have a death wish or no idea they were there to ever go near or in this water. Crocodiles are lightning fast and extremely opportunistic ambush feeders, and they do not discriminate about what they eat. Those guys in the canoes are locals. For what it's worth they know what they're doing and it's extremely rare that they have a problem. I can't remember the last time one of them did. They use those heavy wooden paddles for a reason. Everyone knows aluminum and carbide paddles are cheap and more effective for propulsion, but if a croc gets too close to the canoe, they'll hit them on the head with the edge of the wooden blade and they'll take off every time. God forbid they ever flip or fall out of the canoe trying to do that, though."

"Point made, Alvaro," Elias said. "Alejandro, let's go back up and wait by the plane." As they walked behind Alvaro in single file back up the small slope, Elias remembered that the buffalo herder said crocodiles wouldn't even go near a buffalo for fear of injury. Suddenly, given recent history, that seemed all the more impressive. The guests arrived only a few minutes after they got back to the plane, a group of eight American fly fishermen who spent six days chasing the tarpon at the mouth of the river. Elias and Alejandro greeted them and loaded up their luggage and fishing gear while they gave tips to their fishing guides and said goodbye to the lodge manager.

"This is an unusually clear day up here," Alejandro said as they flew back. The cloud cover was minimal and the volcano smoke was distinctly in view to the north. The ground below leading to the valley revealed virtually no houses or structures except for the occasional farmhouse, barn or other outbuilding.

"Everyone out here has to be pretty much self-reliant," Alejandro said.

"I can see where it would take a lot of will power to want to live out here," Elias agreed.

As they crossed over the barrier mountain and the outskirts of San Jose some of their passengers began speaking.

"Yeah, I told my wife I'd be fishing nine days," one guy said to a member of another group, "but me and my buddy fished for six days and now we are going to spend a few days at the casinos and over at the Striped Marlin and picking from among some of the better looking ladies of the evening. All kinds of fishing are great in Costa Rica!"

Looking at the fat old bastard, Elias figured that the women who would cater to this hairless, pale-skinned example of American excess would really be doing it for the money, if the guy could perform at all. If the lucky winner of his several hundred dollars could fake enjoyment she'd deserve an Academy Award. Far more likely, he wouldn't be able to perform and she'd get paid great money for a good night's sleep.

"I forgot to tell you something, Elias," Alejandro said. "This is something that's not in the employee manual. A lot of foreign guys will ask you where to find a woman here. Even if you know a place, just tell them to go downtown and ask around. We don't involve ourselves in that business here. In fact, the lodge we just left won't let guests bring women out there. The locals out in the Barra don't like it one bit and it makes for a dirty, unsanitary lodge for the owner. A lot of families fly with us to eco-lodges and hotels and surfing destinations. No need to risk losing that work because they hear a pilot talking about where some drunk American can get some action. Everyone knows prostitution is the oldest profession in the world and that it should be shrouded in a bit of a covert environment. Even though it's legal here, Mr. Sanchez wants it left to the passengers who want to find it and out of our day. My favorite two words in Spanish in that circumstance are "no se."

"That's a very practical way to look at it," Elias said. "Thank you for the head's up."

Elias clocked out at 4pm and changed into his shorts and t-shirt in the locker room. He got on his bicycle and headed for the doctor's office where he could get a full blood work up, which was required for him to get continued symbycerol prescriptions. He knew he had to keep up appearances to get the medication, even if he wasn't taking it. Beth knew he needed the blood work to get the medicine and his parents not only knew that as well, but also knew the specific reason why he needed the drug.

"So, are you keeping up with your daily dosages, Mr. Ross?" the doctor asked, after reviewing his nurse's chart of height, weight, oxygen levels, blood pressure and pulse. She also took an EKG and drew blood to confirm his white blood cell count before he could renew his prescription.

"Please call me Elias, and yes, I am."

"The reason I ask is that last month you weighed 79.2 kilograms and this month I note you are at 76.8 kilograms. One definitive side effect of symbycerol is weight gain and very few, if any, people lose weight while on it. This is something of a red flag. You must be cognizant of the fact that we are very sensitive to patients exhibiting covert non-adherence to dosage plans, particularly when treating your condition."

"Well, two things have happened, Doctor. The first is that I'm now working as a bicycle messenger and the second is that I've started eating a much healthier diet. I think a little weight loss was unavoidable. Beyond which, I never weighed over 72 kilograms in my life before this treatment began. I'm still gordo (fat) as far as that is concerned." He immediately made a mental note to put some weights in his shoes, pockets or both at the next visit as he expected to lose significantly more weight without that infernal mind-numbing drug in him.

"That's reasonable, but for most people even a significantly increased exercise regimen does not impact the weight gain caused by this drug. Who are you working for now?"

"I'm self-employed. My girlfriend works for the US Embassy and I get paid to run things like recovered passports and visas around town for them. Sometimes they send me to get take-out meals. I have panniers and a rear rack and bag on my bike for carrying larger items." He knew he wasn't allowed to fly or drive or operate any kind of motorized equipment so he had to have a believable cover story.

"Just be careful on a bicycle in the city, Elias. People drive aggressively here and you know that the side effects of this drug include clumsiness and drowsiness, neither of which will benefit you during rush hour."

"I will," Elias said.

"OK. Everything else looks good with your neutrophils and white blood cells from last month. Your EKG shows no arrhythmia. Because symbycerol is almost 100% metabolized your urine sample shows barely any trace amounts of the drug. Many times it doesn't show at all so that's not unusual. I am putting in your prescription for the next month. If your blood work comes back clear today you can pick up the prescription tomorrow after 2pm. You will stay at 600 mg per day. Understood?"

"Yes, Doctor."

"Fine. By the way, I would prefer to treat you with a long acting injectable, which would preclude any chance of a missed dose. I could give you one or two shots a month that would last 2-3 weeks at a time so there would be no chance of a missed dose. Would you be willing to consider that?" he asked this as a direct follow-on to the issue of weight loss.

"I may, but I'd want to discuss that with my parents first," Elias said. "They were instrumental in getting me on this therapeutic program. I'll give them a call between now and the next visit and let you know. At this point, I feel as though I'm in a good routine and not missing any dosages."

"Sounds reasonable," the doctor said, noting in his records that he suspected Elias may well be a noncompliant psychiatric patient. "You are fortunate that your family located me as I am one of very few physicians in Costa Rica registered to prescribe this drug. Make an appointment for next month with the receptionist and I'll see you in four weeks. Take care and feel free to call me if you feel any indications of a relapse. Here is a card with my personal cell phone," he said, holding out a business card.

"I will," Elias said as he took the card. "Thank you," he said and left the building as quickly as he could without looking anxious.

VII. GOING UNDER THE CANOPY

"I went and got my blood work today so I could continue on my prescription, Beth," Elias told her when she got home a few minutes after him. He put the lab results on the table. "If you want you can look through them you can and you'll see that I'm within all the normal blood parameters so I can keep taking it."

"That's great! You found a doctor who could take you so easily? I thought you were struggling to find one."

"I certainly was, but it's easy now. The airline has a physician and he takes care of everything. When I need a consult with a specialist for this bloodwork, he arranges it," he lied. He always knew he could get in whenever he wanted to the doctor his parents arranged. To keep this charade going he had to go to the visits. Otherwise, he wouldn't get the pills that he flushed down the toilet every day.

"This pilot job is turning out to be a god send," she said.

"So far," Elias said. "I made us some dinner. Well, actually I brought us some dinner. I got coconut chicken with rice and beans and fried plantains for lunch in the Barra Colorado out on the Caribbean coast today and it was so good I thought I'd bring some home for us both. At first, I thought they used some of that spray oil, but I asked and they didn't even know what it was. This is legitimate Costa Rican cuisine and it's really good."

"Sounds great." They sat down at the table he had set.

"This is phenomenal," Beth said, after her first bite. "You

think we can get more of it?"

"Every time I go out there I can get some and I'm sure the restaurant would gladly give us the recipe. By the way, Mr. Sanchez said that once in a while you can fly with me for free if there is an empty seat and we can do an overnight here and there out at one of the smaller airports. I'm thinking we could go to Guanacaste next Saturday morning and come back Sunday so you're here for work on Monday."

"Wonderful. What can we do out there?"

"Well, there are some world renowned eco-lodges and a bunch of places to zip-line through the jungle canopy. There are also a lot of great beaches on the Pacific side we could go to on future trips. You have to share the beaches on the Caribbean side with crocodiles and snakes and jaguars, so I think we'll stick to the Pacific side for your trips. The worst thing that can happen there is a sunburn."

"I can't wait!"

"It'll be a great time."

As he spoke, his phone rang.

"That's my mother," he said as he checked the number on the display. "I'll go outside and talk with her."

"OK."

"Hey, Mom," he said as he walked out the apartment door.

"Elias, we haven't heard from you since you first landed there. How are you doing?"

"I'm fine."

"Well, that's good to hear. I am concerned because Dr. Rojas just sent your lab results. Everything looked good, but he made it a point to note that you had lost some weight. He said that, in the absence of any intervening cause, that is usually a sign that you aren't taking your medication. He did say you are doing bicycle deliveries, so that made some sense to him. Are you taking the medication?"

"I am, Mom. I burned off some fat riding around town. That's all."

"It took a huge amount of effort for your dad and I to find

you this doctor and get him registered and certified to address your condition, Elias. Your medication requires extremely close monitoring for your health and safety. Please make sure that you are following the doctor's orders so that your condition remains stabilized. I wish you weren't so insistent on moving away so far."

"I needed to get away from everything, Mom. Everyone back in New York knows what happened to me and avoids me, so it's as if I'm alone there all the time anyway. Here, nobody knows me so it's a fresh start. Beth works at the US embassy so there is a good reason to have come to Costa Rica."

"She said you are the one who wanted to be there and she could have been situated anywhere that spoke Spanish as a primary language, so I think this is really your choice, not hers. Speaking of Beth, have you sat down with her and explained your situation and condition? It really isn't fair to her if you haven't done that. She should know what the side effects are and what could happen if you don't take your medicine as scheduled."

"Not yet, Mom."

"You need to do that before this gets to be too serious a relationship. You may have already waited too long given that you're living together."

"We've only been dating steadily for six months, Mom. If I tell her how I ended up on this drug she'll leave me for sure."

"You don't know that. The fact is that this is a lifetime treatment plan. If she doesn't want to deal with it she should know sooner than later so you can both get on with your lives. More than likely if you are honest and sincere in your treatment she'll have no problem with it. It's certainly not a genetic issue so having children wouldn't be a problem if your relationship is that serious. You need to be honest and upfront with her. Anything else would be deceitful."

"What you're really saying is that you know she'll break up with me as soon as she knows I spent three months at an inpatient psychiatric facility because you had me involuntarily committed. You want me to have no reason to be here so I come back to New York. That isn't going to happen."

"I know it's a difficult topic, Elias, and I wish it weren't true. But it is true and it did happen and you were at a bad place in your life. Whether or not we wanted to hospitalize you isn't important because we had no idea what else to do. We did what the doctors recommended and you seem to be doing well now."

"Mom, I do what I'm asked to do, but I'm not going to jeopardize my relationship with Beth. She knows the name of the drug I take and she can look it up to see what it is and what it treats if she wants to. Maybe she already has and doesn't let on about it because she knows it bothers me. I'm not going to tell her you guys decided I was exhibiting suicidal behavior and needed to be drugged to cope with life. I didn't believe it then and I still don't believe it today."

"I'm not going to go into the details of how we found you, Elias. It's too upsetting. Just promise me you are following your protocols and that the weight loss isn't because you stopped the medication. Doctor Rojas would prefer you agree to a long acting injectable so that you don't run the risk of missing a dose. Would you please do that? I wish you weren't so far away so we could see you."

"I really don't want to. I promise I'm taking the medication, Mom. Beth and I are going out to eat so I need to go now."

"You aren't driving are you, Elias? You know you're not supposed to drive or operate motorized vehicles with the symbycerol, right?"

"I know, Mom. I don't drive at all and don't even have a driver's license here. Part of the reason I chose to come here is that everything is within walking distance."

"OK. Stay safe. We love you and wish you'd come home."

"Bye, Mom. I love you guys, too," he said, though he couldn't wait to get her off the phone and terribly resented the drug-induced haze he'd been living in until recently. He then went back inside to the apartment and watched the evening news with Beth before they went to bed.

Over the next week Elias flew passengers in the two and four seat Cessna and Seneca planes as well as co-piloting on the twin engine King Air, a seven passenger craft. Except for the twin engine, the small planes were all solo flights for him.

"Can we fly close to the river," one passenger asked as he made a trip out to the Tarpon King Lodge. The guest wanted to start fishing immediately without taking the boat ride from Tortugero, so he paid an extra $600 for a private charter to land at the Barra Colorado airstrip.

Elias radioed the tower to ask and was given approval.

"Home base said fine so hang on and we'll drop down and follow the river out to the runway at the Barra. Make sure your belts are buckled as we could hit a bit of turbulence at lower altitude."

He banked the plane and came in to 250 meters altitude over the river. The jungle ended about 50 meters from the river as the central valley rains had dried up a bit. Crocodiles seemed to be everywhere basking in the sun on the dark sand against the jungle and on top of the silty mud near the river.

"Watch the middle of the small channels," Elias said. "I'm seeing the tarpon rolling as they work their way upstream to Lake Nicaragua, which is where they spawn." Sure enough, even as he spoke, a large tarpon breached and rolled through the brown, silty water, one of the few fish capable of gulping oxygen from the air. Elias wondered what it would be like to be in the water in a place where man was nowhere near the top of the food chain. Immediately following that, he remembered sitting behind the wheel of his SUV in the Poconos parked as close as possible to the steep precipice of a scenic overlook and wondering what the landing would feel like if he drove the SUV over the edge and tried to navigate down the slope between the trees and boulders. He mentioned that thought to his then girlfriend in the passenger seat and, for some reason, she jumped out of the vehicle and he ended up in a pysch ward strapped to a bed the next day.

Still not clear on why that was somehow misinterpreted

as an issue, he proceeded to the Barra and landed smooth as glass.

Beth boarded the plane with the passengers that Saturday for the flight out to Guanacaste.

"I'm really looking forward to this, Elias. Thank you for putting it all together," she said as he stowed her overnight bag in the luggage compartment beneath the passenger space.

"I think you'll enjoy it."

Once they landed and Elias clocked out remotely in the terminal, they walked out to the grassy area next to the runway, making sure they stayed on the tarmac at all times.

"Our rides will be here shortly, Beth. I'm pretty sure you'll appreciate them. I picked out the mode of transportation just for you."

A few minutes later a guide showed up on a horse with two more trotting behind him. All were saddled and ready to ride. The guide wore the all-too-familiar rubber boots that everyone outside the city seemed to sport.

"You Elias?" the rider said.

"Yes, indeed."

"Then you must be Beth," he said as he looked at her. "I'm Mario and I'll be your guide for the day. I'm told you guys need no introduction to horses, so saddle up."

"You've got to be kidding, Elias. This is so cool."

The horses had saddle bags and straps so that their small bags could be carried easily.

"These horses are very small," Beth said. "I've ridden Morgan and quarter horses and a bunch of warm bloods when I went to dressage school back home, but these are even smaller than the Morgans."

"Our horses are all Costa Rican Saddle Horses. They were bred from Arabians and several other breeds to be smaller and stronger so they could negotiate the close quarters, slick conditions and steep slopes on the jungle trails. They can go pretty much anywhere in the country. You'll see them everywhere along both coasts as most families in the villages own one for transportation."

"That's awesome," Beth said. "Where are we headed?"

"Mario is going to take us to the Ecoadventure Lodge in Guanacaste via a jungle trail route so we can see some local flora and fauna. After lunch we're going zip lining in the canopy and tomorrow we will go out on the San Juan river in the lodge's tour boat and see the crocodiles and other animals out there. Believe it or not, tonight we're sleeping in a tree house."

"This is incredible. I can't believe you remembered that I love to ride horses. I only think I told you that once."

Mario led them behind the airport building to the jungle, which started abruptly where the lawn ended. He continued speaking in English but Beth quickly advised him she and Elias preferred Spanish.

"That's wonderful! OK. This is a real jungle tour. There are no guardrails or fences or safety nets. We will be in and near everything, so we need to have some ground rules. Costa Rican jungles are some of the most vibrant and beautiful in the world. They are pristine. We run a safe tour with no injuries over the last 15 years because we do it right. First and foremost, never get off the horse and never touch anything unless I say so. Both of you are experienced riders so that saves time. Know that your horses will start and stop with mine, but you are welcome to use your knowledge to make it easier.

The trees and leaves and vines are all within reach but you must not touch them for a variety of reasons. First, the manzanillo tree looks harmless and it has what appears to be little green apples on it. Do not be fooled. This is the equivalent of the American poison ivy vine on steroids. You touch the leaves or fruit of this tree and you will regret it for weeks as your skin bubbles up and peels away, revealing fresh new skin that sometimes gets re-infected by the rash around it.

Second, everything in the jungle is camouflaged. Most predators, particularly snakes and insects, are ambush predators and they lie in wait for something to come too close. They will also defend themselves. Refrain from touching trunks of trees or leaves or vines as you could get bitten by any number of different insects or animals. Should we stop the horses in a field to look at something, absolutely do not dismount unless I say to do so. Fields are snake country. The fer de lance and the bushmaster are extremely toxic, but there are dozens of other, less infamous, venomous species. The small ones are the most dangerous as you'll never even see them before they bite. The eyelash viper, which is as thin as your little finger at its thickest point, is a perfect example of this. If one of these snakes bites you – and you'll likely never see it coming - it is possible you could lose a limb or die if we do not get you to a clinic fast enough. We do keep a supply of up-to-date common antivenoms at the lodge but to date we've never had to use them.

Insects here can be extremely helpful and also quite dangerous. Everyone thinks spiders are the worst and they certainly can be. That said, heaven forbid you touch a tree or a log without first inspecting it and a 2.5 centimeter bullet ant decides to defend itself and bite you. You won't die but you will then have 24 hours of the most excruciating, mind-numbing pain you can image. It comes in waves and every time you think it is subsiding it comes back with renewed vigor. They are called bullet ants because their bite feels like getting shot. We locals call them the hormiga veinticuatro – the 24 hour ant. They are very common out here."

Continuing on that topic, some predators hide. On the other hand, some prey animals stay in complete view and advertise themselves so predators know better than to eat them. Poison dart frogs are the prettiest creatures in this jungle. They are so decoratively patterned that you almost can't miss them. Just know that their stark coloration wards off predators. If you simply touch their skin you'll likely suffer seizures or risk death. Do not touch them!

Third, if your horse stops suddenly and for no blatantly evident reason, do not get off it or move under any circumstances. These animals live in pastures that have jungle components. They know when snakes or other predators are near, likely by scent. If the horses stop for what appears to be no reason, I will survey the area from my saddle and then dismount with my machete in hand to either move or dispatch whatever is spooking them.

Finally, and this is the most important thing of all. Do not go near the banks of the San Juan river or any of its tributaries or canals. We stay in single file behind me at all times. The horses will automatically maintain a safe distance from the water. So you fully comprehend what I am saying, safe means a distance that a crocodile can't grab the horse and drag you and it into the water, which is something any decent sized crocodile around here can do with ease. Do we all acknowledge and plan to follow the rules? So you know, we created this route as you will likely see some or all of the animals and plants I described."

"Absolutely," Beth said. She looked at Elias. "I love this type of adventure. I did something similar on a photo safari in Namibia two summers ago after I graduated college. You're the best."

"Happy to do it, Beth. We'll obey all the rules," Elias said to Mario. "Let's go."

VIII. SCRATCHING THE SURFACE

"The jungle is so dense I can't see the airport anymore," Beth said when she peeked over her shoulder fifty feet onto the trail. Riding last, Elias glimpsed behind him and confirmed.

"Neither can I. Amazing!"

"This is really more of an animal track than a trail," she continued. "I see why Mario told us not to touch anything because there isn't an arm's length of distance to the vegetation in any direction, including up. With everything so close, the temptation is always there."

"Do not give in to it," Mario said from his position a few feet ahead. He had a strap holding his eighty centimeter machete to his wrist and he held it loosely in his hand while he directed his horse with one hand. Gripping the handle a bit more tightly, he used the blade to lift a branch about half a meter to his right.

"This is the manzanillo shrub. As I mentioned before, if this brushes against your skin, you'll have the most painful hives you can imagine in 12 hours. The funny thing is that good things can grow right next to it. There is a cacao tree and a few banana trees only a couple meters away from it. When you are out here, you have to know what is, and what is not, beneficial."

He continued leading them for a bit before stopping at large palm tree and dismounting.

"You need to learn to keep your eyes open to see how much life is around you. Here is a rhinoceros beetle," and he bent over to the ground and held up a four inch long beetle with three distinct horns. He picked it up by the body behind its mandibles, much like picking up a lobster. "This bug is absolutely harmless despite its sinister appearance. You can usually find them around coconut trees as they bite through the shells to get to the fruit. Imagine that, they can bite through a coconut shell!"

Mario proceeded to flip some small logs and push some of the leaf litter aside with the tip of his machete, always reaching forward as far as possible to keep from any potential harm's way.

"Check this out," he said, holding up the machete sideways for them to see the creature on the blade. "This is a Brazilian Wandering Spider. In Latin it is the Phoneutria. It's very big for an arachnid and very dangerous if it bites you, but normally you'll never see one as they are generally nocturnal predators. I kind of woke this guy up so thankfully he's a bit sluggish." He placed the spider, which was a big as his palm, back on the jungle floor and covered it with leaves. "These animals are not placed here and you never know what you'll find. You should always assume that wherever you sit or stand out here something alive is probably touching you. I think the point I'm making is that this jungle is a vigorous and vital entity," he said as they continued through the dense greenery.

"Is that lizard running on the water?" Elias asked after they startled a reptile from its slumber and it scooted across a small pool in a stream.

"Yes," Mario called from ahead of him. "That is a basilisk lizard. They are also called the "Jesus Christ" lizard as they can run long distances across ponds and rivers and streams on their webbed feet. As you may know, the nickname comes from the Biblical story of Jesus walking across the ocean without sinking. They have no other defense than flight, and they are very good at that."

"Decidedly so."

Beth inhaled sharply ahead of him.

"Is that a sloth?"

"That is a three toed sloth. You are adjusting well, senorita, as you saw that one before me. Sloths are harmless animals so let's stop for a photo opportunity." The sloth hung upside down in a tree not six feet from the path and its brown fur and green algae-covered back provided almost perfect cover in the jungle. If it was trying to run away it was doing so exceptionally slowly.

"Rumor has it these taste so bad nothing will eat them," Mario said. "Like possessing poisonous skin, tasting like crap is also a defense mechanism out here. These guys are so foul tasting they'd gag a maggot. There isn't any other way they could survive. I've heard tell that a starving jaguar or puma may hunt them, but only as a last resort. It looks safe here. Why don't you two stand under it and I'll take your picture?" The two of them posed under the sloth, arms around each other, with the sloth's head pointing down and theirs pointing up, not even a meter separating them, and Mario snapped their picture with Beth's phone camera.

Several hundred meters later the horses abruptly stopped. A fallen tree lay across the path and the lead horse refused to step over it.

"Stay still. This will likely be a bad snake as I described before we left." Before getting off his horse, Mario checked the ground. He slid out of the saddle using only one hand and kept the other firmly on his machete.

"The horses stopped before the log, so I am assuming there is a snake lying in ambush for rodents on the other side. This would be a great spot to catch a meal." He looked over the log. "Yes. There is a relatively large bushmaster here. I will kill this as it is blocking the path and it will not willingly leave a preferred hunting spot. Even if I could get it to move there is no guarantee it wouldn't turn right around and strike one of us or the horses."

"Can we see it before you kill it?" Elias asked.

"No. That is not safe. I will show you very soon. I regret

having to kill it but there is really no other option."

Beth and Elias could not see what he hit when he swung his machete as the blade landed behind the log.

"It is dead," he said. "Give me a moment. I must remove the fangs as these snakes can bite when dead purely out of reflex for a few seconds. After a couple of swings, he reached over the log and lifted, by the tip of the tail, an extremely girthy snake mottled in grey, greens and browns. The head, as big as Elias' fist, was still mostly attached and the fangs were gone.

"This is the bushmaster, one of the heaviest poisonous snakes in the world and with the second longest fangs of all venomous snakes. In your US system, this snake could weigh up to twenty or more pounds and be twelve feet long. The king cobra is the only venomous snake longer than the snake I'm holding. This one is about two meters and ten pounds. Truly a deadly animal but, in reality, it's looking for rodents, birds and other small prey." He put down the snake and scooped up one of the fangs on his machete. "Some of the locals call it the "two-step", because that's how many you have left if it injects all its venom. Fortunately, I rarely find these on the trail. As deadly as they can be they are usually far from people." He held out the two inch plus long hypodermic fangs for them to look at. "These penetrate almost six centimeters into their prey and pump 20-30 ccs of neurotoxin straight into the muscle tissue and blood stream."

"What will you do with the snake body?" Beth asked.

"This doesn't always happen, but we'll bring it the to the river and you'll see. Believe it or not we're only about 1 kilometer from the lodge, which is right on the San Juan River." He pulled a burlap bag out of his saddle bag and put the snake in it and then back in the saddle bag. "We'll be there in about 45 minutes."

With a cacophony of numerous exotic birds and white-faced and howler monkeys escorting them along the trail, they continued until they arrived at the river, moving rapidly and a couple hundred meters wide. Mario spent about twenty minutes describing and pointing out some of the most exotic blooming plants and also noted some otherwise indistinguishable iguanas lying motionless along the banks, completely invisible to all but the most well-trained eyes.

"You know," he said as he looked at the carpet of greenery on the jungle floor where light penetrated and at the edge of the forest, "people have lived out here for hundreds of years solely on what you can pick and eat. It may not be the tastiest menu, but it would be quite easy to identify enough variety out here to live comfortably. I prefer the grocery store myself, but let's see what we can find. You guys stay on the horses and I'll show you a few things."

He jumped down again and, after carefully poking through the living green carpet, lopped off several bunches of shoots and leaves and brought them to Beth and Elias.

"We serve an excellent lunch at the lodge, but this is a local lettuce and with a little balsamic vinegar you could make a fine salad. This," he said, "is the world's only edible orchid, the vanilla pod. Restaurants use this for flavoring and garnishes." He showed them a few wild strawberries and a guava tree.

"In addition to these native plants, you can also find mangos, bananas, plantains, palm tree, cacao trees and arugula growing wild. They are invasive plants brought by farmers over many generations. You need to be really careful about anything you eat as there are also many plants that are poisonous. The jungle giveth and it taketh away!"

He mounted his horse and they rode another fifteen or so minutes.

"There's the lodge," he said, pointing a bit up the bank.

"I brought the snake body for a demonstration of river safety. There's nothing like a live demonstration to drive a point home. You guys want to see why no one ever goes down to the water here?"

"Sure," Beth said.

He reached into his saddle bag and pulled the snake body out of the burlap, carefully moving the cloth until he could grab it from behind the head, presumably still wary even though its fangs were gone.

"Watch this." He swung the six-foot snake by the head like a pendulum and flipped it 10-15 feet into the river. It floated briefly, twisting in the current, and then a smaller crocodile rose up and engulfed it in its jaws.

"Incredible," Elias said. "Won't eating the snake cause the crocodile to die from the venom?"

"No," Mario said. "The venom must be injected directly into the bloodstream to do its destructive work. Digestive juices break it down like any other protein-based type food. The only way that crocodile could get sick or suffer any effects of the poison is if it had a cut in its mouth and poison seeped into its bloodstream. Otherwise, it just got a free meal. I must say that I will never eat this animal, though, because I've seen what its bite can do. Use your search engine and you'll find some gruesome bushmaster bite pictures. Scientifically, I know I would likely digest the poison, but why take the risk if there is ceviche as good as we serve here?"

"I guess the moral of the story is that everything here is beautiful, but nothing is truly dominant."

"Well said, Senorita," Mario replied to Beth as they entered the lodge grounds. The eight cabins were built on the stumps of long fallen hardwoods and had steps up to them. Each unit had privacy screens within the rooms but the exterior walls were all made from sheer bug netting that wafted in the gentle breeze. All of the out-buildings were connected to a central hub via raised concrete walkways with tin roofs that formed a spider web pattern. The hub included a dining room, bar and shower/bathroom facilities designed to make as little ecological impact as possible. All of the buildings had solar panels on them as well as passive solar water heating setups. Several water towers collected water for cooking, plumbing, and bathing. Gravity fed all of the systems with water so that no mechanical pumps were necessary.

Pulling up to a cabin numbered "8," Mario had them dismount.

"OK. Same rules apply here as in the trail tour. Never leave the raised walkways and decks. Be careful where you put your hands – always look first. Even on the decks, always watch your step. We are the environment's guests here. Lunch is in 45 minutes. If you haven't zip lined before you might want to eat lightly!" He helped them gather their bags and then walked the horses back to the central hub where the corral gate stood.

"I would have like to have walked through the jungle a bit," Elias said as he looked around the room. "What about you?"

"With the exception of that spider, I wouldn't have minded," Beth said, "but as soon as I saw that thing I had every intention of staying in the saddle. Snakes and the other animals don't bother me much but I know my limits. It was incredibly cool, though. Unless you know where you're going that jungle is impassable."

"I think we could have worked our way through it if we had to," Elias replied.

"Thank heavens we didn't," she said. "I can't wait to get out on the zip lines. Let's get over to lunch."

Mario met them at the dining room as they finished their meal.

"OK, I hope you guys enjoyed your locally sourced food."

"Outstanding," Beth said. "You were right about the ceviche." Elias nodded his head in agreement.

"Let's go outside and review zip line safety so we can get up in the canopy. Our course starts on this giant kapok tree we are sitting under. Kapoks are the tallest trees in the jungle. They can exceed 65 meters in height. We are blessed that all of our lines run between these giants." He gestured to the skyline where a dozen or so trees towered above the surrounding canopy. "From here, you can see all of the trees we will zip to. We have 11 lines set up and it takes about three hours to complete them. Two of the lines go across the river and back. I will be with you throughout. The most important thing to remember is that you are always clipped in." He held up a harness and showed them the two clip system on a lower demonstration ladder and platform with a short zip line 10 feet off the ground and running about 40 feet between two trees.

"The only time you are unclipped is when you are on the ground with both feet touching the dirt. There are rings every two feet. You start by putting both clips on the first ring. Go up a step and move one clip to the next ring and so on, always making sure one clip is on a ring. When you reach the platform put both clips together on the ring next to the zip line, one clip at a time, and then connect your pulley to the line. Once secured by the pulley, you release your clips, lean back and slide feet first to the landing area. On arrival, before you release the pulley you clip on with both clips to the ring near the landing. I will demonstrate."

Mario then went through the steps live and slid between the trees.

"You guys do it now one at a time. If you do not clip properly each time we cannot allow you to go on the course." Both of them followed instructions to the letter and Mario brought them to the base of the first kapok tree, where another guide waited for them.

"OK. Here we go. This is Angel. He will go first and be at each platform waiting for you to arrive. I will go last and provide assistance if needed on each leg of the course."

"Let's do it!" Elias said. "Do you want to go first, Beth?"

"Absolutely," she said as she began ascending the ladder to the first platform, clipping in religiously at each rung, some 80 feet up the tree trunk.

"Wait here until she takes the first line, Elias. The platforms are small so a bit of separation is good. You can also take pictures of her from below to show how high up in the canopy she is."

"I blew it," Elias said. "She has the only phone. Maybe you could take some and send them to us?"

"Certainly."

They watched until she attached her pulley to the main line.

"Here I go," she called down, and let go and scooted several hundred feet over to Angel, who waited for her arrival on a platform in another kapok. Mario clicked off a dozen or so pictures. "You'll like these," he said. Angel and Beth then scaled a ladder in that tree to a higher platform leading to another zip line.

"Up you go," Mario said, and he followed Elias up to the first platform. "You need to remember to clip in each rung," he said to Elias about halfway up. "You are only doing it every other step and that means you have no safety if you slip."

"I'll do better," Elias said. He deeply resented having to use the clips at all. "Nothing that lives in the jungle has a safety net," he said to himself quietly. "There's no reason why I should be any different."

Mario checked Elias' pulley connection on the first line and then he pushed lightly out over the jungle. Fortunately, the slope of the line was gentle so he could examine the terrain below him as he silently slid along. The deepness of the greenery struck him immediately. The monkeys completely ignored him, likely inured to the presence of people by familiarity, and went about their business of foraging in the canopy.

When he landed at the platform about one hundred meters away Angel had descended to meet him. He reached out and helped Elias gain his footing.

"Before you detach the pulley, you must clip in. Mario radioed me to come down and make sure. It is imperative that you are always clipped in given the heights we are zip lining from."

"Understood. I will not forget again."

"OK. If you do, we'll have to send a horse out to get you and bring you back to the lodge. We simply cannot risk you getting injured."

"This is unbelievable," Beth called from above. "Did you see all the birds and the howler monkeys? I even saw a few white-faced monkeys and a big iguana hanging on a branch. Angel said if I didn't make a sound it would be as if I wasn't even here and he was right. He said there may be a Harpy eagle a few ropes ahead. We have to hope it's in its nest. Even if it isn't there is so much to see!"

"No doubt about that," he called up to her.

"Can I slow down over areas?" he asked Angel. "I think I missed some of the birds and animals Beth saw. I still haven't fully adjusted to looking for them."

"You have a brake on your pulley but you can't come to a complete halt because it is very difficult to start again. Mario would need to come out and push you, and we try very hard not to have two people on a line at any time, even though the tensile strength of these cables is measured in tons, not kilograms." He showed Elias how to use the brake and then went back up to precede Beth to the next platform.

"Wait here for Mario," he said. "The key is to have one guide ahead and one behind and to be one rope apart so the two of you can tell each other what you've seen as you go. I stay ahead of your partner to make sure there are no unwanted animals on the next platform before her arrival."

"I was wondering why there were two of you," Elias said.

"Safety first," Angel said as he clipped himself in to the next ring. "Don't forget to clip in."

Elias watched as Angel and then Beth glided out on the next rope.

Mario arrived as Beth kicked off the platform.

"Angel showed me how to slow down, Mario. Is it OK to do that if I see something interesting?"

"Certainly, but try not to stop. If you do, I'll have to come out on the rope with you and give you a push and then rock myself in motion again. The ropes are very strong but we try to avoid extra weight if at all possible."

"Angel told me that, too. Got it. I won't stop."

Rope after rope had them traverse the area through the canopy. The nesting Harpy eagle highlighted Elias' trip. As he glided past the aerie, the eagle sat brooding on its clutch of eggs. Almost by command performance, the raptor looked at him on the cable and spread her magnificent wings to their seven foot plus span to stretch them before settling back down.

"That eagle was enormous," he said to Mario when they both arrived at the next platform.

"Indeed," he replied. "Harpy eagles can swoop down and snatch and carry away an eight or nine-kilogram monkey without missing a beat."

"Oh my God!" he heard Beth yell from ahead of him on the second to last rope. It was the first time she had exclaimed aloud so it had to be either extra special or extremely scary – or both.

Elias pushed off after Angel radioed back that the rope was clear. He traveled through about seventy feet of the dense jungle and then abruptly emerged from the seemingly impenetrable greenery as the rope extended across a narrow portion of the San Juan River.

He looked down and saw eight or ten buffalo drinking at the edge of the river. Some actually stood in the water or lay submerged in muck with only their heads sticking out. Multiple crocodiles, six of which he could see on the surface, swam back and forth in front of the beasts slightly further off shore in the opaquely colored water. None of the carnivores even tried to attack the buffalo, the majority of whom wallowed in the mud manifestly carefree. Elias slowed to watch the scene, making sure he didn't stop.

"Mario, why didn't the crocodiles attack those buffalo? Didn't you say they would grab a horse and rider and take them to their death in the river?" he asked as soon as his following guide arrived. The river disappeared behind them only a few meters into the jungle.

"I did say that," Mario replied after verifying Elias had properly clipped in. "Horses are nothing like buffalo. Amazing beasts, those buffalo. Several crocodiles will attack a calf or a small female or an old, injured, or weak buffalo if the rest of the herd is not present. If the buffalo is a full grown adult, particularly a bull, the crocodiles virtually never attack. If they do attack, the buffalo will generally inflict a grisly death on them. Buffalo swim like fish and they are highly aggressive when they are put upon in the wild. Did you see how they kept the calves between the adults?"

"I did," Elias said, awed by the seeming indifference the buffalo had for the crocodiles. "It's like they couldn't care less about the risk," he said.

"For them, there is no real risk," Mario replied. "The worst case is a crocodile attacks and injures the buffalo. After the buffalo kills or maims the crocodile in return, it will get to shore with the herd and then, more than likely, heal. They are incredibly tough, durable, healthy and vital animals. The bull will also protect not only the young, but the old and injured, so crocodiles simply stay away. It's getting to the end of the day and that herd lives across the river. As I came after you they were starting to swim back to the south side of the river. We should start on the line before we miss that spectacle."

"That I definitely want to see," he replied. "What about the pumas and jaguars? Would they attack a buffalo?"

"Buffalo regularly fight off and kill lions in Africa and tigers in India. They can weigh 200-300 kilos. No jaguar or puma, even though we call them the "flying chainsaws," would have a chance against a 700 kilo cow buffalo – never mind a bull at 1400 kilos - at a maximum weight of only 70-80 kilos. It would be like a house cat fighting a German Shepherd. The dog might get scratched badly but the cat will get torn apart."

He climbed to the last platform once he received an all clear and pushed off. He ignored all of the nature around him and frantically waited to get back over the river, which took only a few seconds but seemed interminable.

"Incredible," he said aloud to no one but himself as he emerged over the river again. The herd had entered the river and was about two thirds of the way across already. They swum at an angle into the current so they weren't swept downstream. The adults encircled the calves so the current and the crocodiles had no access to them. The largest crocodiles Elias had seen to date patrolled a few feet away from the buffalo, possibly hoping a calf got separately from the others by the current. The bull in front regarded them, almost disinterestedly, and continued to doggedly plie his way across the river. When he reached the bank, he did not struggle to get out on the slippery mud. His immense girth and weight and flexible, wide hooves gave him bulldozer-like traction. Without shaking off the water streaming from his flanks he turned and stood guard until each member of his herd was safely on shore. The group then sauntered into the jungle as a unit.

"Did you see the buffalo swimming in the river?" he exclaimed to Beth. "Unbelievable! They didn't even care about the crocodiles."

"That was one of the most amazing things I've ever seen. I was terrified when I first went out over the river," she said. "Did you know we were going to do that? All I could think was how many seconds I'd last in the water if the line broke or the pulley failed. A little warning would have been good."

"Honestly, I had no idea," which was true. "Mario said we'd go across the river, if you recall. They should have told us what we were going to see when we did. Can you imagine those buffalo? What must it feel like to look the threat of a crocodile in the eye on its own terms?"

"From what I could see the crocodiles were not in control of that situation," she said. "The bull and the cows seemed in total command, almost comically so. I found the interior jungle to be the highlight of the trip, particularly the monkeys. They came within a few meters and watched me. I think the fact that we need ropes, ladders, clips and slings to get up in the trees to watch the wildlife amuses them to no end."

"No doubt about that," he said. "We are intruders in their world held up by strings like puppets."

"I don't know if we're quite like puppets, but Angel told me that the water buffalo are also intruders here, really dominant intruders. He told me past politicians brought them here. They basically introduced an alpha herbivore. They swim so effortlessly and they can weigh three thousand pounds or more in the trophy size. A giant, six hundred pound crocodile, has no chance."

"They are amazing," he replied, intentionally not sharing the research he had already done on the beasts.

Elias rose that night around 1 am without rousing Beth and walked around the tree house. He ran his hands along the bug netting perimeter. Hooks held it at the top and bottom so a breeze would not allow bugs to enter the living quarters and feast on the room occupants.

"I wish we didn't have all this interference between us and the real world," he said as his fingers compressed a bunch of the gossamer fabric. "I'd rather sleep out on the ground and find out what is there and how to deal with it on their terms. This eco-tour only scratches the surface of the real Costa Rica."

He parted the curtain where the Velcro fasteners sealed the room off and stepped out on the deck. Immediately, mosquitos and other bugs began congregating on his skin. Rather than retreat back behind the veils of gnat-proof micromesh, he ventured forward on the decks, looking for a place to hop over and walk on the ground. He found a place to go between the rails and put his first leg through.

"What are you doing?" Angel said, running up behind him carrying a shotgun and with a long machete in a sheath strapped to his leg.

Fabricating on the fly, he replied. "I dropped my wallet earlier and thought where it happened was about here. The moon is bright so I thought I'd look for it. Why do you have that gun?"

"You can never leave the decking. It may seem fine to do, but danger lurks everywhere. We'll look for your wallet in the morning. The gun is for crocodiles. I have my machete for snakes. We guard the grounds twenty-four hours a day because we have to. Please go back to your room. You have mosquitos all over you. Do you want some repellent?" he asked, pulling out a spray can of deet.

"No. I'll go back to the room and search again. Maybe it fell out on the floor or something." He turned and went back to the room, upset that he didn't get to walk down to the river, which really was the plan. While Beth slept on he took her phone from the night table and googled all natural insect repellents and found out that Costa Rican mint was used by the locals to keep insects at bay. He put the phone right back the way he found it so she wouldn't know he used it.

Before breakfast, he went to the dining room ahead of Beth who was getting dressed and saw Angel as he left his shift.

"You were right," he said to the guard. "I found my wallet. It dropped between the night stand and the interior wall. Thank you."

"De nada," Angel replied. "I am happy you found it in the room as opposed to in the yard. Stay safe."

"All aboard," Mario said at the lodge dock a bit later in the morning. Beth and Elias were part of a group of twelve tourists lined up on the dock ready to go out on the river. Only Beth and Elias had taken the trail tour in to the lodge the day before. The other ten people in attendance were all members of the same family. They arrived late afternoon the day before and had only signed up for dinner, a night's stay and zip lining and the eco-cruise.

"Do you do everything here?" Beth asked.

"No," he said with a laugh. "Diego will drive the boat and I'll describe what we're seeing. We switch off responsibilities with every new group of guests. Everybody get a life vest on and carefully hop on the pontoon boat," he called to the tourists. He pointed at the water towards a set of beady eyes about 15 centimeters apart. "Hold the rails when you board, even if you do not think you need to. Stay on the deck and watch your step getting on the boat. That, ladies and gentlemen," he said as he continued to point at the eyes, "is a 3-meter American crocodile hoping fervently that one of you loses focus and slips and falls over the rail. You can barely see it as it lies in wait. The distance between its eyes gives its size away. For over 100 million years they have survived basically unchanged largely because they are perfectly adapted to their purpose of stealth and ambush." Elias stared at the unblinking eyes, wanting to find out how much of a risk it really was and how he could overcome it. The buffalo certainly figured it out.

"Many crocodilian species live in Costa Rica, but the ones you will likely see are the black and the spectacled caiman and the predator I just pointed out. Of those, the American crocodile, Crocodylus acutus, is the greatest threat to larger prey items, including people. The other two species predominantly eat amphibians, reptiles and small mammals they can ambush at the shore or in shallow water. The crocodile can, in extreme circumstances, reach five or six meters in length and weigh 350 or more kilograms. Animals that size are exceedingly rare. It is the apex predator here."

Once everyone got a seat, Diego strung a protective orange cord across the bow and another across the stern so that everyone was under the boat's canopy and safe from falling overboard. Mario cast off and Diego took the boat out into the current, the twin 150 horse Yamahas chugging in rhythm upstream. To the left of the big outboards, mounted on the transom, sat a very large electric motor.

"This is the San Juan River," Mario said as he began his semi-canned spiel. "Its source is Lake Nicaragua and it runs about 192 kilometers to the Caribbean Sea. It has one major branch, the Colorado River, which flows 96 kilometers and also ends in the Caribbean Sea. That section runs through Heredia and Limon Province and the Barra Colorado wildlife preserve, some of the most untouched areas of the country." For some reason, Elias honed in on that piece of information.

"As you can see, the main stream here is patrolled by crocodiles and, to a lesser extent, bull sharks. The ecology is wildly diverse and incudes hundreds, if not thousands, of fish, bird, mammal, amphibian and reptile species. You will find alligator gar two meters long as well as scores of catfish species. The guapote, or rainbow bass, is a prized river catch for anglers as are snook, machaka and the jaguar cichlid, a toothy fish that weighs up to two kilos. Because the water in the river is not clear and moves quickly, we will be going into some of the canals and lagoons, where the water is clear and still. Adult crocodiles do not venture in these areas as there isn't enough large game for them. Therefore, we will see more varied wildlife. With the canvas set as it is over us, we can use the trolling motor to go under the overhanging canopy. You will be amazed at the diversity of life out here."

After a brief run upstream, Diego turned into a canal whose entrance was all but hidden by vegetation.

"Keep your hands and feet in the boat as we pass through the opening," Mario said. "Resist any temptation to reach out and touch the foliage. Look at where the water changes color." Elias and Beth looked down and saw the eddy where the silty brown-red river water magically ended and clear water started. It was a stark line of demarcation.

"When I took high school chemistry, they called a liquid with particles held in suspension a colloid," Beth said. "This isn't quite the same but the dirt and material is held up in the water in a similar way."

"Good point," Elias said. "I recall learning something along those lines, but I never would have thought of the word the way you did."

"We call this the two waters," Mario said. If you have cameras now is the time to take them out." Diego shut down the big motors and used the hydraulics to get them out of the water before starting the electric motor, effectively allowing them to silently cruise forward at low speed.

"The water draws everything in the jungle to it," Mario continued. "Safer water like this draws even more. Today, we are very lucky. To your right you can see a manatee about 20 meters away. Ahead of us is a small pod of river porpoise snacking on snook. Look at the fallen logs on the shore. Those are not all bumps on them. Many of the raised knots are actually iguanas sunning. There are so many birds in this habitat that we have put a chart of the common species – over 200 of them – in the seat back in front of each of you. Given the numbers of birds I won't identify each one, but if you see one you can't ID on the chart, let me know and I'll tell you what it is."

As he spoke a symphony of noise erupted in the canopy directly over the boat. "When we come out from under this overhang, look back and you will see the howler monkeys. They make that sound to intimidate us and warn us to stay away. In their eyes, it worked!"

"Will we be going on land at all?" Elias asked.

"We have a few spots where it is possible, sir, but mostly we will stay on the boat. If conditions allow we will land on a small island where we know a bunch of poison dart frogs live. They're very shy so it's safe to get close to them."

"Sounds good."

"You really want to get back to nature, don't you?" Beth asked, not seeing the inquiry as anything more than curiosity from Elias.

"It's so pristine out here," he responded. "I want to see as much as possible and actually get out into the jungle like we were on the trail."

"With you being able to fly, I'm sure we'll be able to do more trips. This one has been so good I can't wait to do it again."

"Me, too."

"Watch the lagoon shoreline here," Mario continued. All of those openings in the grass along the banks are either adult caiman or juvenile crocodile skids. They slide in and out of the river on their bellies. None of the young crocodiles are more than 3, maybe four feet long. Caiman are generally narrower in body and max out as adults at 1.6 meters. Their snouts are shorter and more rounded than crocodiles so they are easily distinguishable. They live out here because the big crocodiles aren't shy about cannibalism or eating their first cousins." Even as he spoke, several of them spooked by the boat launched into the river, slipping along on the wet mud and hitting the water like torpedoes. A couple of them swam directly under the pontoons, mistaking them for cover.

Right before they returned to the lodge for lunch, Mario asked Diego to beach the boat on an island. He placed a sliding ramp with rails down to the beach. He went ashore and inspected the area where he wanted the guests to gather. After satisfying himself that all was clear he returned to the ramp.

"If anyone would like a closer look at the jungle, let's go and see what we can find." Only about half of the people, including Beth and Elias, came down the ramp. The rest politely declined. Mario led them, single file, to an old stump from a fallen tree.

"Watch this," he said. "If you don't like spiders or millipedes or other creepy-crawlies stay at the back of the group." Using his machete, he flipped a few pieces of wood around the log until he found a tarantula bigger than his palm, fully thirteen centimeters across including the span of its legs. He gathered the tourists who wanted to see it around him.

"Meet the Costa Rican Zebra tarantula! See how its hair is striped around its legs and knees? That's how it got its name."

"Can we pick it up?" Elias said.

"No. It is not deadly but its bite is excruciating – not nearly as bad as a bullet ant, Paraponera clavata – but it will hurt. Moreover, if it urinates on you it'll cause a really irritating rash that lasts several days." After putting the tarantula under some leaf litter, he paused to make sure it was safe and then began his search again, first finding a scorpion and then a centipede fifteen centimeters long.

"The centipede is here because it hunts tarantulas, so the Zebra tarantula should evacuate the environs as fast as it can under the leaf litter while I not unintentionally slow this guy down," he said. "The scorpion is here to avoid the sun so let's put them both back under cover and hope the tarantula we found took advantage of my interrupting the centipede and moves along quickly."

After a short and fruitless search for the frogs, Mario brought everyone back to the boat and they returned to the lodge for lunch. Following their meal, Beth and Elias were shuttled by a smaller boat back to the airport in time for him to prepare for an afternoon flight back to San Jose.

IX. NOT GOING NATIVE

"Can I buy a few of your buffalo?" Elias asked Leonardo when he rode out for milk and cheese a few days after his return. He always went while Beth was at work.

"Why would you want them? Where would you keep them?"

"Well, I would like to buy them and keep them here so they can contribute to your herd and profits. You can keep any calves and all of the milk they produce until I decide to move them. In addition, I would like to pay you to train me how to handle and ride them. Basically, nothing would change except you'd be getting paid to keep the animals and all of the benefits from them until I take them."

"You're serious?"

"Yes. I'd like a big bull and five cows. Name your price."

Sensing that this man on the bicycle might be serious despite appearances, Leonardo pondered that for a moment. "How about $10000 US for the bull and $4000 for each of the cows? $30000 total."

"No problem. Put a bill of sale together and I'll bring you cash tomorrow."

"Pick the ones you want," Leonardo said. "How long do you want me to keep them here before you take possession of them?"

"Probably a few months, but I'm not sure about that yet," Elias said. "Obviously, I'll pay any costs associated with the animals I buy. I'll need your help to pick the best animals. You said you can also make leather products. Can you make a saddle to fit the bull and saddle bags for all six of them? Again, just name your price."

"It'll be $3000 for the saddle and $1000 for each set of saddle bags," he replied, realizing that he might be able to retire because of this blithering idiot, assuming he wasn't talking out his ass.

"And I presume you'll train me on how to handle them and work with them so they look at me as the leader?"

"For an additional $500 a week, sure."

"No problem. That's more than fair."

"I want them to look at me as the leader so I can work with them the way you work with your herd."

Leonardo, an honest businessman, felt embarrassed by how much he was taking this clearly incompetent person for. He also didn't believe he'd see the money in the morning, or ever, for that matter, but he decided to play this out and see what happened. "Then take my second biggest bull. You've seen him and he is only four years old and very placid and trainable. My biggest animal is the dominant male and the one you are buying is around 1150 kilos and still growing. He's already saddle broken, can pull the cart, and is very intelligent, loyal and protective. He drove off a pair of jaguars trying to get a calf last summer by himself. It wasn't even his calf and he was still a juvenile bull. You need to realize that he will come to regard you as the leader, but he does, and always will, have a stubborn streak and a mind of his own. All water buffalo do. If he decides he is going to do something other than what you want, you're farting in the wind to try to force him to do otherwise. You might even find that his decision making surpasses yours."

"I wouldn't want it any other way. It's good that he has a mind of his own. I'll pay you in advance for the animals, the saddles and three months of training. Does that work for you?"

"I'd say so," Leonardo answered, dumbfounded, barely able to keep himself from doing cheetah flips and a dance of joy. He managed to temper himself because it seemed too good to be true.

"Ok," Elias said. "You've got a deal." He offered his hand

and Leonardo shook it vigorously. "I'm going to the farmhouse now to get some milk and cheese before I ride home."

"Are you for real?" Leonardo asked. "Where and how does a guy who rides a bike to get around have the kind of money you are saying you'll pay?"

"Yes. I can assure you I'm for real and so is the money. Don't judge people by the bicycle they ride. I'll be here around 10am tomorrow with the payment. With the banking system here it may take a couple hours for the bank to release the cash to me. All of my funds are here in a Costa Rican bank, but they came from the US, so it's very likely they'll have to verify the use of the money given all of the drug trafficking and enforcement. Make sure you have a bill of sale for me."

"Oh, I will. Tell Miguel the milk and cheese is on the house today. If you come through on this deal the milk and cheese will be free for you as long as you continue to train the animals here. Tell him I said so and he can call me if he wants to check."

"That's very kind of you. Thank you. I will need your full name and telephone number as it is likely the bank will call you to confirm the purpose of the funds. As you know from all the news about drug trafficking in Costa Rica, large cash withdrawals often trigger intense scrutiny."

"It's Russell. Leonardo Russell." He wrote his phone number on a page of the notebook Elias gave him. "I look forward to seeing you tomorrow. I still don't know whether to believe you."

"Rest assured. You can believe me."

Elias rode home, stopping at the bank briefly to check the balances of his accounts in person. He then went directly home, making sure he arrived at the apartment well in advance of Beth.

"You certainly seem happy today," she said. "Did you have another good day at work?"

"I did. You were right. I needed a job to get into the flow of things here. How about you? Are you enjoying the embassy environment?"

"I really do. At first I did not want to come here but each day it gets better and more enjoyable. I get to use everything I learned in school. The only downside is that we only see each other 1-2 days a week other than sleeping."

"Even that will change over time. There's a lot of turnover at the airline, so I think in less than one year I'll be able to pick my schedule. For now, it's looking like more overnights and weekends, but that'll end soon enough."

"Good. I'm looking forward to that."

He left the apartment early the next morning under the pretense of going to work, but it was his day off. "I won't be back until late, probably 8pm as I have a late flight to Limon. Fortunately, I convinced the owner to let me come back in the evening because I'm qualified on instruments. The passengers are only going out there. I have no one on the flight back. The airline calls that a "deadhead flight" and it tries to avoid them for cost reasons. If there were passengers coming back the next morning, I'd be stuck out there for the night."

"Well, be safe and I'll see you tonight," she said as he left the apartment and headed directly for the bank.

"How do you want this money?" asked the teller.

"In cash. Larger bills are better. I'm buying some draft animals."

"So you know, we'll need to check on that. Do you have a name and number for the vendor?"

Elias pushed the notebook across the desk. "I figured you'd need to verify. Here you go."

The teller brought a bank officer over to make the call.

Elias could hear the shocked tone of Leonardo's voice when the officer said the better part of $50,000 US was sitting there in hundred-dollar bill denominations to buy some buffalo and he needed to confirm that the money was being used for that specific purpose. After confirming Leonardo's business ID number for collecting sales taxes, the officer hung up and handed Elias his money, all in crisp new hundred dollar bills wrapped with paper bands holding $5000 each.

"No one has ever come in here to get a bag of money for buying water buffalo before," he said with a bit of incredulity. "Now I have a story to tell people. Best of luck with your venture."

"Thank you," Elias said, and got himself out of the acrid smelling air conditioned office air as fast as he could.

"I have to say, I thought you were kidding me yesterday," Leonardo said as he handed the bill of sale to Elias and received a bag full of cash in return. "I'm shocked that this is real."

"Nope. Like I said. I really want to do this. Can you start showing me how to take care of them today?"

"With what you just paid me, absolutely. Do you have any experience at all with draft animals?"

"I took a fair bit of horse riding lessons when I was younger, but I've never worked with bovines of any type."

"Well, you chose the best place to start, I guess," Leonardo replied. "Water buffalo are the biggest of the bovines, but by far the easiest to handle as long as you respect their independence." He hoped this guy wouldn't get bored or worse, scared, when he saw how big the animals were and ask for his money back. He also questioned why anyone with no experience would walk up to him off the street and spend this much money on something he knew nothing about. He chalked it up to the fact that rich people do eccentric things for no reason. He figured they'd mostly be in asylums if they weren't rich enough to act with total amnesty.

"I have to say I did not expect you to actually show up so I didn't keep the bull we discussed in the separate corral. Let's head out to the field and get him now," he said. "You can help me harness one of the buffalo to the cart." They walked through the gate and into the field. "You'll need to get real boots like mine if you're going to do this. We find a couple snakes a week out here. The buffalo usually stomp them to death and the reptiles seem to stay away from them. You'd never know it, but buffalo can display incredible agility and nimbleness despite their bulk. I don't know how the snakes know it's death for them to go near buffalo, but they do. One of my guys thinks it's the vibration in the ground when the buffalo move. He thinks the buffalo are so heavy the snakes feel the earth shake when they get close. You never know."

"My God," Elias said in audible wonder as they approached the herd. "These animals are enormous." He walked right up to one and reached up to put his hand on its nose. It stood as tall as him at the shoulders and its head was above him. It turned and regarded him without fear.

"Elias, back away slowly from that animal. She is domesticated but does not know you yet and may get aggressive. I appreciate your enthusiasm but discretion is the better part of valor, especially with the calves around. If she hits you with her horns, even accidently, you will, at best, be in the hospital. You have to let them accept you by walking with me at first. The ones you select will learn to become accustomed to you as the leader over time." He walked up to a different mare and bridled her.

"Let's go girl," he said, clicking his tongue against the roof of his mouth, and she placidly fell into step beside him.

"I can't believe the size of the haunches on this animal," Elias said. "Are they all like this?"

"Most are bigger," replied Leonardo. "This is a small female. Look at her hooves. See how big they are. God made them to live in or near the water. They swim effortlessly. They eat vegetation in the water and they will even dive to get it if they need to. Like I told you before, they are not native to this country and, once they are adults, they have no predators here. Originally, they were used as draft animals in India. They called them the "living tractors of the east.""

"That sound you make with your tongue. Can I use the same sound to get them to listen as well?"

"Sure, it just has to be a unique sound that you only use for the purpose of getting their attention. Since your animals will be separated, you can use the same sound and there will be no confusion between the tone you make and I make. From here on, once we put your animals in the separate pasture, I will refrain from using the sound and they will hear it only from you. That will make the transition to your leadership much quicker."

Leonardo attached the cow to the cart and they got on the bench seat. He handed the reins to Elias. "Same as a horse drawn cart. You take us out to the lower field where we first met. You can see all of the cows with the big bull, Zeus. Then, we'll go to a separate field where I have a few other young bulls you can pick from. I'll segregate the animals you select into another field nearby so they can work specifically with you. How's that?"

"Perfect. I don't know enough about them yet, though, to choose. Please pick me a good bull and five strong cows and I'll take your word for it." He snapped the reins and the female buffalo moved forward effortlessly, seemingly oblivious to the weight of the cart.

"With what you've paid I'll give you the top bull after the dominant male and the best five cows I have," which is exactly what Leonardo did. He used a can of red spray paint to make a small patch of color on the rump of the five best animals.

"That has to be Zeus," Elias said, looking at an animal half again larger than any of the others with horns spreading at least five feet.

"Yes indeed. He's pretty imposing, don't you think?" Zeus regarded Elias with a certain amount of seeming disdain, but submissively went to Leonardo to have his ears scratched when he clicked his tongue.

"The bull you pick will behave like this if you put the time in," Leonardo said as he reached up to pat the other side of Zeus' head. The animal exuded power and knew instinctively that he was the guardian and protector of his herd while, at the same time, remained subservient to the, by comparison, miniscule farmer.

"I take it he is the judge, jury and executioner out here if you aren't around," Elias said.

"No doubt. Nothing touches his herd except me or the ranch hands who know him. If you weren't with me, he would not suffer you being this close to his cows and calves. You need to understand that water buffalo do not have a middle gear. If one of these animals acts in a protective mode, you must get out of the way." He gave the bull a sugar cube and patted him on the side of his chest.

"Get back to work, Zeus." When Leonardo turned to Elias, Zeus pivoted and trotted back to the herd with ponderous, powerful steps.

Having marked the cows, they went to the fenced in area containing only younger males.

"These guys have not been with the cows yet. If they had been, it's likely they'd fight for dominance. When that happens they break each other, the gates and fences like tooth picks. We haven't had a fight in years since we made this separate corral for the young males. It's important to separate them, especially since Zeus would kill or injure any or all of these guys one right after the other if they tried to mix with his herd." He pointed at one animal slightly apart from the others.

"That's the one I told you about and that you definitely want. He's gentle as a lamb to the staff and me, but utterly ascendant within this group and he hasn't even been in a fight yet. He is intolerant of any challenge and gives a false charge, which, so far, the other animal always backs down from. You can't see it because you're too new to this, but he outweighs all the others by one hundred kilos or more and size definitely matters in the water buffalo world. We call him Nitro."

"Can we go up to him?"

"Not today. Like I said, I'm going to put him and the cows we picked together for a few days in a separate pasture. I have six pastures fenced off and I rotate the herds through them so I'm never out of fresh grazing pasture. Only three of the pastures have access to the river, so Zeus is always in one of them. If Zeus and Nitro were accidently put together Zeus would pummel Nitro into submission like a naughty child to keep him away from his harem. If they were both full grown adults that would be a battle to see! You should come as often as you can – every day if possible. I'll go out with you each day until they acknowledge you as the leader.

"I'll be here every day around work. Some days it'll be early am and others late afternoon. I have two days off a week and I'll try to be here at least half of each of those days."

"That'll work," Leonardo said. "The more you are here the sooner they'll accept you. Get some boots and a long machete like mine before you come back."

"Will do. Where can I get them?" Leonardo gave him a few outdoor and farm supply dealers, one of which was near the apartment. Elias mounted his bicycle and went directly there.

"Do you make boots with cotton liners?" he asked the clerk. The vulcanized rubber immediately seemed to abrade his skin and felt unnatural on his feet. "I think I'm allergic to the vulcanized rubber."

"No, you'll just have to wear cotton socks inside them."

"I guess that'll work," Elias said, resigned to encasing his feet in the boots, which were, for all intents and purposes, mold and fungus incubators.

He went over to the farm tool section and found the machetes, which were as common in the Costa Rican jungle as pocket knives at US Scout camps.

"I need you to hold these here for pickup tomorrow," he told the clerk when he paid for the items.

"Absolutely, sir. Most of our customers call or order on line and pick up later anyway."

"Thank you," he said and headed home, thankful that Beth's work schedule allowed him to consistently plan around her arrival and departure.

He called the airline as soon as he got in the apartment.

"Mr. Sanchez, any chance I can work 10-6 Monday through Saturday? If needed, I can go overnight to Sundays but I'd prefer that day off." He knew no one wanted those shifts but taking them would give him the opportunity to go to the farm every morning before work.

"Of course," came the reply. "We need someone for those shifts. Thank you."

"No problem."

When Beth came home he greeted her with a kiss and suggested they go out to eat.

"You know," he said, "We should plan to go out two or three nights a week because I'm going to be working those extended shifts I told you about. It'll give us more time together until my schedule settles out."

"That's a wonderful idea," she said. "I think we've both found our callings here."

"I couldn't agree more," he replied.

X. GOING DOWN THE WRONG PATH

"Are you serious?" Leonardo asked six weeks later.

"Yes."

"You want to sleep in the pasture tonight with the buffalo? Why?"

"I've been working with them every day for almost two months and I can get all of them to bed down. You taught me how to ride them all with your saddles and I've actually taken naps against Nitro's back during the heat of the day. They even come to me on command now. I'm pretty sure it'll be no problem."

"Look. I've helped you learn about the animals and how to train them, but this seems kind of crazy. What if Nitro rolls over in the night? He weighs significantly over a ton already. You'd die a horrible death and he wouldn't even notice."

"I'm a spiritual man, Leonardo. I try to walk with God. I doubt very much that being crushed by a buffalo is how I'll leave this earth. Let me do this and I'll sign whatever you want to release you from any liability."

Leonardo shrugged in dismay.

"I'll go write something up, but I'm begging you not to do this."

"It's OK. I'll wait out here for you to come back. By the way, Miguel had me go into the leather shop to check out the saddle and saddle bags he's making for me. They look phenomenal. I asked him to treat them with as many protective treatments as he could because I expect them to get soaked quite often. I even brought him some mink oil, a water resistant treatment made from a North American animal a lot like the giant river otter here. Oil rendered from its fat makes leather impervious to water if you treat it enough times."

Miguel does great work. Your saddles and bags are made from some of the thickest, supplest, hides we have. They'll last for generations."

"That's what I'm hoping for."

Leonardo went back to his cart and his buffalo took him back towards the farm house. Elias mingled with his herd, talking to them soothingly about his day.

"Lots of passengers on the flights the last few days. They all think they experience all that Costa Rica has to offer when they take a canned eco-tour, but they miss the whole experience sleeping in their hotel rooms and sitting on their canvas covered boats. Taking pictures from the deck of a pontoon boat is not experiencing nature. It's just seeing something that you're actually too scared to really be a part of. You and I," he said as he gestured to the six animals chewing up the grass around him, "we know what it's like to commune with the world in its natural state with no barriers between us and whatever is out there."

He brought the herd over to the jungle where he could identify some coconut and mango trees. Gathering the animals around him, he ventured into the canopy to pick and gather some fruit for his dinner. When he emerged Leonardo was in the field watching him come back to the higher pasture.

"Did you just go in the jungle?"

"Yes. I saw some coconuts and a few mangos I thought I'd eat for dinner and figured as long as the buffalo were around me there would be no problem."

"You are loco," he said. "Sign this and please don't go in the forest on my property again. Otherwise, you'll force me to write another waiver about the jungle. I'm a farmer, not a lawyer. I'll send someone out to check on you in the early morning.

You want us to bring some coffee or rice and beans then?"

"No. I'll be fine. I have to head back to San Jose after I get them out grazing in the morning anyway. But thank you."

Leonardo shook his head, hopped back in his cart and returned to his house. As soon as he was out of sight, Elias took off his boots and socks and put a pair of thin, open-toed beach sandals on his feet.

"Much better," he sighed as he flexed his toes. The buffalo wandered aimlessly and fed while he tagged along with them. The group loosely followed Nitro, who often stopped feeding, picked up his massive head, and instinctively surveyed his surroundings in the verdant greenery to do a brief safety check. As Leonardo had put Elias' herd in one of the pastures with river access, Nitro nonchalantly headed to the water, with his group of cows and Elias in tow. Without slowing his plodding pace, Nitro casually walked directly into the river, submerging up to his neck and feeding on the water weeds and greenery. Once every minute or so, his whole head submerged as he chewed the weeds off the river bottom. He often surfaced with his horns covered in dangling, bright green weeds, looking like a poorly woven holiday wreath. The river current, though fairly strong, did not seem to impact him at all. The cows followed him in one by one and began feeding as well.

"It's like an air-conditioned buffet for water buffalo," Elias thought. Leonardo told him that there were crocodiles everywhere in the river, but he did not see any and his animals clearly did not seem to attract them, though he knew they could lurk an inch from the shore undetected. They might even be swimming between his animal's legs for all he knew.

As darkness began to gather, Nitro led the group out of the water and back up the slope. He did not seek shelter but went to an open area in the middle of the field. The cows all laid down in something of a circle and Nitro knelt and went on his side last after one final surveillance of the field, his body completing the geometric shape. Anything that approached would have to go through one of the buffalo.

"Hey, buddy, I'm going to sit down and put my back against you while I sleep tonight," Elias said to the bull. "Rest easy. We'll both keep an eye on everything. Wake me up if you need me for anything." He sat down and leaned back against the beast, which probably didn't even know he was there.

Elias vowed not to move throughout the night and kept that promise to himself even after he found out that the very ground was alive with bugs. He discovered all kinds of insects crawling on his legs and up his back. Mosquitos did not seem to be as much of a problem as he'd expected, but he did suffer some bites. Animals called out from the jungle edges and he could hear some of them walking in the field, the long grass rustling with their movements. With his hat pulled over his eyes, he disregarded them. Nothing in this jungle would threaten the buffalo.

He slept in fits and starts and woke whenever Nitro stirred, which was quite often. He realized that the buffalo were more active at night than during the day. They preferred the cool air of the night to get back to the serious business of eating. He rose after what felt like several hours and ambled to the river in the glow of the full moon, again with his harem in tow. This time, crocodiles were already on the bank. Elias held back about 150 feet from the reptiles while Nitro dismissively walked through their midst and into the water. The crocodiles in his path made way, not grudgingly, but quickly and with absolute deference to his clear mastery of them.

"What would it be like to be able to walk in the den of death and be both indifferent and unscathed?" he thought as he watched the buffalo start eating the water weeds. "For them, it isn't even a den of death. They own those crocodiles."

"What the hell are you doing?" he heard Miguel scream at him a few hours later, snapping him out of his sleep on the grassy bank. "Those crocodiles are everywhere and you are sleeping in the high grass where we find snakes constantly. They are probably in the grass around you right now. Get over here! Did you take off your boots? What are you thinking?"

"I just woke up," Elias said, "and the herd was hungry last night so they came down here and I followed."

"God protects the innocent and stupid," Miguel said, with more than a little unmasked scorn. "You are either one or the other. Worse, maybe you are both extremely stupid and extraordinarily innocent. That certainly wouldn't surprise me one bit. Get your boots on and I'll bring you to the road so you can ride your bike back to San Jose. Leonardo said you had to get back to work this morning."

"Sadly, I do," Elias said. "Keep an eye on the herd for me until tomorrow."

"We always do. You are, far and away, our most valued customer. Oh, being a witness to your adventure out by the river almost made me forget. Do you have time to see your saddle and bags before you go? I finished them yesterday afternoon. Considering what you paid, this is the best work I've ever done."

"Absolutely, I've been waiting for those to be done."

Miguel detoured over to his workshop, a separate small building, or bodega, near the main barn. They went in and he showed the saddle bags and saddle to Elias, who ran his hands over the thick leather. The stitching was all done in handmade buffalo leather rawhide and the cut edges and flat surfaces, though plain, had a sheen of water repellent oil on them.

"Where did you get these buckles and hasps?" Miguel asked about the hardware Elias supplied him. "I've never seen anything like these. Is there anything special about them?"

"First of all, these are gorgeous," Elias said. "As far as the fasteners and bridle and clips, once you gave me the list of metal parts you needed I had everything made out of a special silicon bronze alloy by a shop in San Jose. It's a marine grade metal that will never corrode or break down, at least not in our lives or the lives of our grandchildren and great grandchildren. It's impervious to saltwater and requires no buffing. I had the raw metal imported from a marine metallurgy shop in the United States. I told them to send all the extra metal to you when they finished making the parts, so you should receive it soon. There's enough for several more saddles and bridles."

"I didn't even know such products existed. I know the saddles may look a little plain, but a lot of detail went into these," Miguel said. "I filled each stitch hole with your oil and let it sit several days before stitching with rawhide that I also immersed in the mink oil for several days. Each surface and every cut edge was treated six times before the pieces were assembled. If you do one additional treatment every year, these items will last several lifetimes. Watch this." He took one of the bags and held it underwater in a rain barrel outside the door. When he pulled it out the water simply beaded up and ran off.

"You can do that for months or years and the water will always bead up like that. The mink oil you brought is the best product I have ever used for that purpose."

Elias reached into his backpack and pulled out $500.

"Take this, Miguel," he said. "It's not much but work like this is priceless."

"Much appreciated," Miguel said, and pocketed the bills. "Until you pick them up, I will continue to add oil treatments so they will be as fully permeated as possible." Not surprisingly, Miguel found that the extra money made Elias' outlandish behavior suddenly somewhat more palatable. Eccentric rich people can buy acceptance for their lunacy if they have enough money, he figured.

"Perfect," Elias said. "Given the weather here there is no way to treat them enough times," and he left the shop and rode back to San Jose.

XI. THE WEBS ONE WEAVES

Elias rode to the airport so he could clean up, shower and shave before going home to Beth. He felt there was no need for her to know where he spent his free time. He felt no twang of remorse that she thought his free time was supposed to be work time. If she thought his happiness came from work, then so much the better.

As he left the locker room, Mr. Sanchez came up to him. Given it was a Sunday and Sanchez regularly attended church, his uncharacteristic scowl and baleful gaze at Elias clearly foreshadowed something unpleasant coming his way.

"Elias, do you know how national health care works in Costa Rica?"

"No."

"Given the events of the last few hours, I suspect you likely know it as well, if not better, than me, but let me explain it for you to be sure. When you see a doctor anywhere in this country the visit is recorded under your ID number. In your case, that is a state number assigned through us at the time we applied to get you a work visa. When you are from another country, your Costa Rican ID number is linked to your Social Security Number. Are you starting to see where I am going with this?"

"No," though he knew perfectly well and decided he might as well play it out to the inevitable end at this point.

"Well, since you want to play dumb, I'll just spell it out,

then. All of your medical records in this country and abroad are connected and viewable by any medical professional in Costa Rica, of which our company doctor is one, and your medical records include the anti-psychotic medication that you intentionally failed to tell us about."

"My medical records are private," Elias said.

"Not in Costa Rica they're not," Sanchez said angrily. "You perhaps could get away with this in the U.S. with all of its silly privacy laws, but not here. You purposefully deceived us and we relied on your assertions of fitness when we gave you a job. Thankfully, no one suffered injuries by virtue of your trickery. You are terminated as of this moment."

"But I'm one of your best pilots."

"You are, or should be, taking symbycerol, a drug our physician said is used to treat suicidal people and that is only prescribed after more conservative treatments do not work to prevent suicidal thoughts and actions. It also completely compromises your reflexes. According to our doctor, you shouldn't be driving a tricycle with rubber bumpers in a fenced off vacant lot, never mind piloting a plane with passengers in and out of the central valley."

"The bottom line is that we have notified the physician who is monitoring that medication and giving you your monthly blood work and dosages. He called me frantically and told us to terminate you immediately. As we speak, he is contacting your family about the gravity of your psychiatric situation. I suggest you take any belongings you have here and leave immediately. I will call the police if you do not."

Elias silently gathered his personal items from his locker under Mr. Sanchez's watchful eye. He put them in his backpack and pedaled away from the airport, not towards the apartment, but back to the farm and outdoor supply store. He thought he formulated a course of action as he rode, but it had already occurred and developed almost subconsciously over many weeks and now he needed only to implement it.

"I need some dry bags, the kind you use on a canoe or

kayak if you think your bags will, or could, fall into the water. I want the best ones. Price does not matter. From what I understand, nothing in the best ones gets wet even if they are completely submerged for a week."

"We have a variety of those," the clerk said. "Come this way." He brought Elias to a display and he purchased twelve of them, one for each side of the saddle bags of his six buffalo.

"Before I pay, can you give me demonstration on how these work? I don't have the luxury of time to figure it out on my own."

"Of course. We actually have a real life scenario we show with these." He pulled out his cell phone and put it in one of the smaller display bags. He then squeezed out the extra air from the bag, folded the open end over onto itself three times and then clasped the opposing buckles to ensure a watertight seal.

"Give me one minute, sir. I'll be right back." He returned with a bucket of water.

"Put the bag in the water and submerge it for as long as you like. Squeeze it if you choose. After a few minutes of holding the bag under and pressing at various angles on all sides of it, he pulled it out of the water and handed it back to the clerk.

"See," he said as he pulled his bone dry phone out of the bag. "Completely dry."

"Wonderful," Elias said.

Satisfied now that they would work, he paid cash for them.

"What time do you close? I think I'll likely be back here later this afternoon to pick them up."

"We close at five."

"That should work."

Elias left and cycled to the apartment. He found Beth on the street loading her possessions into her new car. He pulled over to her.

"Stay away from me," she said a lot more calmly than he expected. "Your parents just called me and gave me a little bit of history about this minor medical condition you said you have. Apparently, most medical professionals do not consider it minor. I took your word on your condition and you outright lied to me about taking your medication. I should have looked it up and regret that I didn't. You seemed like such a nice guy, and I had so much fun with you, but you are a liar and a fraud and possibly a danger to yourself and others. I hope they fired you at the airport."

"They just did," he said truthfully.

"Good. The apartment is yours. For the time being, I'm moving in with one of the other embassy women at her flat. I can't live in this place knowing how you deliberately duped me. I tried to get out of here before you arrived and almost pulled it off. This is my last trip. I'm begging you not to try to explain anything. Every word out of your mouth would presumably be another lie. I can't handle any more of that. I prefer that you just let me go. I almost bought you a phone this morning. Thank God I didn't. Right now, I don't want to ever hear from you again. I hope down the road that changes." He stood silently and granted the request that he not speak.

Her behavior clearly showed she did not, and perhaps could not, understand his motivations. With his head unimpeded by the drugs he was operating at a much higher level every day. Using his feet, he backed his bicycle away from her so she could pass unhindered.

"Oh, and by the way, I checked my browser history at your father's request and there's a lot of searches about symbycerol side effects and Costa Rican water ways and edible native plants and water buffalo and other bizarre, off-the-wall, topics. I sent them all to your parents. They said they'd send them to your US doctor electronically for review. Maybe they can decipher whatever it is you are doing. I certainly can't. If you do not want people to know you are using their computer, you should at least have the common sense to delete your browser history. Given your education you should know that. Oh, and your father said he bought a ticket on "the next jet smoking" to get you and bring you home. He's pissed, but not as much as I am

XI. THE WEBS ONE WEAVES | 99

distraught and upset." She marched past him and got in the car.

"I'll leave the apartment phone on until tomorrow because your parents asked me to so they can try to communicate with you, which is something you should definitely do. Then, because it's in my name, I'm shutting it off in the morning. You need serious help Elias. I hope you get it." The car revved slightly as she started it and drove away. Elias was disgusted by the fumes the motor created.

He went inside and the phone began to ring immediately. On his way to answer it he picked up his Aramaic Chumash from the night table and tucked it under his arm to take with him.

"Hello, Mom," he said without even knowing it was her. "Who else could it be?"

"Elias, I told Beth to call me as soon as she saw you there. Is she still there with you?"

"No, Mom. Thanks to you she is gone for good. I'm 4000 miles away and Dad and you are still doing everything you can to screw up my life. You must both be proud." As they spoke he wandered around the apartment, picking up a few pairs of shorts and some t-shirts and a light raincoat.

"You caused all of this, Elias, not me. They call it a sin of omission if you care to know. You lied to Beth by not explaining your situation and letting her make an informed decision. You lied about taking your medications. You lied about your job and you probably have lied about everything else. You know full well you shouldn't fly and yet you took a pilot's job because your current flight license hadn't expired yet in the United States. How could you possibly think they wouldn't find out? Everything is in the public domain now."

"Did you do this to me, Mom? Did you tell everyone so that I'd be unable to work at something I love? She didn't say it, but I got the idea Beth already knew everything about my medical history and this was an easy way out for her. I think you do these things to me on purpose for some bizarre reason."

"I did not. The airline doctor saw your prescription and your medical history on his computer when he punched in your

ID #. He called your specialist and, after they spoke, the specialist called your father and I. The specialist already knew something was wrong when you showed up five pounds lighter at your appointment with him. You need to come home so we can get you some help."

"None of what you just said would have occurred if you left me alone. No way am I coming home," Elias replied.

"Where will you live? How will you get money? You have to come back so we can help you get your treatments going again."

"I inherited plenty of money from Uncle Joseph, probably more than any five or ten people would ever need to live comfortable lives. That's all in my name and I wired it down here when I moved. I won't be going back to the doctor."

"You did what? Why?"

"That's my money and I didn't want anyone to try to get a guardianship or conservatorship like you threatened you were going to try to do. Now you can't touch the money because it's not in a US bank and there's no reciprocity with Costa Rica, which is one of the primary reasons I came here."

"So what are you going to do? You can't just be alone all the time and not take your medication."

"I've got some things to do, Mom. I won't have a phone or an email address that I can check regularly. Every once in a while I may call or drop a line if I can get on a computer or a cell phone. "

"It sounds like you're abandoning your family," she said, beside herself with angst. "We're the ones who love you and want to help you."

"No. You abandoned me to those doctors who tied me down. That's not love or anything close to it. I've got some things to attend to here and I will not be accessible most of the time."

"Please tell me what you're going to do so we at least know where you are."

"I can't, Mom, because I don't know where I'll be day to

day. Tell Dad he can come here if he wants but I will not return with him under any condition. I'm going to go now and I'll contact you if and when I can." He hung up with her screaming on the other end of the line. As he walked out the door he heard the phone's incessant ringing as she desperately tried to call him back. He didn't even slow down.

It had been a full day and it still wasn't even noon. Against all of his principles, he turned around and went back in the apartment and used the phone as soon as it stopped ringing to call a livery service to meet him at the apartment with a cargo van. Upon its arrival, he put his bike in the back and went to the outdoor supply store, where he picked up his dry bags, a compass, four three meter square tarps, a selection of rugged plastic containers from a few ounces to a couple quarts, three pairs of tweezers and nail clippers along with a personal grooming kit, four tubes of toothpaste, several hundred meters of thin, but strong, parachute rope, two extra machetes, a sharpening stone, a portable water filter with extra filters good for 25000 gallons, a sealable water bottle, a stowable aluminum cookware kit, a flint and striking stone, waterproof matches, a powerful, metal-rimmed, magnifying glass, a few topographical maps of Costa Rica and a few water-proof books on the local flora and fauna, as well as what among them was edible.

"Take me over to the Price Mart, please," he told the driver after he loaded up the van.

He found some boxes of stone ground all natural crackers, a few jars of peanut butter that had "roasted peanuts" and "salt" as the only ingredients, and he cleaned out the trail mix aisle except for any package with added sugar.

"Please take me to the nearest fishing store, or a store that has fishing gear," he said when he got back in the van.

The driver nodded and took him to an upscale outdoor sport place in the business district of San Jose. "I need two sturdy telescoping rods and reels, a big box of assorted hook sizes for bait, a couple spools of extra line, and a few boxes of metal spoons and spinners of different sizes." Along with the hooks and lures, the clerk found him a couple of two-meter travel rods with spinning reels that collapsed down to less than 30 centimeters. Jamie paid in cash and went back to the van.

"Ok, here's the address we're going to so you can drop me off," he said when he got back in the van. The driver brought him to the buffalo farm and it wasn't even two o'clock. "Please wait for me here," he said to the driver. "I'm going to get someone to help me unload."

As he walked up to the house, Miguel came out of his workshop.

"Hey, can you get a cart and help me with some stuff I brought here today. I can't possibly carry it all to the field."

"Sure," Miguel said. He hitched up a buffalo to a cart and had it at the van in five minutes.

They unloaded everything from the van into the cart and Elias gave the driver a $100 bill for a $20 fare.

"Let's go to your bodega and load up the saddle and saddle bags and take them down to my buffalo. I think I would like to see how they look fully laden."

Miguel knew Elias was a bit eccentric but saw nothing wrong with that request. The equipment had already been tested for fit and comfort as he made it and each time he had simply brought them back to the shop afterward.

"Happy to," he replied.

The leather saddle and bags were feather-light to a buffalo, but weighed between 15 kilos at the lightest for the saddle bags and 25 kilos for the saddle. Miguel was at the cart and did not see when Elias took all of the remaining cans of mink oil and put them in the cart as well. They rode through the verdant field under a cloudless sky, which occurred very infrequently in the San Jose valley. Usually, cumulous clouds were always perched around the rim of the valley, but today, the sun shone unfiltered.

"This is a great day to take a few pictures of the animals with the saddles on them," Miguel said. "I could post them on my website and maybe get some more business, though I doubt

I'll ever make any as fine as these again."

The thought of being on social media revolted him, but he needed to keep moving.

"That's a great idea, Miguel. Once they're saddled I'll get out of the frame and you can take a few pics with your phone."

"Thank you,"

As soon as the herd saw them, Nitro emerged from the shelter of the jungle canopy where he had been resting in the heat of the day. The cows lazily wandered behind him. Not wanting them to get overheated in the sun, Elias had Miguel bring the cart into the shade cast by the adjacent jungle.

"We can offload here in the shade," Elias said, and he spread two tarps and they put everything on them.

"I'm going to saddle up the herd," Elias said. "If you really want a picture give me a few minutes."

"You want some help?"

"At this point, no, Miguel. I think they have learned accept me as their handler and I want to reinforce that by doing everything myself from here on. I also need to prove to myself that I actually can do it alone." He started with Nitro. The bull came immediately at the click of Elias' tongue. The animal smelled pungently of the jungle and the water that he waded in.

"Hey, there, boss man," Elias said too quietly for Miguel to hear. "You ready to go for a walk or a swim tonight? It's a big country and there's a lot to see. I'm thinking you and the ladies could use some new pasture and some different surroundings. Don't take this wrong, but this place belongs to Zeus and you need your own kingdom. If you stay here too long the two of you will have to duke it out and he's clearly a lot bigger than you. I have a better idea than letting that happen. Let's see how all of this gear looks on you guys fully loaded." Nitro looked back impassively but stood still while Elias struggled to put on his saddle and bridle, succeeding after about ten minutes. He then worked his way through each of the cows, getting incrementally more efficient each time. As he finished the last pair of saddle bags he relented on being in the photograph.

"You ready to take a picture or two, Miguel? The saddle and bags are incredible and they look great on the buffalo."

"Yes sir." Elias posed in front of the group and then to the side of them while Miguel used his phone to take photos.

"I hope this leads to a lot of leather work for you, Miguel. You deserve it. Thank you for making these for me. You can go back up to your bodega. Please take my bike back up there with you in the cart. I brought all my stuff because I'm going to camp out here tonight and tomorrow night. Don't worry. I'll be fine with the buffalo to protect me."

At this point, Elias had spent enough time in the field that Miguel didn't even think twice about the request. "OK. I'll let Leonardo know. You have a good night and I'll swing by in the morning."

"Sounds good. See you then."

Elias watched until the cart disappeared over the hill crest and then began to equally distribute all of his items into the twelve dry bags soon to be dangling against the animals' sides. He put as much granola as possible into the heavy duty re-sealable containers. His estimates as to capacity were spot on as the dry bags easily fit into the leather saddle bags so that he could cinch the thick leather straps and fasten the buckles, thus precluding any of his gear from floating away. He also took off and packed his t-shirt and boots and donned his pair of light sandals, so that all he had on was an old pair of faded blue gym shorts.

"OK guys, most days I'm going to let you tell me when you want to start roaming, but for today and the next few days I'll take the lead until you get used to it." He took Nitro's bridle and led him through the tall grass to the river's edge as dusk approached. The water surface already looked like black oil. Anything could lurk an inch away and no one would know.

"What do you say, guys? Are you ready to roll?"

Whether he was unconcerned or uncaring about what might be waiting for them, Nitro looked at the water and plodded directly in, waiting in the shallows and watching until all the cows joined him. With his wide splayed hooves, he did not sink appreciably into the muck given his bulk. Even at the edge the bottom was invisible. Elias knew the whole area was rife with crocodiles and bull sharks and had, not fear, but exhilaration as he entered a domain that he did not dominate because of his species. He waded out to the bull amidst the cows and climbed into his saddle and the group started foraging in the weeds, inching steadily closer and closer to the moderately swifter, deeper current. He tied his sandals into the bridle strap so he wouldn't lose them.

The bull suddenly and spontaneously came to the conclusion that he did not need to return to shore. He looked back at the cows and grunted and the whole group stepped into the deeper water and began drifting and kicking their feet lackadaisically with the current, instinctively clustering in a tight group, like a small school of gigantic, mammalian, herring. Any swimming effort was done by design and only to stay close to the other members of the herd. As a result, the buffalo expended very little energy. Nitro, always the lead animal, was buoyant as a cork, and Elias sat in the saddle, dry from the waist up.

He did not carry a watch. He'd left the one his parents gave him when he graduated from college in the apartment. Whether it was five minutes or two hours, at some point after darkness fell he stopped checking the surface swirls and eddies for predatory eyes as the buffalo bobbed along effortlessly. He did not guide them. At times the water became shallow and they would remain in place and forage before setting off again, seemingly deep-rooted primitive survival urges compelling them to always act as a group. The moon and stars rose and Elias found himself dozing intermittently in the saddle and to his own surprise, totally at ease. The unmistakable snap of crocodile jaws closing a short distance away roused him briefly, but the herd neither reacted nor seemed to care, so he ignored it as well.

Without a flashlight, he found that his eyes became accustomed to the darkness. When monkeys howled in the jungle, he could look in the trees and occasionally see silhouettes. He began to see crocodiles in the water and on the banks. None of them appeared interested in the buffalo, though he suspected that while those animals feigned indifference, some of their brethren likely skulked much closer, perhaps even under the swimming bovines. If they got too close or tried to attack, he believed his herd would respond accordingly.

The moon and stars moved around in the clear sky and sometime before dawn Nitro led the group out of the water to the shore. He picked an area that appeared to be grassy, but abutting the jungle only a few meters away. Elias saw no houses or structures or lights. In fact, he hadn't seen any for what he felt was quite a while. The herd neared the shore and began the march up the bank. The mud was softer here than where they entered the river and Elias could hear the suction as they pulled their hooves out of the ooze that futilely tried to restrain them.

"You guys have a good night?" Elias asked the herd. "Everyone should be full and ready for a nap. I know you guys prefer to travel at night so we'll go whenever you are ready in the evening and stop when you say so. We've got plenty to eat and drink here so let's get some rest." He wrestled all of the saddles off and got them to bed down in their circle, with his gear in the middle.

"Miguel would be proud of his work," he said with admiration as he watched the water bead and roll off the leather and pour out from the vents at the bottom of each bag. Until that moment of revelation he did not know why Miguel put two small vents in the corners at the bottom of each bag. He went to the inside of the circle and put his back against Nitro to sleep. The bugs did not seem that bad and even with just his shorts on, the air temperature was around 70 degrees and the bull's body provided ample additional warmth via convection through Elias' back.

XII. GETTING INTO THE ROUTINE

"We've got a lot to do today, guys," he said to the buffalo at dawn. "While you guys get out there and eat and drink I'm going to repack all the gear so I know which of you is carrying what items. Then, I'll rub another coat of mink oil into the leather. I think I'll do that at least every other day until I use it all up. Then, if we get to a town where I can order some I'll get more, though I have no idea where I will ship it to. We'll figure that out when the time comes."

Nitro's agenda differed from Elias' proposed schedule. He went to the water and stared back at him, digging at the bank with his left front hoof to demonstrate his impatience.

"Or, since you're the leader as it regards herd movements, we can gear up immediately and move down the river a bit more." He had trained the animals so much in the preceding weeks that they stayed with Nitro until he saddled them all up. At that point, without ado, Nitro then went directly into the current and started swimming, leaving Elias on the shore with the cows.

"Hey," he called to the bull. "We're a family. We're going to need to work some more on group coordination, organization and working as a cohesive unit." He waded into the water with the cows and found he could ride one of them just as easily as the bull, even without a saddle. When he checked around at the other cows, he noted that the cow he rode didn't even sink lower in the water with him on her back. Their natural buoyancy and strength made his weight, at best, an inconsequential nuisance. The cows caught up with Nitro's lollygagging tempo in a couple minutes. They fell into their usual "V" formation around him and, without checking his surroundings, Elias hopped off the cow, swam over to the bull, and climbed into his saddle.

"You and I stay together, buddy. I don't want to tether you at night, but we need to stay as a group. From now on I'll saddle you last to keep that from happening." As he finished speaking a very large crocodile decided to approach the group, perhaps because Elias' swimming figure presented an appropriately sized prey item and it had followed after them. The smallest of the cows spied it and wheeled on it as it came within biting distance. She rose the front end of her 700 kilo body in the water and slammed her front hooves on it. The animal thrashed about in shock, stunned, and floated away, moving but clearly injured.

Elias' pulse didn't even go up. The herd turned to the direction where the animal came from, saw no other threats and then continued to proceed down the river. Just a few minutes later a large field ringed by jungle appeared as they rounded a bend. Nitro brought the group out of the river so they could eat, drink and rest during the day.

"OK. I understand now. You all needed a better place to graze and sleep. I shouldn't have threatened to tether you, Nitro. Our mutual freedom remains the most important part of this excursion. That was wrong of me. I will trust your judgement going forward. If I take off the saddles do you think you can stay here for a bit? I have a lot to do."

He took no answer as the same thing as getting a yes. He took off the saddle and bags about 100 feet from the river bank. "You guys go eat. I'll call you or get you in a while."

The animals didn't wander far, staying in a group and moving back and forth along the tree line and coming back to the river repeatedly to drink some of their required 130-150 liters of water per day. Appropriately named, Elias knew from his research that water buffalo never wander more than a few miles from a reliable water source.

"I need to reorganize." He started by pulling two of the tarps out and spreading everything out. "I should always be able to get what I need when I need it." The dry bags all worked. Even fully submerged in the river for most of the night, nothing felt remotely damp.

"I want to get everything broken out by category, but I don't want to give one animal more to carry than the others." He suddenly realized that Nitro's name came from the ranch before he bought him, so he was stuck with that, but the cows had no names. He knew each of them from distinct markings and behaviors, but they needed names. He pondered that for a bit as he sorted through his gear. He used his poetic license and came up with a solution. "We'll go alphabetically. How about Abby, Bessie, Cassie, Dolly, and Elly?"

Over the next hour or two Elias categorized and repacked. He put the most likely to be used items in Nitro's saddle bags so he would have quick access to them. His herd milled about around him, alternating between eating, wallowing in the mud at the river's edge and drinking. Any time an animal came up to him he would stop and pet it and talk to it. He found that the cows lingered around Nitro at all times, so as long as he remained close the herd would follow suit.

"You need to let me know in advance if you want to get moving, Nitro," he said as he rubbed his nose. "I have to get you guys packed up and that takes a few minutes. Maybe we can just agree that we'll travel at night and rest by day. You OK with that?" The bull continued sauntering about, possibly staying because of the soothing nature of Elias' voice or because the man had spent a couple months conditioning the herd to always follow him. It may simply have been that the bull had sufficient pasture to graze on.

His stomach began rumbling and Elias pulled out a bag of granola. Before he tore open the bag, he remembered that he had the book on edible plants. He re-stowed the bag and pulled out the book. Donning his sandals, he walked to the edge of the forest carrying the book and the machete. His herd apparently watched him as they came over to stand with him.

"Thank you, guys. I appreciate your concern for my well-being. Let's see what we can find to eat." Within a few feet he found some of the local lettuce Mario had shown him and a mango tree. He gathered some of the lettuce and a few of the riper fruits and went back to the tarps, buffalo in tow.

"It'll take some time, but I'll get better at this," he told the herd. "You guys are already good at what you do, so I need to catch up and learn to adapt to this environment. I'm not going to eat the granola right away. I'll keep it for a time when there is nothing to eat available in the jungle and I'll learn to fish here and catch some food as well. It'll be awhile but I'm sure we'll get where we need to go." He ate his lunch and then rubbed all of the saddles and bags with mink oil and let them bake in the sun so it absorbed into the leather. While they sat in the bright afternoon light he perused the book of edible plants and walked about trying to identify some of them.

"This isn't so hard," he said as he followed the herd around the perimeter of the field. "Everywhere I look I find something edible." He found fruits and legumes including grandilla, carambola, mammon chino, guabe and pejibaye growing wild. He recognized many of them not from the book but from the street vendors who sold them at intersections in San Jose. "Those guys must make good money," he said. "Their inventory costs are nothing. They just go in the jungle, pick a couple bags of fruit and sell them on the street. They undoubtedly don't collect or pay sales tax and render unto Caesar what would rightfully be his, either."

He picked a couple grandilla to eat during the evening travel. Returning to the tarps, he pulled out his chumash and read the Aramaic verses for about thirty minutes and then saw clouds forming. He stowed the book in its dry bag and then stowed it in Cassie's saddle bag.

"Time to load up," he said. He clicked his tongue and

XII. GETTING INTO THE ROUTINE | 111

Nitro ambled over with the cows in tow. As he finished cinching the last bag the skies opened up, instantly drenching him. The rain, which occurred most every day in Costa Rica and totaled almost four meters per year, was as warm as the ambient air, so apart from getting soaked it was only a minor inconvenience. Elias learned from training them in the field that rain, no matter hard it fell, only served to cool the buffalo off.

"Time to go Nitro. Lead on." The bull strolled along with the flow of the eastward bound river, seemingly enjoying the rain. When he ran out of field, he took the cows down to the river's edge and they kept moving nimbly through the mud and shallow water. Between their wide splayed hooves and massive shoulder and haunch muscles they didn't even slow down or change gait. On the contrary, Elias had to climb in the saddle at that point as he became effectively immobilized in the mud, nearly losing his sandals to the sucking black ooze. The buffalo pushed through grass and low hanging jungle vegetation until, after a brief pause, the bull took them into the stream, the rain pelting the river nearly into a froth all around them. Clumps of foam churned up from the mud and pollutants coming from upstream glided past them, pushed by the wind and water.

"Visibility is not too good out here right now," Elias said to the group. "You guys seem to know that as well," he continued, noting that the herd pressed together to maintain contact with each other in the torrential downpour. "If I were in the Caravan we'd be flying on instruments, but out here you guys are the instruments and the vehicle all rolled into one."

With the rain came a surge in the water levels and current in the river. As the river flowed through San Jose west of the herd, trash and other man made detritus drifted by them. As time went on larger and larger objects came down the stream until Elias noted large branches, logs and even trees freshly downed that appeared felled by the current undermining their roots along the shore.

"What do you think, Nitro?" he asked. "I'm thinking we may want to go to shore to avoid getting hit by one of those trees. I suspect they could hurt you guys if we're not careful." Nitro evidently did not share that concern and continued on for what felt like another two hours, weaving around several large tree trunks before finding an opening in the jungle that he liked enough to bring the herd to shore.

"Much appreciated," Elias said through the still driving rain. Surprisingly, he found that the water and the rain were basically like taking a warm shower, and he was not cold in the least. After gathering the herd together, removing the saddle and bags and getting them to bed down, he pulled out one of his tarps, sat against Nitro, and spread it over himself in the middle of the group, all of whom were already asleep.

He roused a few hours later when the bull rolled onto his feet away from him, causing him to abruptly fall on his back. Dawn colored the sky and the rain had stopped in the night.

"What are you doing here? How did you get here?" a male voice asked him.

Elias walked around Cassie and saw a man standing there, his small house directly behind him. The rain had been so torrential that Elias did not see the modest edifice when they came ashore, though it wasn't even a stone's throw away.

"I came out of the river sometime in the night with the herd," Elias said.

"That's suicide. The crocodiles take everything."

"Not these guys and not me if I'm with them," Elias replied. "These water buffalo are the baddest bovines in the world and they are designed to travel at night in water. They are more or less nocturnal."

"Look, I've lived here my whole life and there is nothing they won't eat if there are enough of them and they are hungry enough."

"I guess we'll see."

"What are you trying to do?"

"I'm beginning my journey as a pastoral nomad. I plan to travel the water ways and trade milk and meat and leather for the things I need while I grow my herd."

"Where's your boat?" the farmer asked as he surveyed the shore, still not believing Elias' word that he drifted with the buffalo.

"I already told you I don't have one. I saddle the bull and ride him in the river."

"Then you are going to die in the river."

"If that's God's will, but I don't think so."

"Look, the river here is still a bit narrow. Once you join the main stream of the Colorado, the water is faster and deeper and the crocodiles can be 5-6 meters and weigh 200-300 kilos or more. They will rip these cows apart."

"These are not cows," Elias said, pointing out the horns on both the bull and the cows. "These are water buffalo. The females all weigh over 700 kilos and the bull weighed 1150 kilos when we left. I suspect he weighs more than that already and he's likely on his way to something approaching 1400 kilos. The dominant bull at the ranch where I bought him dwarfs my bull. They can swim all day and eat grass, leaves, and water vegetation. They'll even dive for it. No crocodile or group of crocodiles around here will take a chance getting hurt trying to eat them."

"Are you that sure," the farmer said.

"Yes. I walk with God."

"God doesn't protect prey from predators and I don't believe he plays favorites. People often lose sight of that. He made them both, after all. He doesn't likely favor one over the other. You're not right in the head."

"Do you want me to leave?"

"No, there's plenty of forage and water here for your animals and if you give me some milk I'll make some food for you. Maybe if you stay here for a bit and think it over you'll stay on land and hire a barge to bring you back where you came from. What is your name? I would like to know that for when you disappear and the authorities come looking for you if you continue."

"I'm Elias. Thank you. That's very kind of you. You don't

have to make me food. I like to catch and find my own. Bring me a bucket and I'll get to work. Buffalo milk is protein and fat rich. I think you'll like it a lot more than cow's milk from a nutritional standpoint."

"OK. I'll go get one. We are going to stay outside here and cook around the fire today as one of my neighbors found an army ant nest a bit up river. They are moving this way. We don't know if they'll get here today or tomorrow. Do you know anything about army ants?"

"No, but the name unquestionably doesn't sound good."

"Well, names can be deceptive because these bugs are greatly beneficial. They nest at night in a ball. I read in a book that Americans call the nest they make out of their own bodies is known as a bivouac. The soldier ants create the outside layers to protect the workers and the queen at the very center. Anyway, they rest at night and move with great vigor during the day, eating everything in their path. This ant colony is heading our way along the riverside and I'm hoping my house is in their path."

"Why would you hope for that?"

"You'll see. Just wait until the sun rises and the temperature goes up and they become active. Then you'll come to know why we always welcome them. People who live near the city try to stop and them and lose out on their benefits." He handed Elias a large white pail. "I'll take whatever milk you want to give me. One of my friends makes cheese so we'll drink some and give the rest to him." He pulled out a cell phone and dialed. "Roy, you think you can make cheese with buffalo milk?" He listened momentarily and then said "Ok" and hung up.

"Roy says buffalo milk makes some of the best cheese in the world. He can't wait to get some of your milk because the fat and protein contents are so high he'll be able to make twice as much cheese with the same volume of milk. He said some of the finest mozzarella cheese in the world is made from buffalo milk – mozzarella di bufala."

Elias was shocked and slightly repulsed that the man had

a cell phone.

"I only recently found that out, too. I've had a lot of that cheese myself. I may be able to fill two or three of these buckets," he said, "so while I work on this one bring me a few more. Whatever milk you don't need or your friend Roy can't use please give to your neighbors and friends who need it. The cows will make more and I don't like to see it go to waste."

"That's very generous of you. Thank you."

"You're welcome."

Fortunately, the day turned out to be extremely hot and humid and the buffalo were more than content to laze in the shade around the river's edge. Though the mud was not deep enough to fully immerse themselves, they rolled around in the muck until they looked like they had been dipped in chocolate ganache. The farmer brought down the extra buckets just as Elias filled the first one from Abby and Bessie. He stopped milking a few inches from the top so none would slop over when the farmer carried it.

"Hey, if the herd will stay here without you why don't you come to the edge of the jungle with me and watch the army ants work their magic. They are almost here. Do you have boots for walking through the grass?" He looked at Elias standing in just his old shorts with his beard starting to grow out. "In fact, do you have any clothes other than your shorts?"

"I do but I'm fine with just the shorts and sandals."

"If the crocs, bull sharks or snakes don't get you the Costa Rican sun will cook you like a roast or give you skin cancer, my friend. You should wear lightweight, long sleeves and a hat to protect your skin like I do. You simply know nothing about living out here. Come along then."

Elias heard the low decibel crunching sound emanating from the jungle many meters before he got to the trees.

"What is that sound?"

"The army ants are collecting food for the nest. That is the sound of their mandibles crunching as they cut things into bite size pieces. Look, here they are." As he finished speaking a column-like line of large black ants emerged in formation from the leaf litter on the jungle floor. As soon as they were in the field, birds of many different species began swooping in front of them and picking up the insects and small rodents and reptiles fleeing before the swarm like seabirds picking off baitfish driven to the ocean's surface by predatory fish. The ants marched with unwavering purpose on a direct line to the farmer's house.

"Perfect. Don't step on or near the line because that might inadvertently change their direction. These guys bite and it'll hurt a bit. Let's go to the door of my house and you can see what happens when these insects visit." They carefully walked beside the lead ants up to the house. The ants amassed and poured in through the windows, doors, cracks in the floor boards and any other entry they could access. As the house stood on pilings about 70 centimeters high, the initial assault included scaling those structures. Once inside, the ants fanned out, rapidly scouring through every crevice from the floor to the ceiling. They raced with purpose through the cupboards and closets and any opening large enough for them to enter. Elias watched, fascinated, as the thronging soldier ants killed cockroaches, mice, small lizards and even a baby bird from a nest in the eaves. All were dispatched with extreme prejudice and then methodically cut up by the workers to be carried back to the queen.

"When they leave, my house will be as clean as it can be. The ants leave nothing behind. They will march until dark, then nest for the night and start moving again in the morning."

"Amazing," Elias said. "That is awesome! These guys serve as Mother Nature's housekeeping service."

"It certainly saves a lot of cleaning time. The key is to not try to deter them. They just do their job and leave. The whole process only takes about 15-20 minutes and then it's as if they were never here."

The farmer and Elias went back down to the river to his herd and found a number of neighboring residents gathered at a respectful distance from the buffalo. All had come by boat, some from a fair distance.

"What's going on here?" Elias asked.

"Some of these folks would like some milk if your animals can produce some more and others came to see the man who floats down the river with the crocodiles. You are somewhat famous for your bravado – and more so for your folly."

"I travel with my herd," Elias said. "As long as the forage is good and they want to stay here I will milk the cows for the people. The cows are more comfortable when that is done regularly anyway. I will get about 7 kilos a day from each animal so that's 35 kilos total. Have them bring buckets of some sort and I'll do what I can. Oh, you don't need to make me lunch today, either. I saw some mamon chino and pejibaye in the jungle and I'll pick some of those later. I could use some fire wood as I plan to fish a bit from the shore. Are there any machaka here?"

"I'll get you some wood and yes, there are machaka as well as guapote and catfish just off the bank. I'll bring you a bit of bait when I get the wood."

"Thank you. I don't think I need any bait. I have plenty of lures and I'd like to try them out."

The farmer shook his head back and forth. "You float with buffalo and fish with lures. You'll get eaten doing the first and starve doing the second. Lures are for sport fishermen who want to "give the fish a chance" and only for a last resort if you are living off the land as you seem to want to do. Bait is for a man trying to catch a fish and eat. I'll bring you bait."

"Thank you," he replied.

"You seem like a smart man, Elias," he continued. "I can see you will not change your mind about traveling in the river with your herd. It's almost certain that you will encounter an animal hungry enough to attack and try to eat you. At least listen to a couple warnings. Anything that floats in the river – vegetation, logs, trash – can and usually does serve as a raft for snakes. We pull logs out of the river to cut into lumber and we are always careful as you'll find snakes quite often in knotholes in the wood. Also, the closer you get to the ocean, the more bull sharks there are in the river. They are here, too, but usually a bit smaller and fewer in number. They eat everything, including crocodiles, so I think they'd look at your buffalo as a hot lunch. Please think about these things. Perhaps the worst thing is that you said you travel at night. That is when the predators are most active. It is also when you can't see them approach."

"I don't think they'll be a problem," Elias said somewhat dismissively. "As I said, I walk with God."

"God will always try to help you but, especially out here in the jungle, he expects you to protect yourself as much as you can, amigo. Common sense can be anything but common at times. In your case, it is utterly nonexistent."

"Protecting myself is what I'm doing with the buffalo," Elias said. "I'm going to work on my saddles and bags and then start milking so send people down in a couple hours."

"Will do."

"By the way, does your cell phone have internet service?"

"Of course. My laptop in the house does, too."

"May I use your phone to look something up?"

"Sure." He handed his phone to Elias, who went to his email account. He had ten emails from his mother and five from Beth. They were all sent to him and cc:ed to each other.

He skimmed them, culling various sentences from each. "Where are you?" "We're worried." "No one has seen you since Beth left the apartment." "Without your medication you could suffer psychotic episodes and exhibit unusual or suicidal behavior." "Are you alive?" He found that one humorous as he could hardly answer if he weren't alive. In the last few days he had never felt so alive. He hit reply to all and tapped out a message to the last one. "I'm fine. Will write again when I'm able. Bye for now. Elias." He deleted his browser history and handed the phone back to the farmer and went to apply another coat of mink oil to his leather gear. After he completed that task he milked his cows for a group of people with buckets. They offered to help, but he declined.

"These animals must always know that I'm their caretaker so I am the only one who handles them or cares for them.

That's how it has to be."

While he milked the cows, the farmer brought him a small pile of dry firewood and kindling in the form of coconut husks. He also brought a few small pieces of cooked chicken meat and skin to use as bait. "The fish will strip this off your hook almost immediately, so use little pieces and keep the line taught. May I show you once?"

"Sure," Elias replied. He pulled out the telescoping rod and reel and set it up with a slip weight and hook.

"This is incredibly convenient," he noted with regard to Elias' telescoping fishing rod. "I wondered whether you had a fishing rod and where you kept it if you did. You don't need a weight here," said the farmer, when he looked at the rigging. "You should get some fine steel leaders so you don't lose all your hooks. Most of the fish here have strong teeth."

"OK, I'll get some. How do you cast without weights?"

"You don't. This river is alive. You just reach out the length of the rod and drop it in." He demonstrated and the bait barely disappeared under the layer of silty top water when the line went straight out and the rod bent almost double.

"This'll be an alligator gar. Too big for dinner for you but I'll keep it for my family and friends if you don't mind. These are the best tasting fish here. It's like eating a shrimp and lobster casserole."

"Fine by me," Elias replied.

The farmer checked the line and rod strength and pulled the four foot, fifteen kilo fish to the shore. Primordial in appearance and protected by armor-like scales and skutes on its back, it looked, appropriately, Elias thought, like it had alligator jaws and they snapped repeatedly. Fortunately, the hook was in the corner of the mouth or it would have severed the line in an instant. Elias took a step forward and reached to grab it by the tail.

"No," the farmer said. "There are crocodiles here and they will opportunistically grab hooked fish. I will use the line to pull it a bit away from the water." He did and then stretched forward with his machete and killed the fish by burying the blade in its head. He then pulled it towards him and picked it up by the tail.

"Now you try. Set the hook as soon as you feel a tap so the fish doesn't swallow the hook and cut the line when it bites. That will give you the best chance of hooking the fish in the corner of the mouth where it can't bite through the line. Just be careful of how close you get to the river while you fish. If you don't get something, please let me know and I'll give you some fillets from this gar. Always wash any scent of fish off you before you get in the water to travel, which you simply should not do in any case. If you don't, it's like rubbing yourself down with bacon grease and sitting in a lion's cage and asking it to consider becoming a vegetarian."

Elias had fished many times in Scouts as a boy so he drew on that experience and caught a machaka on his second try. It weighed about one kilo so he emulated the farmer and pulled the fish in to himself across the bank using the line and dispatched it with his machete. He made a fire ring back where the herd rested and put a tarp up with two poles he cut at the jungle's edge and used his saddle and bags to hold the back side of the tarp down. The lean-to would shelter the flames so he could cook when it rained.

"Now let's try to light a fire the old fashioned way," he said to no one. He got out his flint and striker, bunched up some of the dry coconut kindling and struck sparks into it. It immediately caught and then burned out before lighting the larger pieces of wood. Remembering his Scout days, Elias used his machete to chop up smaller pieces of wood into shards from mere splinters up to pieces an inch or so in diameter. This time he put the kindling down, the splinters on top of that and then the slightly larger pieces, forming a classic log cabin box around the tinder. Instead of striking the flint again, he used his magnifying glass to focus the tropical sun into a beam directed at the coconut husk and the splinters and soon he had a good fire going. He figured keeping the flint for cloudy weather, rain or night time use would make it last longer. He decided to ask the farmer for some additional husk kindling and he'd keep that in his dedicated camping dry bag.

While a flat rock he found and intended to use as a cooking surface heated in the flames, Elias cleaned the machaka with his machete and scaled it by scraping the machete against the grain of the scales. The herd settled in around him, but at a respectful distance from the fire. Normally they would be itching to travel, but the cows were getting milked regularly and they were content. Nitro, who appeared to take queues from the cows, seemed to know there was no reason to move as yet. Elias used his machete tip to slide the heated stone to the edge of the fire pit after about an hour, during which time he ate a couple pieces of his fruit. He dropped the whole cleaned fish on the baking hot rock and its flesh instantly started sizzling and popping. As dusk approached the rain began falling and the farmer came out with a tattered old umbrella.

"You can sleep in the house you know. We have plenty of room and bug screens."

"Thank you, but I need to stay with my animals at all times. You want a piece of fish? It's almost done."

"Thank you but I just ate the gar fish with my family. Have a good night and I'll see you in the morning."

"Sounds good."

Left to himself, Elias ate all of the machaka with his fingers and then flipped the rock back into the flames to burn clean so that there would be no scent to draw rats or a jaguar or a raccoon under his tarp encampment. After a few minutes he left the shelter of the tarp and slept with his back against Nitro, one of his other tarps covering his body while the rain drummed against his uncovered head, pounding his curly brown hair flat.

The sky had cleared and the rain was over when he awoke to the bull's movements. He had no idea of the time, but the fire was completely out and the cows were all impatiently waiting in the dark.

"I guess it's time to move along," he said to them. He put

his gear on them and Nitro, whom he intentionally saddled last, walked straight into the river with everyone else in tow. Elias hopped on him as he waded into the current. Still exhausted from his fitful sleep in the rain, Elias wrapped his right hand around the bridle and drowsed with the lower half of his body submerged, completely confident that his animals would keep him safe as they alternatingly swam and drifted through the murky water. The buffalo always stayed tightly together with the bull in the lead. Dolly and Cassie seemed to consistently hold positions at his flanks with the other three spread out behind him so that the six animals formed a living wedge.

Elias napped sporadically throughout the remainder of the night and was still somewhat groggy when the sun came up. He woke fully to see boats drifting with his herd in the current.

"Please keep back from the animals," he called to them in alarm. "Don't let the propellers anywhere near them. You could hurt them."

Knowing that he spoke Spanish at that point, they started calling out to him.

"You must get out of the water. Look around you, there are crocodiles everywhere. The ones you can see aren't really the issue. It's the ones beneath the water, which are likely far more numerous, that will attack your animals' legs and drag them under."

Sure enough, he scanned the water and saw no less than ten crocodiles drifting and keeping parallel to the sides and back of his herd. The closest one, also the largest, stared at him from the left side about fifty feet away.

"They are no problem," he called back. "It's you guys who could cause injury to the buffalo."

"We came out to help you. Do you want us to save you and bring you to shore?"

"No, stay back. The buffalo will decide whether and when to come to shore."

"You are insane," one called to him. They all pulled back and began videoing the scene, figuring that a graphic film of this

American getting eaten alive might sell for a few dollars.

After another 15 minutes of swimming, Nitro turned towards a field he spied on the river bank. He swiveled directly into the crocodiles on that flank and accelerated into them to keep the current from pushing them past his desired landing point. Whether they sensed his immense size advantage, strength, or lack of fear, all but one scattered. The big crocodile waited until they were nearly face to face and then backed down from the bull, pivoting in the water and swimming away when he suddenly realized this animal's nearly five foot horns, head and shoulders alone outweighed his 250 kilos. The cows behind him, each also two to three times his size and sporting three foot horns, cruising in phalanx formation with Nitro made it all the more intimidating.

"Please get back," Elias called to the boats. "Let us move to shore without you injuring the animals." Suddenly realizing this nut may have a point, they all backed off and let the animals get to the shallows and effortlessly power up the slope to the field. The boats came to shore and tied off on the dock and any available trees and rocks.

Elias didn't want or need to hear he was demented once more. Without the symbycerol dimming his senses he saw everything clearly.

"Anyone want to trade," he asked the group of men and children approaching in Spanish. "I can supply you with milk if you can get me some dry coconut husks for kindling and I need a few steel leaders for my fishing rod."

"Are you kidding?" one asked. "That's what you want."

"Those are the items I need," he said as he unloaded the herd's bags. "Please stay back from my buffalo. They only know me and that is the way it has to be."

"I have some steel leaders, but they cost a lot and I'll need to get more than some milk for them," one local said. He pointed over to where three young men, likely his sons, were urging two yoked cows to pull out a stump that wouldn't give up. It was one of fifteen or twenty visible in the field. "I live there beyond the field in that house and I can bring the leaders but what else do you have? Those wire leaders are hard to come by."

"Do you want those stumps gone from your field?"

"Yes, but my team can't get them free."

"If Nitro takes them out can I have 4 leaders in exchange?"

"Sure, but how can one of your animals do it if two of mine can't?"

"My animals are not cattle," Elias said. Bring the biggest harness you have and we'll see if we can get it over his head. Unfortunately, no amount of adjustment or manipulation could get the harness over Nitro's head and shoulders. He brought Bessie over and it barely fit her.

"Nitro," he said to the bull, "Bessie and I have some work to do. I know you'd rather show off a little but the equipment won't fit the likes of you. Do me a favor and bring the rest of the ladies out to the field to eat. Bessie will be back in an hour or two. The bull snuffed derisively and wandered off with the remaining cows, dropping a big pile of dung as he did so.

"That wasn't very polite," Elias called after the bull. "OK," he said to the young man, "Let's hook up the first stump." He held Bessie in place so there was slack to work with on the chain. The vast majority of the trees in the flood zone of the river all had extensive, but shallow, roots as water in the lowlands was never more than a foot or two below the surface.

"We hitched?" he asked the young man.

"Yes."

Elias took hold of the side of the harness and clicked his tongue the way Leonardo taught him at the farm. Bessie moved forward and the chain went taught. She stopped, initially unused to the resistance. The young man smiled, unabashedly happy that this odd beast was stopped at something his cows couldn't do.

"Don't let Nitro think he's the only one who could do this, girl. Gender equality is a good thing," Elias said encouragingly. He clicked his tongue again and Bessie reset her legs in a wider stance for balance and strained forward, her broad, flexible, hooves digging into the soft mud but not losing purchase while her sides suddenly turned to rock hard muscle. The stump popped out of the ground like a jack in the box, leaving the young man's jaw against his chest in awe.

"Come on. How did she do that?" he asked.

"One water buffalo is stronger than two yoked oxen and these roots are shallow," Elias said. "The yoke doesn't give you the full strength of both animals as they always pull in slightly different directions. Let's get the rest of them so Bessie can rejoin the herd and graze and get some water in her. She's likely tired and hungry after traveling so long." In 45 minutes, much less time than he thought, they had pulled all the stumps up. None of them offered anything more than token resistance.

The young man's father came out and gave Elias fifteen steel fishing leaders and a box of hooks.

"I said I'd remove the stumps for four leaders," Elias said.

"I thought you had no chance of doing it at all," he said. "Keep the leaders. I've never seen anything like that in my life, and I doubt I ever will again. Usually, we have the cattle pull while we cut the roots on one side until the stump gives. Your cow simply tore them out of the ground. Unbelievable."

"Thank you," Elias said. It was only 830 am. "If anyone has some dry coconut husk I can use for kindling tell them I'll trade milk for some. Tell them to come around 10 am so Bessie can get some food and water in her before then."

"You're sure that's all you want?"

"Yes."

"Ok. I'll call a few of my friends in the area."

Elias walked out to the herd and mingled with them as they grazed, went to drink and resumed foraging multiple times. Satisfied that they were content, he went and treated his saddle and bags with oil and read his chumash until people started showing up with buckets. The herd, never far from him, came as soon as he clicked his tongue. Nitro stood alone in the shallows of the river, munching water weeds and drinking. He looked oblivious to the occasional crocodile that patrolled, albeit at a respectful distance, near him, but Elias thought he might also be letting the predators know that he was here and they should beware his wrath. As each cow was milked it would go back to him and begin doing the same. When Elias finished with Elly she waded into the water and began eating her way through the vegetation over to Nitro, Abby and Dolly.

    A large crocodile lying in ambush lunged from below the surface weeds and grabbed her by the horns and neck with its jaws simultaneously with her effort to submerge to eat. Bursting to the surface and baying loudly, she swam fifteen or twenty labored feet sideways until she found purchase on the bottom. Then, she backed out of the water, inexorably and resolutely dragging the crocodile with her up the slick river bank while it tried ineffectually to twist and wrench her into deeper water, quite possibly failing at that endeavor for the first time in its adult life.

    Elias jumped up with his machete and raced over to save her. Before he arrived, Nitro exploded out of the weedy river and slammed headfirst into the crocodile, detaching its grip. The bull slammed his head down on the reptile repeatedly and stomped on it with his front hooves as it initially tried to return to the water. Though buffalo horns curve backward and he could not gore the animal from that angle, the blunt, crushing horn and hoof blows killed the crocodile with grotesque efficiency. When it finally stopped moving, Nitro paused petulantly, borderline contemptuously, over the reptile's flattened and shattered carcass as if to make sure it was dead, almost posing for effect, and then started to bring Elly over to the other three cows. With his testosterone levels into the stratosphere, he strutted right beside her, less than a foot away, glaring around for any other animal, crocodile or otherwise, insolent enough to test him.

    Elias clicked his tongue and Nitro and Elly halted in the water in front of him. He waded out and checked Elly's head. Fortunately, the top jaw of the crocodile clamped down on her left horn and there were only a few superficial scratches on it.

She did have a few punctures and some blood from where the lower jaw teeth went in her neck, but she seemed unfazed. He checked the wounds and let her go feed. "You are a tough young lady, Elly. Go get some lunch and forget about this."

"Good work, Nitro," Elias said as he patted the bull and checked him for wounds as well. "I think she had it under control, but you are the protector and you did your job. I'm happy you got there before me. From now on the cows travel in pairs or with you."

The farmer's son who had pulled stumps with him approached as Elias sat down to finish milking. He saw that this barely clothed stranger acted as though nothing had happened.

"Your animal just pulled an adult crocodile out of the water from deep water and the big one killed it like squashing a bug. Normally, once they grab a cow like that in the water it's over. I've never seen anything pull a full grown crocodile out of the water like that. Your cow was submerged in water over its head when that crocodile bit her. Under normal circumstances, it's a done deal. That's amazing by itself. Then the bull annihilated as if it were helpless. I could not believe how fast it ran to get there to help her. Though it's illegal to kill them, that one animal had taken several pigs and a cow in the past year and we hadn't been able to shoot it because it has been so elusive. That animal was a menace."

"Not anymore. Water buffalo are built differently," Elias said, "and Nitro will not suffer anything touching his herd. Water buffalo can sprint at almost 50 kilometers per hour. He, and the cows, are family oriented. Elly probably didn't really need any help, but Nitro made short work of the problem and kept her from suffering more injuries."

"I noticed. You mind if we cut up the backstrap and tail from that crocodile? It'll feed a lot of people. I may take the hide and make some leather from the sections the bull didn't ruin."

"Go ahead. Too bad it attacked the wrong animal." He didn't think to ask for some of the meat or leather for himself.

"Were you really going to try to save that animal with only a machete? That would be like using a flyswatter to drive off a jaguar."

"Absolutely."

"You likely would have died, either from the crocodile's jaws or from your own bull going right through you to save the cow."

"I doubt it. Even enraged, he knows I'm the alpha. Anyway, Nitro beat me there and it's over."

"And after seeing that attack you'll go back in the water with them when they are ready to travel again?"

"Of course. In fact, based on what just happened I see no need to worry about that in the least. I'm only worried about some idiot boater drifting too close and chopping up one of my buffalo with a propeller. People are the problem, not the sharks and crocodiles."

"I can't believe I'm saying this, but you are starting to convince me. Don't get me wrong, though, I'd never even consider what you were going to do and, you know, something about you just isn't right."

The man walked away shaking his head, leaving Elias as he finished milking the last cow. He wanted to tell him that wading out to the bull to check on his cow's condition with the cow's blood in the water was basically an unintended suicide attempt, but he knew it would fall on deaf ears.

XIII. SMALL DETAILS

The herd abruptly decided to leave the next day around noon, almost immediately after he finished milking the last cow. The temperature rose well into the nineties and the humidity spiked as well. The river water offered the only available respite from the oppressive heat. Nitro snorted at the river's edge, impatient for Elias to get his saddle on.

"I know," he said to the bull. "You want to get out in the water where it's cooler. We'll go, but you need to watch out for people and their boats at this time of day. Whenever they come too close, I'll get off the saddle and warn them off if need be. I won't let anyone hurt you guys. You maintain your travel rate and watch the cows. Sound good?" Nitro stared at him, only curious if he had a treat for him and if his saddle was cinched.

"Look, before you go, please listen," said the farmer's son. "You are only a couple miles from the confluence of this river and the Colorado, which runs about ninety kilometers straight out to the Caribbean. The crocodiles are bigger and more plentiful, as are sharks and other threats. The current flows much more swiftly and you will encounter dangerous eddies and whirlpools. Trees and other debris move with great speed and momentum in the river and submerged limbs stuck in the bottom can pull you under and pin you against the current until you drown. If you go out there in rainy season, and that could start any day now, you and your animals will be swept along no matter how well they swim. It could happen that you go the length of the river and then get pushed into the Caribbean Sea, unable to make it to shore against the tide and current. Please reconsider doing this. This is not the action of a sane man. If this is about machismo, you have proven more than enough merely getting yourself in one piece this far from San Jose."

"I'm not here to prove anything. I walk with God," Elias said, repeating his mantra. "My herd and I are in harmony with nature. My animals are more than up to any natural challenge they'll face in the jungle and on this river and I will help them deal with people who do not seem to get the simple fact that they should stay away."

"Look, if I can't convince you to stay here or travel with your animals on land somehow, then I will hope that I see you again in the future."

"It's likely that I'll be rotating through here again, but we'll see. Gotta go now," Elias said as the herd stepped to the edge of the river. "I need to stay with them at all times." He dove off the bank behind them and swam into the animals' midst, rising up and climbing into the bull's saddle.

As he left in the daytime, boats followed him constantly, the pilots and passengers waiting with morbid anticipation for the gruesome attack that everyone assumed was soon coming his way. After some period of time, they all left and returned home, likely to conserve precious fuel.

"Nitro, I know we've talked about this several times, but we have to think about traveling only at night from here on," he said. "People simply won't leave us alone. They're OK when we are on land and we need them to trade, but they pose a danger to us out here in the water. What do you think?" The bull continued to coast through the water effortlessly, sometimes just drifting like a bobbing cork, as much at home in the murky river as he was in the mud at the shore or in the jungle among the vines and vegetation. Without tigers, hippos, elephants or rhinos or a larger male water buffalo, Elias figured the bull stood alone as the herbivorous master of this place.

The river current slowed and got shallower as it continued to widen for most of the afternoon and the buffalo found they could lumber along the river bed, eating weeds and water vegetation and drinking huge amounts of water even in the center of the river. The generally waist-deep, lethargic, water allowed them to laze around and stay cooler while selectively eating the most succulent plants. At times, they bunched together and laid down in the water with only their heads and horns poking through the surface.

"You guys are all over the place today," Elias said, not realizing that the animals were following a pattern of weeds that they enjoyed the most. The bed, though connected, zigzagged across the bottom of the river and they ate the most appetizing parts and kept moving, leaving the pulpy, woody shoots to regrow. Here, the buffalo ate quite judiciously, singling out the most delectable greenery. In a pinch, though, they would eat tree leaves, shrubs, grass and anything green in the jungle.

All of the animals' backs were so broad that he could stand up on them while they swam. He did so while they rested in place, digging his toes into Nitro's hide for stability so he could see further along the banks for a spot to land. "Guys, I see a nice patch of grass and some fruit trees on that bank," Elias said, pointing to the north shore for their benefit. "Why don't we take a break and go up there so I can get some lunch and do some reading. I'm sure there's good grazing up there as well." He sat back down and tugged at the bridle to get Nitro to lead the rest of the herd to shore, but he stopped swimming and tried to look over his shoulder at Elias, clearly indicating his displeasure.

"I know. You're happy out here but I haven't eaten at all today. Let's go out on the bank for a while and then we'll come right back into the river. I promise. I won't even unsaddle you guys. I only need enough time to get some fruit. I won't do any reading until later." He clicked his tongue and tugged on the bridle again and the bull reluctantly abandoned his watery feast and effortlessly climbed the slick bank.

Elias slipped out of the saddle into the grass and took his machete from Nitro's saddle bag when all six animals were grouped up.

"OK," he said, pointing at a nearby tree. "Here's the deal. I'm going to cut a few mangos off that tree then hop back in the saddle and away we go. Wait here for a couple minutes and we'll be back on our way."

He held his machete and walked through the tall grass to the base of the mango tree, ever vigilant for snakes. He knew the locals wore boots because they were so well concealed that they seemed almost invisible, but he confidently strode forward. The grass ended at the tree line as abruptly as it began on the bank. A bunch of fruits already lay in the leaf litter below the tree, but he saw some low hanging mangos that appeared perfectly ripe hanging from a branch a foot or two from the bole of the tree. He rose up on his toes and tried to cut the branch holding them but missed low by an inch or two. He knew he could reach the branch if he balanced himself so he put his left hand on the tree trunk and swung, cutting the branch and screaming in agony at the same time.

He dropped the machete and grabbed his throbbing left hand by the wrist in his right hand. He watched three or four one inch-long bullet ants dig their mandibles into his palm and the webbing between his thumb and index finger, possibly for the second or third time. He collapsed to the ground, knees first, as the poneratoxin, a neurotoxic peptide, worked its way up his arm. The bugs completed their bite, released their jaws and fell to the ground and scampered away as Elias experienced the initial phase of the widely acknowledged most painful bite in the insect world.

As he endured spasm after uncontrollable spasm on the ground, he recalled from his clandestine internet searches on Beth's computer that the bullet ant bite, according to an authoritative bug bite pain scale he found, would bring waves of progressively excruciating, virtually disabling, pain for the next twenty-four hours. It would not, to his tormented chagrin, kill him, though. He agreed with the so-called experts who said that it felt like being shot as he rolled around in the brown leaves, praying that he didn't experience the double whammy of a snake bite as well. If his jangled memory served, the bullet ant, the tarantula hawk and the warrior wasp were the three most painful bites in the insect world, with the bullet ant being the original member of that infamous club.

Shuddering in abject torture, he managed to click his tongue and the herd, which was only a few meters away, casually meandered over to his nerve jangled body. Unable to get to his feet or use his left hand and sweating profusely, he pulled himself up Nitro's saddle strap with his right hand and threw himself into the saddle, slumped over, knowing exactly why he had been stung. He felt a newfound respect for the indigenous tribe in the Amazon basin that used bullet ant stings willingly administered to thirteen-year old boys to celebrate their passage into manhood. They captured the bullet ants and sewed them into straw mitts with the mandibles pointed forward. During the rite of passage ceremony, the male candidates put the mitts on and received dozens of bites while they sang and chanted to try to endure the pain. "I'd rather stay a child if this is what those kids have to face to become a man."

"I'm sorry, guys," he said to the buffalo in a strained voice. "I put my needs ahead of yours and this is a deserved punishment and the bites are my penance." He gritted his teeth in agony. "My arrogance in putting my needs ahead of yours led to this. From now on I know that attaining harmony requires that I listen to you guys first. You can't walk with God if you put yourself first. This won't happen again. I promise you that I have learned my lesson on that once and for all."

Unperturbed by his distress, the herd moseyed back into the river, casually working their way around the weed beds while Elias quivered in recurrent surges of pain throughout the afternoon and evening. He tried to remain vigilant but found himself fading in and out of consciousness. He had the presence of mind to wrap his right hand in the bridle strap to keep from falling out of the saddle. Searing pain rattled him awake frequently so he could throw up from the agony until nothing but bile could come out, interspersed among several dry heaving wretches. Crocodiles, hearing his heaving and smelling the vomit in the water, approached the herd but the buffalo repeatedly drove them off so they could continue foraging. Oblivious to Elias, the herd knew the feeding was too good to abandon. Sometime, long after darkness, they emerged from the river and came up on the bank. With only his right hand, Elias semi-deliriously managed to undo their saddles and bags and bed them down as a downpour started. Unable to function through the increasingly intense waves of pain, he laid back against Nitro without a tarp and spent the night getting pelted by rain, the discomfort of which served to slightly lessened the throbbing from his hand.

XIV. CONCESSIONS

When the sun came up Elias was on the ground in a mud puddle, shivering in pain despite the high temperature of the ambient air. The buffalo stood around him at varying distances. His hand still hurt but he could function marginally better, not because the pain had abated, but because he had acclimated to the searing torment. He went to the saddle bags and found a bag of granola and ate the whole thing by the handful, shoving the calories down his throat. With his left hand still compromised and spasmodically shaking, he bit the cellophane wrapper open while holding the bag in his right hand. To eat, he pinned the bag against his stomach with his left forearm and scooped the grain mixture into his mouth with his right hand only.

"I appreciate you guys sticking with me through this," he said to the herd. "I was in some pretty tough shape. I'm still pretty messed up now. Then again, most people in the medical community think I'm messed up all the time. I hope you guys don't think that way." They didn't seem to hear him. As a group, they stared out at the river.

"I take it you guys are ready to go. I'll never question that again." He strapped on the saddles and bags using his right hand as much as possible and they entered the river. Due to his delirium from the night prior, Elias did not realize how close they were to the confluence with the Rio Colorado. After a few twists in the river he saw the much larger main stream approaching.

"I assume you guys are ready for this," he said. "You guys are my family. I trust your judgment." He expected the buffalo to get tossed around at the confluence but the water was not as turbulent as it initially appeared. It was definitely deeper and murkier, but the animals handled it without issue. He scanned the shores and the water around him and, because the herd was immersed in water up to their necks, he appeared to be a periscope for them. The villager from up the tributary was right. The crocodiles were noticeably bigger and more aggressive out here. They approached within inches before turning away and looking for an easier meal. Even Nitro looked around a bit more warily, though he still proceeded unscathed in the middle of the river, one hundred meters or more from shore.

A concrete dock appeared in the distance next to a field and the herd began working their way across the current towards it. Elias could not formulate a specific reason why, but he would have preferred to stay away from such an obviously man-made structure. However, the buffalo had gained his unfailing confidence the day before and he did not dissuade them from their course. He watched during the approach and saw a series of buildings and a sign that said "Porto Lindo." The animals went straight to the concrete incline and walked up, likely the first time a water buffalo herd had ever used a boat ramp on the Colorado River. By the time they reached the top of the 15 meter slope a group of residents had already gathered.

Elias had grown tired of the people muttering about him and his sanity in Spanish at every populated stop, thinking that he more than likely did not speak the language based on his appearance. He decided that from here on he would speak first in Spanish so fewer people would feel free to throw jabs at his perceived lunacy that they thought he would not comprehend.

"How are you all?" he said, pointing past them to a grassy area beyond the buildings. "Unless you mind, I'm going to bring the herd out to the field over there to graze. If anyone would like some milk, bring a bucket and I'll milk the herd once they rest a bit. If anyone has some rubbing alcohol or ointment or anything for a bug bite, I'll gladly trade some milk for a bit of it. I got stung by some bullet ants yesterday and would like to disinfect the area. It really hurts." His tactic worked in that he was so fluent that the murmuring insults he usually heard were silenced.

"You are welcome to use the field. I'll see what I have for the bites," a woman said. "My name is Rosie. Please do not go in and out of the river too often with the children around. In fact, please don't do that at all. We don't want them to think for a single second that what you do is safe or right. We've spent our lives teaching them how to respect the river and what is in it while keeping a safe distance from the water. You clearly either do not know or, worse, do not care about those risks and it sets a bad example for the young ones. No one here ever gets stung by bullet ants because we know how to avoid them. Avoiding needless and unnecessary risks does not apparently seem to be one of your strengths."

Still getting recurrent, throbbing, pain from his bites, though significantly less than the first 15 hours that he could barely remember, Elias declined to explain that with God and the world's baddest bovine animal protecting him he felt no fear. "We usually travel at night or whenever the herd says it's time to go. When it's time to go from here, I'll ask them to either leave while the children are in school or to wait until full dark to go to the river so the kids do not see me leave. If the grazing is good here and they are milked it is likely they'll stay here two, maybe three, days. Is that ok? I basically travel whenever the herd shows me it's ready to move on."

"Fine with us," she said, "though I hope you don't actually take advice from your cows. The land out here is owned by the country so you are free to do as you please. Some of my friends upriver called and said we might see you here if you survived your journey. I didn't believe them. Neither did anyone else. We all thought it was some kind of joke or prank. That's why I talked to you about the children."

"I understand why you are concerned and I will tell the children not to go near the river, but I'm really tired and the stings still hurt a lot, so I'm going to set up camp and get some rest. As I said, please give me a few hours for my hand to hurt less and then I can milk the herd. If anyone makes cheese around here, they'll probably want some. Cheesemakers love the fat content of buffalo milk. Oh, and please tell people, especially the children, not to approach or feed the buffalo. There is no risk of injury, but I am their only handler."

"The young ones know better than to approach any animal they do not know. I'll get the interested people in the area to come by for milk," Rosie said. "I'll bring you something for the ant stings in a few minutes. Please wear boots in the field if you have them. We have a lot of fer de lance snakes around here."

Elias starting walking into the grass with his sandals a couple meters behind the buffalo. "I'll be fine as long as I let them lead," he said. "Snakes clear out when they feel the buffalo nearing them." As he finished taking off the herd's bags, Rosie came through the field in her own boots and gave Elias a tube of antibiotic ointment and a bottle of rubbing alcohol. "If this doesn't take down the swelling soon you should go to the clinic up the road. The river water is dirty and you could get an infection if the bites swell too much and bursts the skin apart. Exposed flesh in this humidity gets infected fast."

"Thank you," Elias replied, immediately cleaning the stings with alcohol and applying some antibacterial ointment to the affected areas. It didn't occur to him that he was using a man-made product – a concession to the modern world - to help get the pain to subside and reduce the possibility of a pus-filled abscess. "I'll see how this does over the next day or so. Can I trade some milk for a couple pieces of chicken I can cook and maybe use a little bit for fishing bait?"

"Sure. I'll send it out with the kids when they bring a bucket for milk."

"Much appreciated."

As she walked away, Elias turned to the herd. "Things go a lot smoother and better when I don't try to impose my needs over yours."

He made a fire after cutting some wood, including three six foot poles an inch or so in diameter, with his machete and cooked the chicken that Rosie's children brought him, then he filled buckets and pitchers with milk for several locals. Many of them showed him pictures on their phones of him in the river from social media.

"You're the most famous crazy man that we know," one child of around 10 years old said.

"Am I crazy if I keep doing it and I never seem to get hurt?" he asked in reply.

"If you keep going in the river the way you do, then yes. My dad says it only takes one hungry crocodile to grab you – and there are thousands of crocodiles in the river. We hope you stop."

"As long as I live the right way, I believe I'll be fine," Elias replied, nonplussed by the logic of the children, "but don't any one you ever do what I do. You and your parents don't understand how buffalo behave when they are threatened. Do I have your word that you will never do what I do? Your parents do not want to see you get hurt. They know how dangerous the river can be."

"Yes," they said in unison.

"Good."

Despite more than a few offers to sleep inside at one of the local's houses, he set up his tarp and made a fire where he cooked dinner with the herd milling contentedly around him. He treated the saddles with mink oil and read from his chumash and then studied the topographical maps, not so much concerned about where the trip went day to day but how he could turn it into a big loop. His hand, so bitterly painful only a few hours prior, had subsided enough for him to sleep. He took that as further proof that he needed to let the path go where it would, without his input whenever possible. As darkness fell, the buffalo clustered around him and bedded down, though it was only around 630 pm.

"Thank you for letting me know it's time to sleep," he said to them. He cleaned his work area under the tarp and left the shelter of it to sleep against Nitro as the evening rains began.

He woke before dawn when the herd roused and went to the river to feed and drink. "You guys ready to move on yet?" Watching their meandering as they sought good grazing among the weeds he realized from their body language that they wanted to stay so he went back to the tarp, started a fire with coconut husk and, as it burned down to embers, he returned to the river with his collapsible fishing road, a couple small pieces of chicken, and a few lures. Only a few casts produced a fat guapote so he went back to the fire, tossed in a flat, round, rock he found near the bank to get hot and added some more wood and coals around the perimeter of the stone so it would evenly heat. After scaling and gutting the guapote, a truly odd looking fish with striking colors and a bump over its head, and making sure all of the unused parts burned up in the fire, he sharpened his two machetes with his stone, always honing the blade away from his body. He tested the edges by scraping them lightly against his thumbnail, satisfied only when an impossibly thin layer of nail that he could practically see through peeled up in a translucent curl.

Before he put the fish on the stone to cook, he spat on the rock to make sure it was hot enough to instantly evaporate his saliva. Otherwise, if the rock's temperature was not sufficiently high, the flesh would stick and burn and, as a result, he'd lose some of the precious nutrients. He placed the fish on the rock by holding its tail, and dropping it the way he used to deep fry chicken in oil in his mother's cast iron pan. Then, he waited until it browned on the bottom, lifting the tail with the machete to check its progress. Without a watch or timekeeping of any kind, checking time and again was his only recourse. Once brown, he flipped it over and repeated the process until he knew it was cooked through. Even then, he ate from the back of the fish, cutting off a few inches of meat near the tail and using his machete as a spatula and serving tray. In this way, the thicker section of the fish continued to cook. He ate with his fingers, picking the fish clean and leaving nothing but the naked bones, which he meticulously pitched into the fire to be consumed so no odors would remain to draw in animals.

Not realizing how hungry he was after the trials and tribulations of the ant stings, he ate the entire fish, leaving nothing but the gill plates and bones, then walked to the edge of the jungle with the herd and found a coconut tree and some mangos. He did not touch the trees this time and watched his feet constantly. If he couldn't reach a fruit, then he took that as a sign he should take something closer. Returning to the tarp, he cut up and ate two mangos and half of a coconut, finally satisfied. The sun was fully up just above the tree line and the village was starting to move. A bus boat, 15 meters long and narrow with a shallow draft and covered by marine canvas, sat at the ramp waiting to bring the children of Porto Lindo to school down the river in the village at the Barra Colorado. The boat's width, or beam, was just wide enough to have an aisle and a seat on each side of the aisle against the gunwales. Elias watched the kids come out of the houses in their good school clothes. They waved to him and he responded in kind as they walked down the one road to the ramp.

"Why do you have such a good boat ramp here?" Elias asked Rosie when she came down for some milk. He noted that with the river at a low point, eight men with shovels were working in the muck, facing the shore, and excavating accumulated silt from the front of the dock and ramp and pitching it into the river over their shoulders. Two men with shotguns stood on the dock watching the water behind the men digging zealously. "What are those guys doing? Looks like the two guys with guns are either parole officers or drew the easy job."

"The river is our highway, but a dock is not a natural occurrence so the river and the jungle always want to take it back. Those men are digging up and removing the silt that piles up during high water periods and stops boats from landing. The men with guns are watching for crocodiles, something you do not seem to care about. Two of the guys in the river rotate to sentry duty every half hour or so that no one labors in the heat all day without at least a few breaks."

"This is the last road before the ocean on the Colorado River," she continued. "The ocean is about seventeen kilometers east of here. Anyone who lives beyond here uses this ramp to take the bus back to Cariari or San Jose or wherever. It's about thirty kilometers of gravel before you get to pavement, then another fifteen kilometers to Cariari. San Jose is about a three-hour ride assuming the roads aren't washed out. That happens quite often given the amount of rainfall we get here. Both sides of the road have intermittent steep drop offs, so you have to be careful."

"Why would people want to go back there?" he asked. "You have everything you need here."

"We have everything except good doctors, dentists for the children, clothes for school and other basic necessities," she said with a strong, unmasked tone of sarcasm. "We also like the occasional ice cream. We pack it in dry ice and newspaper and bring it out here for the kids' birthdays. If we could afford to live closer to those things, we would have moved already."

Elias handed her the bucket of milk. "If you didn't eat the ice cream you wouldn't have such a need of the dentist."

"True, but the parents and kids are willing to take the risk to have a nice birthday. Life should be fun, especially for the children. I think the only thing adults owe the world is that the young have a good childhood."

"Agreed," Elias said, contemplating his own childhood.

The buffalo seemed to enjoy the village environs and they showed no signs of being ready to move on, so Elias milked all of the cows and had more than enough takers for every drop of the milk. As he finished, a four-wheel drive SUV pulled down to the end of the road. It stopped in a cloud of dust, which would soon be mud again when the evening rains came.

Elias watched with a bit of surprise as his father got out of the vehicle and immediately came to the edge of the field to get closer to him. He made no effort to return his wave or leave his camp and go to meet him as he was intently building a tripod using lashing knots he'd learned in Scouts to heat water over his fire. He made it from the three poles he'd cut and a length of parachute cord, utilizing a clove hitch to start, a series of wraps and fraps and two half hitches to complete it. With the lashing completed six inches from the top of the three poles, he spread the tripod legs around his fire pit and then hung a length of line from the top to the handle of his aluminum pot and began boiling water. When it became clear that Elias had no intention of crossing the field to him, his dad's driver had to restrain his father by the shoulder and make him put on boots before he stormed across the field to the tarp that served as a kitchen, study and milking center for his son.

"I can't believe I was able to find you, Elias," were the first words out of his mouth. "I don't know why, but I figured you'd at least come greet me after I made the trip all this way. Look at you. You look like a homeless person." Crouched sitting on his haunches and wearing only his shorts and with his beard and hair well on the way to being shaggy, he undeniably looked like an itinerant vagrant. He looked around at the makeshift camp. "I see you remembered most everything I taught you in the Scouts. You know you are still the youngest kid in the troop to earn Eagle Scout."

"Hi, Dad," he said in English. "I don't have need of a mirror so I don't know what I look like. That would be vanity, at least that's what you taught me when I was a boy. That said, I'm far removed from being homeless. I'm more at home than I've ever been, to be perfectly honest about it.

As far as being the youngest Eagle in the troop, you pushed that on me. I wanted to move along with my friends but you kept pushing the ranks on me to get through them. It wasn't about checking the box to say I was an Eagle for me. It was supposed to be about enjoying the camping and the activities with my friends and getting ranks and badges because I wanted to. Instead, you made it a chore like homework or SAT class or riding lessons. Everything always had an ulterior motive. "You have to be the best Elias. You have to try to be first. This will help you get into college. I won't live that way anymore. You can chase everything like it's some kind of vendetta of achievement. I'm not. Anyway, I mistakenly thought you'd be proud of how well my campsite is set up. Not that you care, but I lost a lot of friends who saw I got treated differently all the way through to my Court of Honor. I did all the work and I earned it, but I would have rather earned it along with my friends."

"I could care less about your campsite organization at this point. That part of life ended long ago. Time to get over it. You say you lost some friends, I'm sorry about that. Your mother is losing her mind back at home right now. She's basically paralyzed with fear that you were either dead or about to die. I figured I was coming out here to maybe find your remains, but more likely there would be nothing left when the crocodiles or whatever else lives out here finished with you. You are all over peoples' social media accounts floating around in this river full of crocodiles like a second-rate carnival act. You are making us look like idiots to our friends. The people you grew up with don't even look at us, never mind talk to us. Do you have any idea how risky this whole charade is? The locals all tell me there is virtually no chance of survival." He carefully avoided the term suicidal. He used his phone and took a picture of his son without asking. "I have to text a picture of you to your mother so she knows you're alive. I shouldn't send this because she will be horrified at your appearance."

"I walk with God, Dad," he replied. "I am safe for that reason. I also have the buffalo to protect me from any predators. I don't believe anything in this river will take them on, at least not with any success. To date, they make way for us rather than stand their ground or attack. Predators can't get me unless they get through them first, and that is highly unlikely. I feel bad if your friends look at you differently or don't talk to you anymore. Like I said, that happened to me, too. I guess karma has a way of coming back at you."

"I don't think you have any idea what you are saying. Those animals you have are a snack if a bunch of crocodiles decides to come after them. For whatever fortunate reason, it just hasn't happened yet. You need to come back home and get back on your medicine before something terrible happens. Moreover, you are swimming, not walking, with God. Is God a lifeguard in your delusional world?"

"I just said I am at home, Dad. That poison you had those doctors put in me clouded my vision and now I see the world clearly. I read my chumash daily and I am going to live with my herd along the waterways, trading for what I need. That's all I want."

"You know you need more than that. Don't play games with me. That's why you moved all your money here. You know you can fall back on that whenever you want. It's a complete safety net and you are well aware of that. We found you because I hired a private investigator to find the location of the IP address when you replied to our emails. For days we've followed this godforsaken river getting various reports about you from locals both in person and on their social media. You know full well that's possible. You studied computer science. Answering that email was like asking us to come help you, whether it was a conscious decision or not. Now I'm here. Please, come back with me and let us do that. You're worse off than I thought if you think this behavior is "seeing the world clearly.""

"Like I said, I am home. I'm a citizen of the world now. I'm not going back with you to live locked in a room in a haze of drugs again. Contrary to what you've convinced yourself to believe, if I thought for a instant you'd actually try to find me I wouldn't have answered that email at all. Whether you accept that or not is your choice, something I never had until recently. You are welcome to stay here until the buffalo are ready to move, which I expect to be tonight or tomorrow. I move with them when they are ready to go, which historically occurs after dark. I'm sure you can find a place in the village to stay the night. You need to be aware that I will leave as soon as the animals tell me it's time to go, and that could happen at any time and without notice. In fact, that is what usually happens. If you see the need to follow me in a boat, please stay far enough away from the herd so that you don't ram them and hurt them. They can fight off or discourage hungry crocodiles. They can't fight off a steel or aluminum propeller."

"You're going to walk in that river with these buffalo in the middle of the night?" he asked incredulously. "And you think the buffalo will tell you when it's time to do that? What is going on in your head?"

"I do it night after night, Dad. God and the water buffalo protect me."

"God isn't in that river, Elias. Crocodile and bull sharks are. Sooner or later you'll be next on the menu."

"I sincerely doubt that, Dad. God is everywhere. I am perfectly safe out there. Even if I were to get attacked by an animal in the river, that would be a better fate than living half-dead on symbycerol. I'm going to have lunch soon. I plan to catch a fish and pick some guava and carambola in the jungle. They seem to grow wild here. I think they aren't indigenous plants to Costa Roca, but they continued to thrive and spread after the old fruit plantations shut down."

"Oh God, you're not going in the jungle, too, are you? What the hell is wrong with you. Everything in there can kill you. You have more money than anyone could possibly need to live a comfortable life. Please just buy your food like everyone else. Even the villagers here buy their food at the store. You might be eating tainted fruit or vegetables and not even know it. Worse, the insects here can be deadly. Your mother is terrified you'll be torn to pieces by crocodiles or a jaguar. My guide said it's more likely you'll die alone in the jungle from a disease you get from mosquitos than by snake bite. Do you even have repellent?"

"No, I don't have commercially made bug repellent. Once in a while I find some Costa Rican mint and that works to repel bugs at least as well as deet. Moreover, I spend a lot of each day in the jungle looking for food and staying with the herd. I've had no major problems. Do you want to eat with me or not?"

"I can't eat what you are eating. I'll be sick for a week. My guide said your system has to adjust for a bit to the local food. I find it hard to believe that you aren't convulsively puking and crapping constantly now. That river is polluted. That's not just silt. Don't you see all the trash floating down on the current from the city? It's a giant raw sewage line. Swallowing a drop of that will give you cholera or giardia or some other crazy as yet unnamed and unknown shit. I will sit out here with you, though, if that's OK."

"Suit yourself," Elias replied and he went about his business. At least now he understood why he experienced rampant diarrhea for the first week or so out here. In the beginning, he thought the water filter wasn't working but he followed the instructions religiously and boiled the water after he filtered it. Fortunately, the lower intestinal disaster had abated recently as relieving himself in the saddle while half submerged was awkward at best. He stood on the bull's back and basically shit on him to preclude an all too personal attack from the infamous candiru catfish.

"Look, buddy," he said to the bull at the time. "I'd happily tread water beside you and relieve myself, but you know how the candiru locates its food? It swims around scenting the water for uric acid and swims full bore right at that chemical. Usually, it's in the gills of a passing fish and the candiru latches on and sucks some blood out of the host's tissue. I know everyone says it's urban legend, and maybe it is, but since I'm pissing out uric acid, that skinny little three-inch fish with retractable, backward facing fins is going to do what God intended it to do. Namely, follow the uric acid and wiggle into my urethra and lodge itself in my dick and stick its fins out so it can't be removed. You have to get a surgeon to hack it out. Needless to say, I'm more worried about the candiru than I am about any predator in the river. The doctors said I'm suicidal and I disagree. That said, suffering the fate of the candiru easily eclipses suicide."

Snapping back into the present, he watched his father's

driver bring a folding chair and several bottles of water out for him. His dad sat under the tarp in the shade of the sweltering heat, his head mostly in his hands as he begged his son to return to the United State throughout the day, all to no avail.

"Everything we've done has been for you, Elias. You are our only child and we don't know what else to do."

"You've done more than enough as far as I'm concerned. Why not just enjoy the evening until I leave?"

His father fell silent in reply.

As twilight approached, the herd, as predicted, gathered down at the water and looked back at Elias.

"Time for me to go," Elias said to his father, who openly began sobbing. He ignored his father and packed everything up into the dry bags and placed them in the saddle bags.

"Are you going to make me sit here helplessly and watch you wade out there to your death?"

"I'm truly sorry you do not have faith and confidence in me, Dad, but the herd is saying it's time to go. They make the decisions and I help them. Beyond which, I'm not making you do anything, which is a far cry from what you did to me. You can watch or you can leave. The choice is yours. Helpless describes my situation the last few years until now." He put all of the buffalo's saddles and bags on the animals and fastened all the straps that held his gear in the saddle bags.

"I wish I could say it was good to see you, Dad, but it isn't. You refuse to accept that I am following God's design and that you knowingly tried to keep me from doing that in that forsaken hospital. Instead, you let people who didn't even know me lash me to a bed and poison my mind."

"You tried to kill yourself, Elias! Just like you are trying to kill yourself now. Why do you think you were on those medications? We had no choice. The airline you worked for here wanted to have you arrested and prosecuted for deceiving them about your condition. They didn't send the police after you because we said you were mentally incapacitated without your medicine. Beth, for some unfathomable reason, still thinks you are a wonderful person but knows you are compromised and need help. If you don't care about yourself, come back to keep your mother from dying of hysteria. For the love of God, please come with me!" he cried as he carefully followed his son to the river, picking his way around clumps of grass. The herd was already milling about in the current next to the ramp and Elias didn't even slow down when he got to the end of the bank. He waded out to Nitro and climbed in the saddle.

"You are asking to die," his father plead again from fifteen feet away from the water's cloudy edge. Even his love for his son could not overcome his fear and draw him closer.

"Actually, no, I'm not. It's quite the opposite, really. I'm begging to live." He patted the bull between his shoulders and clicked his tongue. "Ok, buddy, let's go wherever you want." Nitro began moving out into the deeper water until the bottom dropped out from under him and he began swimming. Elias turned back to his inconsolable father. "Tell Mom I said hello and that I continue to pray for the strength to forgive both of you for what you did to me. I still don't have that strength. I'm really not sure I ever will. Please don't follow me. I know I said earlier that you could rent a boat and do that, but I really don't want you around if you plan to complain and whine constantly about what other people might think. I'm way past caring about what others think. There is no way I'm going back with you to the United States – or anywhere else for that matter. I'm home here. Stay safe heading back to the city. The people here say that road you drove in on can be treacherous and has frequent washouts. Be careful." He turned back forward to face the unknown stretch of river and gradually disappeared into the night.

XV. THE DANGER ZONE

Usually, Elias saw a man-made structure or two along the banks or slightly hidden, recessed in the foliage, every kilometer or so. All civilization, however, seemed to be on hiatus once he left Porto Lindo. The rains held off on this evening and the water flowed without so much as a ripple, except those created by the herd. His father, the self-appointed scoutmaster, had taught the troop that if you don't use a flashlight as it gets dark you can actually see extremely well at night, particularly on a moonlit night like this one. "Wouldn't he be proud to see me using that lesson?" he said with derision.

Changing tone to a more cathartic voice, he spoke to the herd. "Serene out here tonight, don't you think, guys? Obviously we're going to do whatever you want, but I think it might be nice to head out to the coast and then turn south along the seashore. The old fruit companies dug canals that run parallel to the beach so they're will be plenty of water and forage for all of you. Since those companies planted lots of fruit trees that are supposedly still growing out there I'll be able to get what I need as well." He did not receive an answer so he took their silence as a tacit agreement.

After an unknown amount of time, he began to see tarpon rolling as they migrated up the river to Lake Nicaragua, where locals said they spawned.

"Looks like the crocodiles and bull sharks will have their fill tonight of something other than buffalo," he said, knowing that most of the tarpon would make it through to breed. "You know, guys, the guides at the tarpon lodge down by the ocean told me those fish aren't necessarily rolling to evade predators, though that would help them escape, I think. Tarpon can breathe air so they roll to gulp oxygen and keep on their journey west. It's over 100 miles upstream to Lake Nicaragua. What do you all think of that? It's pretty amazing to me. They've been doing that for tens of millions of years, and the crocodiles have been trying to catch them for just as long. It's a giant balancing act between predator and prey. You guys are a total unknown to them. No way they expect something your size and strength to swim amongst them with such impunity."

As usual, the buffalo heard his words but didn't answer him. They seemed perfectly at ease and moved from the current to the shallows to feed and then back out to the deeper water several times. In one spot against the bank Nitro found some very tasty weeds in about seven feet of water. Unable to reach them standing, he dove down and filled his mouth before coming up for air, repeating the process two or three dozen times in succession. Elias struggled to hold his breath long enough each time even though his head was the last thing to go underwater. To stay attached to the bull he took a last second gulp of air and laid forward in the saddle and reached his arms as far as he could around Nitro's prodigious neck.

He knew they had been out afloat for a significant amount of time from the stars' changed positions when the herd found a sand bar – perhaps a small island - in the middle of the river. The bull led them up on the loose, granular, surface.

"You want to stop here for a bit?" Elias asked. "Fine with me." He knew the river could rise and fall rapidly but there had been no unusual amount of rain locally, just the normal torrents, so he took the saddles off and they bedded down on the sand. He figured that, in a pinch, if flood waters came surging down from the central valley he could flip the saddle and bags on Nitro alone and ride him bareback to the shore. The animals bedded down in an unusually compact circle and Elias took his accustomed position against Nitro in the center of it.

He woke with the first movements from the bull. The pre-dawn sun glowed slightly in the east. Nitro shifted his prodigious bulk but did not get up. Elias stood in the circle of still sleeping buffalo and surveyed his surroundings. He gazed over to the shoreline on both banks and noted the river was at least a kilometer wide, even taking into account the width of the now apparent island. He looked around immediately outside the circle of buffalo and realized adult crocodiles littered the sand, the closest about fifty feet away. He counted fourteen of them inside his limited field of view. Likely, many more were invisible to him and patrolled under the surface near the shore. The shortest appeared to be about two and one half meters and the longest was about five meters.

"I guess I get why we slept in such a compressed group last night now," he said without a hint of concern. "I thought everyone got cold and huddled up." He noted that though Nitro was still laying down, he was wide awake and fidgeting restlessly. "Good to see you stayed on duty, my friend," he said. With fishing for breakfast out of the question, he went to Dolly's saddle bag and got a bag of granola, munching on it methodically until the animals all decided to rise. Usually, they got to their feet one by one, but today, given the proximity of the reptiles, they rose in near unison with Cassie the first to her feet. Elias thought it looked as if they'd moved in a premeditated manner.

"What's on the agenda today?" he asked them as he put the empty wrapper back in Dolly's saddle bag. Nitro, the last to stand, glanced at him as he rolled to his feet from his side and then promptly proceeded to stomp around the area, kicking up sand and mock charging the crocodiles one by one with his head lowered and the business end of his horns ready for action until they all scampered and slid into the water, even the largest ones ultimately reluctantly conceding the ground to this gigantic, and clearly unimpressed, bovine.

Elias waited with the cows for Nitro to return to them. When he did the bull immediately looked to the shore on the south side of the river. "Time to move to the mainland, now? No problem. Let me put the gear on." Elias found himself not scared, but fascinated by the thought of where the crocodiles went. Were they just off shore, hiding an inch below the dirty surface water, or were they still swimming a half mile away? Either way, the herd was moving to the shore. He mounted Nitro and the herd stepped into the water.

Almost as soon as the bottom fell out beneath him and the bull began swimming, the surface in front of them exploded as multiple crocodiles lunged at him, two of them fortunately only locked on each side of his back curled horns. They likely expected to drag him under to subdue and drown him, not comprehending that this animal swam as powerfully as any predominantly land-based animal can, could dive for a significant period of time to graze on the river bed and also possessed the buoyancy of a Styrofoam float. Elias watched unafraid, altogether fascinated, as the crocodiles futilely yanked downward repeatedly and attempted a death roll, but did not succeed in even making the bull's neck bend in the slightest degree.

After a slightly delayed reaction at what he likely perceived as the insolence of the reptiles, Nitro bellowed angrily and shook them off and gored one as it slid over his horns, tossing the nine foot animal over Elias' head like flipping a coin, its blood spattering down on him. It landed on top of Dolly and she added insult to injury by goring it a second time and, equally effortlessly, heaving it airborne again. With the bull stretching almost three meters from nose to rump, Elias easily leaned back in the saddle, a good five feet away from the confrontation. Without excitement or emotion, he observed the action unfold, curious how it would end. The twice gored reptile thrashed weakly in its death throes up against the shore. Elias looked back and saw that it was ripped wide open across a third of the width of its abdomen. Its entrails bulged out of its thoracic cavity. The other crocodile appeared to have its lower jaw broken or dislocated, probably self-inflicted when the death roll failed to budge the bull and all of the torque ended up exerted on the animal's own jaw instead of its intended prey. Any others of their reptilian brethren lurking beneath the water looking for a meal did not elect to further the attack.

"Bad mistake on their part, Nitro. The local animals have no idea what they're dealing with when you guys come along. I'll bet word gets around fast in the crocodile community. That little display should clear the way for you and everyone else in the herd." Whatever the reason, the crocodiles all kept a respectful distance thereafter.

A greater threat presented itself when all of the morning fishermen and commuters from the Barra Colorado came out on the river and formed a small flotilla around him, crowding the animals.

"That's the guy we've been hearing about," one called out to a friend. "Supposedly, he's come all the way from San Jose by swimming in the river with these beasts."

"Luck only lasts so long," came the reply. "He better get out of the river at the airport or he'll get swept into the ocean and some of the sharks out there are bigger than his herd. If they don't get him the offshore currents will."

"Luck is when you survive for a day," the first man called back. "This guy has reportedly been doing this out here for weeks, maybe months. That's something else entirely beyond luck. Luck happens once or twice, not every day for a month. I have no idea what to call this. Hey, buddy," he called to Elias. "If you can do it, please get out at the airport."

Elias looked around and realized he had come all the way to the Tarpon King Lodge. Its dock stood out as the highest structure in the area. The fields around the runway just past the lodge at the airport served as a pasture for livestock, a playground for the children and an adult meeting place for all of the local residents.

"We'll see if the buffalo want to get out there," he called back. "I just ride and they go where they please."

"You better hope they "please" to go to the airport or you're in trouble soon."

"That's all I keep hearing," Elias replied.

"You're beyond being the luckiest man in the world, or maybe these animals are something special for you to still be alive."

"Luck has nothing to do with it. I walk with God."

"Whatever. I hope you get out at the airport." The man pulled out his cell phone and began videoing the spectacle. Like everyone else, he figured sooner or later someone would film this guy getting dismembered and eaten.

Nitro drifted past the lodge with the boats and a number of crocodiles in tow, all moving apace with the herd. As he turned the slight bend and saw the huge airport clearing and extensive grazing opportunities, he turned to starboard and made a beeline straight for it.

"That animal has a lot more common sense than you," the first guy called out. "I just have to talk with you once you're ashore to find out why you're doing this. There's an army of crocodiles on the shoreline where you will land so be careful."

"The crocodiles are not my biggest concern," Elias said. "With a few exceptions, they usually know better than to get too close. It's the propellers on your boats that bother me. Crocodiles typically have enough common sense to learn to stay away from the buffalo. Propellers can maim or kill my animals and men are in charge of them." He recalled what the farmer said a few days prior. "Common sense is anything but common in most men. Unlike the crocodiles and sharks, that scares me."

Though he knew this shoreline fairly well from his trips to the lodge, he let Nitro pick his landing location, which turned out to be in the shade of the trees at the eastern side of the opening. Usually, they touched ground in places with only a few hundred square meters of grass. Here, there were a few square kilometers of grass spread out around the runway. The builders had cleared hundreds of meters in all directions from the tarmac. The villagers extended that area by building their homes against the runway clearing. As long as his herd could amicably share the expansive area with the local animals, Elias figured they could spend several days here if needed.

With everyone in the boats behind him, there was no one on the shore to greet him. The herd found purchase on the muddy bottom and walked up the slope towards the field. A few feet before the grass, while they were still on packed dirt, they all froze in place, staring at one spot in the greenery a couple meters ahead. Elias knew what that meant from his eco-tour with Mario.

"I guess there's finally something that you guys actually need me for. Hold still. I'll take care of this. Everybody relax." He removed his machete from its clip and got off the bull slowly, checking the ground as he touched the brown soil in his sandaled feet. He looked to verify where the buffalo were staring and then moved to the demarcation line of dirt and grass, parting the long stems with his machete tip until he found a fer de lance coiled and seemingly at rest.

"Sorry, my friend," he said, and quickly swung the machete and chopped the animal in half. He knew from his reading that this type of snake would attack as soon as it became aware of his presence so he wasted no time dispensing it. He regretted killing it so inefficiently while it bled out. On the eco-tour, Mario chopped the head nearly off and death was virtually instant. The two halves of this animal, once well over a meter long, writhed about, the head still every bit as dangerous as it was when the snake was fully alive. Elias waited for it to settle down a bit as its life ebbed away and then pinned it to the ground just behind the head with the machete blade. Satisfied that the business end of the snake was immobile, he pressed down and severed the head, thankful that he spent a lot of time honing the edge on the blade as it passed through the unresisting spine of the snake. He went back to Nitro and got his other machete and, using that to hold the head still, opened the jaws and severed the fangs with his first machete.

"Not the most skilled way to do it, but well done, nonetheless," said the man from the first boat. "Always try to get as close to the head as you can so the animal can't strike even when it's lopped in half. I watched you from the bow of my boat on shore before coming over. I would have helped but you seemed to have it well under control. I'm Mateo."

"I'm Elias," he replied. "Is this field open to anyone with a herd? Can my buffalo graze here, assuming they get along with the other animals?"

"Anyone can use it. Like everything in the Barra, this is government land and the residents all take advantage of it. No one owns it so no one can throw you off legally. We're so far away from the central government no one back in San Jose really cares what we do. What few police we have are dedicated entirely to stopping drug trafficking, not some guy in the river with a herd of animals. If anyone gives you shit tell them to go see Mateo. I'll clear it up for you."

"I like the sound of that," Elias replied as he carefully picked up the snake remains and tossed them in the river. An alligator gar came up and swallowed the three pieces in seconds. "Is there a spot where I can set up my tarp and build a fire ring?"

"Sure, anywhere along the inside of the chain link fence perimeter is fine."

"That would be great."

"Hey, not to change the subject, but do you know anything about one freshly dead crocodile we found washed up against the dock of the village on the north side of the river and another maimed one that we shot this morning to put it out of its misery? Both of them were quite large – one over three meters and the other over four meters."

"They might be the ones that attacked my bull early this morning when we started traveling. They bit his head and he gored one in the guts really badly and broke the jaw of the other one."

"Those are the ones. You're saying this one animal did that?"

"Yes," Elias said impassively. "They grabbed his horns right after he started swimming this morning and he protected himself and the herd. He threw one over his head and one of the cows gored it a second time, but the major damage was already done." He walked over to Nitro to check his horns. "See, they scratched his horns a little bit right here. You ok, pal?" he asked the bull. Mateo took his cell phone from his pocket and clicked a picture of the barely detectable scratch.

"That's nothing. You can barely see it. That's all they did? Usually, they crush the bones when they bite. Were you in the saddle when that happened? By the way, these are not cows, are they? I've never seen such huge animals. I wondered how they swim so well but seeing their hooves I get it now."

"Of course I was in the saddle. I always travel with the herd. These are water buffalo. The bull weighs close to 1200 kilos and he's still growing. The cows are all 700 kilos or more. As you can see, they all have horns and are quite formidable when threatened."

"You suffered no injury? By the way, your cows weigh far more than our bulls. Your bull is something out of a circus. I did not realize how big their horns were until I saw you walking next to them."

"No. The crocodiles never got near me. They'd have to go through Nitro under me and the cows all around me, which is altogether a very remote possibility. The buffalo swim packed together like a school of bait fish as you saw this morning. One of the cows stunned or killed a crocodile further upstream and the bull dispatched one that attacked Elly on the riverside. She could have handled it alone, but he got overzealous and crushed it pretty much into pulp. My animals are normal size and temperament for their breed. Why are you so interested?"

"I'm 58 years old. I have lived here my whole life. No one ever goes in the water here because the risks are so great. The crocodiles probably take five or six people a year along with many cows and an occasional horse. They may take more people than that because some folks simply disappear without a trace. My cousin sixty kilometers up the river said a loco American was floating down the river with six buffalo. I, and everyone else around here for that matter, thought it was a joke and didn't believe it. You're like a mythical figure, a story we could tell our children and grandchildren. I figured the pictures and videos that I've seen on social media were photo shopped. Now, I'm dumbfounded, but I believe."

"I guess truth is stranger than fiction. Please humor me with one correction. I lived in the United States for most of my life, but I consider myself a citizen of the world. It's still early, so I'm going to set up and milk the herd. You want some milk? If your phone has internet access and I can use it for twenty minutes, I'll give you a big bucket of milk."

"I make cheese so that would be appreciated. "I'll get a bucket and come back in about an hour. You can use my phone then. Also, crocodiles are protected but we can butcher up the one the bull killed and the one we euthanized. I guess technically you could say he killed them both. We did that animal a mercy. How about if I bring you some backstrap or some tail meat from it for dinner? You can grill it up on a spit over your fire. It's the best meat you'll ever eat. Slice it thin and cook it through so it's dry and you'll be a crocodile meat convert for sure."

"Much appreciated. Sounds good." While they spoke, a crowd of fifty or so local residents had gathered around the animals.

Mateo looked at Elias a bit more closely. "Aren't you the pilot that brought guests out here to the lodge for a short while? Alejandro said you left the airline but no one knew why. At first I couldn't tell with the long hair and beard, but I recognize your voice. I'm one of the guides at the lodge. I used to meet you at the plane to pick up and drop off guests and their luggage. We must have crossed paths thirty times easily. I complemented you on how fluent you are in Spanish the first time we met."

"I'm sorry," Elias said truthfully, "but I can hardly remember most of my life before I entered the river in San Jose. I remember this place, but not a lot more. I don't consider myself overly spiritual, but it seemed like a new beginning of sorts.

Now, I focus only on caring for my herd and continuing my journey."

Mateo didn't answer immediately because he knew for sure he'd had multiple interactions with this man. Everyone up and down the river said there was something distinctly wrong with this guy. He now formed the same opinion from his first-hand encounter.

"Well, think about it. Maybe you'll be able to remember later once you've been here for a few hours."

"OK. Hey, when you leave, please ask your neighbors to respect the animals and keep their distance. I am their only handler. It has to stay that way. I have to maintain their confidence in me without interference so they look to me for guidance when needed. If anyone wants milk and has nothing to trade, I'll give away what they produce to families in need when I can if you let me know who they are."

"I will," Mateo said. He told the people to stay back as he went to get the bucket. To make sure they understood, he also told them that the bull killed and maimed two adult crocodiles at the same time. "Any animal that can do that is just as deadly as the crocodiles, even if they don't eat meat," he told them.

XVI. LOCAL WONDER

Before setting up camp at the river end of the runway, Elias closely monitored the behavior of the herd. He hoped they would be satisfied to stay here for 3-4 days so he could go through everything in his bags and replenish any items he needed to continue his journey. Fortunately, they seemed completely at ease in this, the largest expanse of grass they had seen since they left the ranch. He noted that they totally disregarded the local Brahma cows and bulls, which appeared to be reciprocal indifference on their behalf. They looked like puppies next to the water buffalo, so Nitro likely felt no need to assert his dominance as he would have with his own kind.

Satisfied, he walked back to his bags, stacked against the chain link fence that encircled the entire runway and grounds. Mateo stood waiting for him with a metal handled, white bucket.

"So, this is where you will set up?" he asked.

"Yes, it's near the water and the field, so the herd can drink and eat with little effort and I can watch them easily."

"Well thought out, my friend. You realize you've traveled by floating and drifting and swimming all the way from San Jose to here in what might be one of the most dangerous waterways in the world?"

"I don't look at it that way."

"Can I ask how you do look at it?"

"Sure. My ancient ancestors were pastoral nomads in the Middle East, following the waterways around their region and selling and trading meat, hides and milk with villages and settlements that they met along the way. That's what I plan to do. The herd guides me and I follow them. I make suggestions to them so that we keep close to waterways and generally stay on the route I'd like to follow, but they seem to innately know where the water flows. I don't see any danger in what I'm doing as long as I stay with them and they stay with me."

"Did you knowingly guide them into the tributary that brought you in to the Colorado River?"

"No. On the first day I brought them to the water's edge and they decided to get in and start swimming. I climbed into the saddle and they moved until it was time to bed down. After that, some days they'd travel an hour. Other days they'd go eighteen or twenty hours just floating along with the current and eating vegetation in the shallows or growing on sand bars. Sometimes they travel at night and other times in the day. Most of the time, they seem to prefer moving in the night, maybe because it's cooler."

"Did these nomads herd water buffalo?"

"No, they had goats and sheep and some cows."

"So their animals couldn't simply disregard, stomp, gore or overpower the Nile crocodiles they came across."

"Probably not."

"Well, you certainly have an advantage over them, thank God. That's probably why you chose them, I guess, and probably why you are still alive."

"Again, I never thought about it that way. I just walk with God and let Him send me where He wants."

"Well, keep trying to do it as safely as you can. If not for the safety they provide, then you must have picked these water buffalo for some other good reason. If you didn't specifically select them for their abilities, then random chance gave you animals that even adult crocodiles in this river would mostly rather avoid than attack. Nothing except the lottery is blind chance in this world. I'd say you knew full well the attributes of these buffalo long before you got in the river with them." He reached in his pocket and got his phone.

"You want to use this now?"

"I'd appreciate it. Thank you." Elias took the phone and first checked the balance in his bank account, making sure he didn't save the password on the device. The high seven figure balance was still there and untouched. He then deleted his browser history and went in and checked his email. After sifting through and deleting the inevitable spam he had one email from Beth and one from his mother.

The one from his mother was nothing more than a rehash of the visit with his father and how she felt he was heading towards a violent death. He skimmed through it, replied that he was fine and deleted it.

Beth's correspondence contained a more thought out and personal note.

"Elias: I wasn't sure where you went and, at first, I didn't care because you lied to me repeatedly. That hurt more than you'll ever know. With a bit of time, I now realize your behavior is out of your control even more than is normal for the average person – whatever that means. I also owe you an apology for not telling you I knew everything about your condition from your parents before we ever came to Costa Rica. They told me to keep it quiet until you decided to share it with me. I guess you never felt comfortable enough to do it, but I kept hoping because I really liked you. They are incredibly controlling people. In some ways I understand why you've taken such a rash course.

None of us really know where we are going or what we are doing, so we try to create frameworks where we think we do have a bit of foresight. After your parents told me how your father found you on the river a few days ago I searched in my browser for buffalo floating guy and found many pictures and videos of you making your way down the river. In a very visceral way, I'm terrified for you. In another way, however misguided you may be, I see that you have taken control of your daily life in a way most people would never even consider risking. I don't want to restart a relationship with you even if you come back as I believe – in fact I know - you need extensive help. Your medications – whether you are on the right ones or not - and constant monitoring are critical to your well-being and ability to cope with the day to day world the rest of us live in.

With that said, I pray daily for your safety and I will drop an occasional line to see how you are. Write me if you wish. Call me if you want. Please try to stay safe. Beth."

He re-read the email. Beth's comment about Elias controlling his own life made it seem that she was markedly closer to understanding him but still lacked the insight needed to verbalize his purpose. Using his grimy thumbs, he deftly tapped out a brief reply. "Beth: I left the contradictions and problems of the daily world of man behind me. They are shallow and meaningless. My parents want nothing but to control me. The pettiness of man's day-to-day world is in my rearview mirror, to analogize to the car you wanted. I walk with God now. I'll write once in a while if I can and may call if the opportunity arises. I hope you find happiness and I am truly sorry for causing you anger. That was wrong of me. Elias."

Again, after he logged out of his email he deleted his browser history and handed the phone back to Mateo.

"Much appreciated, Mateo. Thank you. Let's get you some milk."

"Before we do I want to suggest that after you set up your camp with necessities that you store your bags and the rest of your gear in one of the lodge staff's houses. People will steal from you if you leave your bags on the ground out here."

"You really think so?"

"I know it." He pointed at the house closest to Elias' equipment, less than fifteen meters away. "Luis lives there. He is the mechanic for the lodge. Put your bags on his porch and no one will touch them. Luis has a reputation for swift justice when crossed. That tends to keep bad people away. Here, I'll help you." Leaving just the items he was using, they brought the saddle bags and Nitro's saddle under the porch.

"I should have thought of that before the animals landed here," Elias said as they finished the fourth, and final, trip. "Most men can't be trusted. The worst kind are the ones who deceive themselves into thinking they are somehow doing good against someone else's wishes."

He started a fire with his magnifying glass and while it burned to coals, he used his machete to make a spit from a branch for the crocodile meat Mateo brought him. Once that was all set up and the crocodile meat slow roasted while suspended above the embers, he filled Mateo's bucket with milk from Abby and Cassie. He tasted the milk and nodded his approval to Elias.

"This is incredibly rich. It's almost pure fat. I'll bring you some cheese tomorrow if you are still here."

"I expect I will be for as many as three or four days. The herd seems satisfied here and has unlimited food and water."

"Sounds good." He pointed at some women approaching with buckets and bowls and pitchers. "As you can see I did what you asked and sent some people who could use some milk over."

"Great. Please tell them I'd appreciate it if they'd bring me some dried coconut husk to use for lighting fires when they come back tomorrow."

"Will do," Mateo said. "Tonight, a few of the men in the village would like to meet you and hear about your journey. Can we sit by the fire with you for a while?"

"That's fine. I bed down with the animals when they sleep, which should be shortly after dark."

"You mean you go to bed when they do?"

"No, I actually sleep with them so that I am always available to them."

"You sleep on the ground with them?"

"Actually, I sleep with my back against the bull."

"All I can say to that is "wow." I'll be back with the guys around five."

"I'll be waiting."

With most of the day ahead of him and the herd inside the chain link fence enclosing several square kilometers, Elias went through his usual routine of treating the leather, this time at Luis' house, then retrieved some driftwood from the riverside for his fire and put some water through his filter and stored that in its accompanying two-liter bottle. He sat under his tarp and read his chumash and ate the crocodile meat, which turned out to be incredibly good tasting. Each time he took some off the spit to eat he'd immediately add more to cook. While the meat popped and crackled over the fire he also picked some fruit from trees lining the outside of the chain link. He thought the two kilos of meat Mateo gave him would be too much but he ate every bit of it during the course of the day. Much of it turned out to be water weight that cooked off in the thin slices, leaving the meat with an almost jerky-like texture.

"I'll bet this animal never thought it would wind up at this end of the food chain," he said as he licked his fingers clean after the last piece.

Throughout the afternoon he kept a watchful eye on people, especially the children, as they neared his herd.

"Please do not touch or feed them," became his mantra. "They always need to know that I am the source of their food and well-being so that they respond to me if and when needed."

Crestfallen, the children would walk away. Elias regarded them as kindly and innocent, but also as a nuisance to his purpose.

Mateo returned promptly at five with seven other men from the village. All worked as guides at the lodge. They brought folding chairs and some rum and Mateo, not having a guest at the lodge that day, made some cheese in the afternoon and brought it with him. After setting up around the fire, conversation began in earnest.

"The guys told me you floated through the river to get here," the eldest guide, Javier, said, more in the tone of a question than a statement.

"I did."

"Did you see a stretch where the river narrowed and the tarpon kept rolling?"

"Yes, we slept on a sand bar right before the end of it."

"That sand bar has more big crocodiles than any other place in this river. They always lie in wait there when the river is low so they can catch the tarpon as they cruise upstream to Lake Nicaragua. We call that area the bananas, but it really is a gauntlet for the tarpon. The river splits into three branches that flow for two or three kilometers and then they rejoin into one once more. If you look at it from above it looks like a bunch of bananas, thus the name. It's extremely dangerous because it creates a perfect ambush spot for the crocodiles. Maybe they were full of tarpon and chose not to bother you."

"Makes sense. There were a lot of them all around us when I woke up this morning. They were everywhere."

"What did you do?"

"Nothing. The bull thought they were too close and drove them all off. A few of them didn't go far enough away and he killed them when they bit his horns as we swam off the island."

"Mateo said that. I honestly didn't believe it. Did he drag them out of the water and kill them on land?"

"No. we had just started swimming and when they latched on to his horns he shook his head and gored one and unwittingly broke the jaw of another one. I'll never know for sure, but I think when it tried to roll, Nitro didn't budge and so all that force went into its jaw and caused it to snap. He threw the one he gored right over me, probably two meters over my head."

Javier thought about that.

"Where were you when this happened?" asked Leo.

"In the saddle on the bull," he said matter-of-factly to their stoically unchanging faces. Elias pulled out his topographical maps and spread them on the ground in front of him as the men sat wondering if they should run away or get this crazy man committed.

"You could give me $500 to wade out to my waist and back to shore in this river and I would say no," another guide, Gael, said. "It's an absolute certainty that you'd get taken and eaten."

"Guys, I need to get down into Panama – or as close to it as I can - and then go to the west coast and circle back up to where

I started in San Jose. Can you look at these maps and help me by showing me waterways I can travel in or near?"

"You want to stay in the water and make a circle for hundreds of kilometers in crocodile infested waters? Why?"

"This is how I live. I travel the waterways with my herd and trade for what I need as I go."

"You know," Hugo said. The crocodiles aren't the only risk out there. I assume you know about the bugs and snakes and sharks and jaguars, but there are also pirates and drug dealers and plain old bad people along the waterways and they have camps hidden in the jungle. The jungle may not be comfortable, but it is a great place to hide if you don't want to be found. They are heavily armed and have no mercy or tolerance for lone people trespassing in their areas. You need to avoid them as well."

"People are always the biggest challenge, but I do what I can," Elias said. "The worst thing that happened so far is when the bullet ants stung me. That transpired because I made the herd leave the water before it wanted to. I'll never force them to change action again. That was a lesson that came with consequences. I spent the night puking while riding in the river. Not to change the topic, but this cheese is wonderful, Mateo."

"It's because of that buffalo milk you gave me. It's the best base imaginable. I'll get more for you tomorrow if you would like it."

"Absolutely. I don't mean to seem greedy, but please bring me a bit more crocodile meat if you have it as well. Bring your bucket and I'll get you more milk."

"No problem."

As he spoke, Javier had been perusing the maps. The guides were accustomed to crazy Americans, so, even though in their estimation this guy was completely off his rocker, they just went with it. They knew there was no negotiating with crazy. They found that truism cut across all cultures and nationalities.

"Look here," he said to Elias while pointing at the map in

the gathering twilight. "These canals run parallel to the ocean through Limon almost all the way to Panama. I can show you a trail through the jungle to get to them. You could take the Sixaola and Terraba rivers back to the west coast. It would take a while as you'd be fighting the current, but these are both slow moving rivers and easily navigable for your animals. Once you got to the west coast, you could then work your way north and start again at the San Juan. I wouldn't recommend it, but then again, I wouldn't recommend what you've done so far, either. What you shouldn't do is float to the mouth and go south walking on the beach. With the currents at the mouth even these beasts could get washed out to sea. Beyond which, I doubt they drink salt water."

Elias watched as Javier traced the route and compared it to the scale of centimeters to kilometers.

"That would work," he said. "I need it to take 4-6 months so I could make 2-3 circuits a year."

"You're going to do this again?" Hugo asked.

"Oh yes," Elias replied. "I plan to live a nomadic existence and move from place to place doing exactly what I'm doing here."

"Sounds risky," Javier said again, "but I never would have thought you'd make it here so maybe I'm wrong. No offense, but I'd never do it."

"Seems to be going just fine," Elias commented. The herd had approached lethargically in the darkness as the group talked and the guides sipped rum, from which Elias abstained. The animals acted logy, gorged on forage from the field and the river weeds.

"Time for me to hit the sack," Elias said. "Feel free to stop by tomorrow night if you want."

"We will. Is it ok if we bring a few guests from the lodge as well? Not surprisingly, everyone keeps asking about you," Mateo said.

"I don't mind as long as they don't try to touch the animals. See you tomorrow." He walked over to the herd as the guides watched and clicked his tongue. He petted Nitro's muzzle and pushed down on top of his snout. Responding immediately, the bull laid down and the cows followed suit, forming a circle with their horns facing out. Elias walked between them to the inside of the circle and reclined against the bull's immense back, completely obscured from the guides' view by his bulk.

"I have no idea what to say about this," Javier said as he and Mateo walked down the runway to their homes. "The guy seems completely harmless, almost like a child. He's naïve as hell. Someone has to look out for him. We know who around here would try to rob or hurt him once he is back in the jungle. It's bad enough that he'll be dealing with the wildlife without any training or experience. He learns as he goes, which is a recipe for disaster. I'm going to let those people know that if they, or any of their friends, go near Elias we'll give them a warm reception when they get back to the Barra."

XVII. LOOKS CAN BE DECEIVING

The rains deluged in the central valley where San Jose sat and the resulting water poured out into the flat land via the San Juan and then the Colorado rivers during the night. Elias woke before dawn and saw that the water had risen and covered all the way up to the area enclosed by the fence. Yesterday's dry ground was under a foot of water. The bulldozers and backhoes that raised the land for the supposedly once military runway made the area into a temporary, artificial, island. The rest of the land at sea level around them was immersed in water that ranged from shin to knee deep.

"It's different world than yesterday," Elias said to the herd as they happily began foraging in the water, able to both eat and drink at the same time. He knew now why all the houses were either built on pilings or up close to the runway, which appeared to be the prime real estate. "Looks like you guys are ok with it, though." He made a fire and read his Aramaic verses by its light as the sun rose.

"Hey, here's the cheese and meat you asked for," Mateo said as the guides walked by in their boots to go to work. They wore boots and carried their sneakers or sandals in their hands. "This water will recede during the day as the rains in the valley stopped yesterday afternoon according to the weather report. By nightfall, everything should look as it did yesterday. If you have boots, consider wearing them as the snakes will come up on the runway rather than be eaten by the gar, sharks and crocodiles."

"I'll be ok with these," Elias said, pointing at his feet as he sat in his sandals.

"Suit yourself, my friend," Mateo replied. "It has, against all odds, worked for you thus far. We'll see you tonight with a few guests. You know, today's waters will recede quickly, but this is only the first major rain of the season. The next storms will bring waters that do not completely abate for a couple of months. Take that into account when you leave."

"Thank you, Mateo. You and the guides have been a great source of guidance. Most people kind of ignore me when I ask for information."

"That's because most people can't imagine what to say to someone doing what you are planning. I see Americans all the time and this is loco to me, too. The further you go along without incident, the more acceptance you gain for your method. No one will ever imitate it, but you make it appear more and more possible with each passing day."

By the time he cooked the meat and had breakfast the flood waters had already receded to almost normal levels. "The water flow out the river mouth must be tremendous," he thought as he finished the block of soft cheese. "I think Javier is right about using the canals."

He took his chumash down to the river bank near the landing dock and sat on a rock ten meters or so from the rapidly moving water. Yesterday's lazy current was nothing but a memory compared to today's rapidly swirling eddies and mini whirlpools and vortexes. While he read, residents suffering from various maladies began trickling down to sit on the benches near the dock. Some were tethered to oxygen tanks that they dragged through the grass on little wheels. Others appeared to have AV fistulas and ports on their forearms, likely for dialysis. A few had toe or foot amputations. The wheezing sound of emphysema came from a few folks determinedly chain smoking. Also sprinkled among the group were folks with vision impairments. They wore the dark, boxy sunglasses that

Elias thought appeared characteristic of post-cataract surgery, though he assumed they may also have been victims of diabetic vision loss. A couple of men and women had the jaundiced, yellowy complexion of unchecked alcoholism, which explained the altogether too common empty rum bottles he saw floating in the river.

"What's going on here?" he asked the nearest person to him.

"The hospital boat comes here three or four times a week to take care of things the local clinic can't handle," the woman replied. She looked around at the group. "If there is an emergency we also have a high speed ambulance boat for situations requiring immediate response. We have a lot of sick people here, more than a population this small should have. Some of these people have diabetes and need dialysis or wound care. I have high blood pressure and cholesterol and need medication for that. The men you see in the glasses mostly all work as guides for sport fishermen out in the sun all day, resulting in cataracts. All these young kids – really everyone in the village - needs dental work because of the sweets they eat. There's just a whole bunch of medical issues that we can't handle here without outside assistance."

"Has it always been this way?"

"Not when I was young. Back then no one came out here and so no one had access to cigarettes, soda or candy or the things that cause these problems. Once we had them everyone wanted them – but no one seemed to perceive the value of a toothbrush, floss, mouthwash, tooth paste or, more importantly, moderation. We went overboard and now a lot of us have one health issue or another."

The hospital boat, the largest vessel by far Elias had seen since he first entered the river, came into view while they talked. It was really more of a giant tri-hull pontoon boat with about a 17-meter length and a 7-meter beam. The pontoons allowed it to move around even in shallow water. It was powered by three enormous 400 horsepower outboards rather than an inboard diesel so the space on board could care for more patients. The outboards also gave the craft a shallower draft so it could operate in the dry season when the river was low. Perhaps most impressive, it had a lower and upper floor.

"You know, if you cut all that man-made stuff out, you guys would mostly be healthy again. If you never had it before your bodies weren't able to gradually adjust so it's like eating and drinking poison. Processed white sugar just isn't good for anyone, especially if you've never had it in large quantities before."

"It's pretty addictive stuff, though. At this point, most people can't give it up even if they try. Cigarettes are significantly worse. People get emphysema treatments then walk off the boat and light up right on the dock."

"You know what a lot of Americans call cigarettes?"

"No. What do they call them?"

"Coffin nails," Elias replied.

"That's certainly appropriate," she said.

"How does everyone pay for all these treatments?"

"We are all under the national health system, so it's free."

Elias did not bother telling her that the free Costa Rican health care system cost him a job that he loved. He turned and checked his herd visually and then watched as the walking, rolling and limping wounded boarded the vessel now moored to the dock. He counted thirty-two people. Not one had a snake bite or animal wound or other jungle-related trauma. The locals knew how to deal with those perils so they were as extinct here as polio. Every single person he saw had a self-inflicted malady.

"Everyone keeps telling me that the snakes and crocodiles are the biggest risks out here," he said to himself when the last of them had boarded. "It seems that man is the biggest risk to himself no matter where he is. The danger wildlife poses out here is a distant second to greed. Making money by getting people hooked on these insidious products is much worse. It's actually evil because the profiteers know what they are doing and persist even when they know what is happening. I'm starting to hope the herd decides to move on soon. There's a dark side to every bit of light here in this place."

Nitro and the cows whiled away the morning grazing until Elias milked them. Then, they found a deep patch of mud in the shallows on the river bank and immersed themselves, wallowing in it to stay cool and bug free. Elias watched them bury themselves right up to their necks and lay there, eyes closed and seemingly asleep in the rank smelling mire. Nitro always positioned himself so that he remained between the cows and the river, shifting easily around in the black sludge whenever the cows moved so that any predator would have to go through him to get to the other animals. After about two hours of that the herd wandered further into the river to rinse off and then came ashore to start eating again along the runway.

"Aren't you worried about the crocodiles attacking them in the mud or the shallows? They can't escape from the mud if they do," one of the local men said to him while they were still in the mud.

"I'm no more worried about that than the buffalo seem to be," Elias replied. "Look there," he said to the man. "You can see a couple of crocodiles hanging around a little way offshore. Don't be misled. They aren't out there waiting for an opportunity to attack the herd. You might think that, but you should not. If they wanted to they could have tried an assault or an ambush at any time. They're patiently waiting for the buffalo to leave so they can move back in safely. Buffalo move through mud the way we move through air. Believe me. Those crocodiles know full well they are overmatched." The local shook his head and left.

Mateo came by at lunch and picked his bucket of milk up from Luis' icebox. As part of his compensation, the lodge gave him a cooler to keep at home and let him fill it with ice from the lodge ice-making machines.

"I have a couple hours while the guests eat lunch and rest before the afternoon fishing from 2-5pm. I'll get another batch of cheese started today so you can have some tomorrow. How's the herd doing?"

"Well," Elias replied. "I suspect they'll be itching to move on tomorrow night. This is the longest they've stayed anywhere."

"Well, we'll be back for dinner and have a few guests with us. We'd offer to have you at the lodge if you want to come, but I assume you wouldn't want to leave the herd that long."

"You're right. I need to always be with or near them so I'll make sure I have a fire going."

"We'll try to bring you dinner."

"OK. See you then."

He gathered some more wood for the evening fire and then walked beside the runway with the herd. He checked Nitro again for wounds he may have missed after the crocodile attack, but thankfully found none. He also checked all of the other cows to see if they had been bitten or injured in the water but they were all free of both wounds and ticks. Elly's bite wounds were all but gone. The extensive wallowing had freed all of the parasitic insects from their hides. He noted that the whole herd appeared to have gained significant weight and strength since they left San Jose. Constant movement agreed with their constitution. When they went to the river to drink he caught a catfish using a tiny piece of crocodile meat for bait and cooked it for a slightly late lunch.

"Imagine that, using crocodile to catch catfish!" he said aloud. "Now that's a reversal of roles if ever there was one."

Later that afternoon he went to the local store, also located against the runway on the higher ground on the opposite side of the asphalt from his camp.

"You have any granola?" he asked the clerk.

"Next aisle over on the shelf near the freezer." Elias walked over past the old unit, its compressor laboriously chugging and struggling mightily to deal with the heat and humidity of the jungle while it maintained the ice cream supply in something approaching a solid form. "People are paying for this stuff, which couldn't even be here without this electric monstrosity, and then getting diabetes and high blood pressure and heart disease," was all he could think. "Weren't they all better off without this? They should be required to put a skull and cross bones on these products the way they do with cigarettes." Without reading the labels to check for added sugar, he scooped up all of the granola they had and brought it to the counter.

"How about fishing gear?" he asked. "I need some lures and hooks and line for fishing in the river, lagoons and canals. What would you recommend?"

The clerk, a young man Elias estimated to be about twenty, looked up from his phone, his thumbs moving a mile a minute. He already had the start of a significant pot belly and his arms looked like light brown wood putty and had no definition.

"No idea. I haven't fished since the last time my father made me go when I was ten years old. All our fishing equipment is on that wall," he replied, pointing at the side of the store to his left. "You can buy whatever you want."

"Are you originally from here?" Elias asked.

"Yes, I was born here and have been here my whole life."

"But you say you have no idea what to use fishing in these waters? I thought a lot of people here made their living fishing."

"They do. Hey, my dad and my uncles are all fishermen and farmers. I'm going to school to get out of here and move to San Jose and get a life and a desk or office job that doesn't break my back. I don't want to be out here fishing and growing carrots and squash when I'm thirty or forty or fifty."

Looking at him and thinking of the condition of the people on the hospital boat Elias thought, "Given your appearance you'll be lucky to make thirty, forty or fifty." Instead, he said aloud. "Fishing and farming are great lives and keep you close to God and nature. It's also great exercise. Those aren't the worst things in the world."

The young man gave Elias a sullen look of superiority. "Hey, I'm not taking advice from a crazy man floating down the river with a bunch of cows and saying God is protecting him."

"Hard for me to dispute that kind of logic. I can't blame you for that," Elias replied, knowing full well that he, of all people, had no business acting as a life coach for anyone under any circumstances. He walked over to the fishing display and bought packages of steel leaders, line, hooks and some surface poppers, jigs and spoon lures he'd seen people casting from the banks at various times. He brought them all back and put them on the counter.

"Where do you keep the toothpaste and brushes?"

This time the clerk didn't even look up. He pointed to the second shelf in the middle aisle of the three aisle store. Elias followed his finger and retrieved 4 tubes of fluoride toothpaste, four toothbrushes and all the floss they had.

"Last things, do you have sunscreen or medical kits? A guy upriver warned me that I'd burn up in this sun and I should have listened to him."

"We don't carry medical kits and the sunscreen is all gone. It sells out to the guides at the lodge the second we get any here. How are you going to pay for all this?" the clerk asked, noting that this scraggly patron wore only shorts and sandals and had no pockets or bag of any kind that might hold money.

Knowing exactly how Costa Rica and its economic and tax systems worked, Elias replied. "I assume you have a state ID and account numbers and a bank registered account to accept payment."

"Yeah."

"OK, what's the total and let me use your phone to log in and send you a wire. You'll need to give me the bank details."

"You know how to do that?"

"Certainly I do. Why wouldn't I? What's the total?" he replied, holding out his hand for the phone.

"Are you paying in cash or colones?"

"I have sub-accounts in both US and Costa Rican currencies. Let's use dollars if you can accept US currency. It's easier for me and I don't have access to the exchange rate at the time. I assume you charge a premium on that anyway."

"We do. The total is $207.88."

"Fine." He took the phone and exited the young man's video game, paid the bill by wire using the bank information the clerk provided on an index card and then deleted his history.

"Check your account," he said.

The clerk skeptically did so. "You're all set," he said with an instantaneous, newfound, respect for this apparent madman after he checked the balance. Though he moved a bit clumsily due to the amount of items, Elias swept everything up off the counter in his arms and left the store to pack everything away in his saddle bags. With each passing hour, he realized it was getting closer and closer to the time to leave this place. He wouldn't press them but he hoped the buffalo would draw the same conclusion.

"You want any help moving all that stuff," the clerk called after him with a now unchecked eagerness to assist.

"Nope. I'm all set on my own. I'd rather drop something or make two trips than take help from someone who thought I was deranged until they discovered that I had a few bucks. Thank you anyway."

He used the rest of the afternoon to treat his saddles with oil yet again, noting that he only had enough for two or three more applications before he needed to order more. He thought he might ask Mateo if he could have it shipped out here to his house and he'd get it the next time he rotated through. Around 430, Javier and the guides returned to the village to change.

We're just going to let the guests clean up and then we'll be over for dinner," Mateo said.

"Great, Mateo," Elias replied. "Hey, Javier, can you show me where the trail to the canals starts? I think you said it's close and I'm pretty sure we'll be leaving tomorrow night. If it's convenient and has forage, I'll show it to them and see if they'll take that route to the canals rather than going out to the ocean and walking the beach until we hit the nearest canal. The water was screaming down the river this morning."

"Of course," Javier said. By far the oldest of the guides, he appeared to be about seventy. He, like Elias, only wore sandals. "Come with me."

He led Elias around the fence and into the tall grass and walked, purposefully, towards a spot in the jungle that looked like any other. He never once looked like he stared down at his feet while he walked through the half meter tall grass.

"Everyone else here is in boots and screams at me that I'm going to die from a snake bite. I see you wear sandals like me. From what I saw when the hospital boat landed this morning, candy, cigarettes and rum take more lives than the animals. Are you worried about snakes?"

"Nope. I've lived here my entire life. Sure, there are snakes, but they make way if they hear you coming and as long as you watch your step just a bit you should be fine. I see them all the time and I've never been bitten yet. I saw a few walking here with you. I assumed you saw them?"

"No."

"You are young. Your eyes should be better – or at least better acclimated to being out here. Maybe you haven't lived out here long enough yet. Inexperience can be dangerous out here. You need much more practice." He pulled up some weeds with his left hand and gave them to Elias. "This is Costa Rican mint. Remember what it looks like. You can rub it on your skin and it will repel biting insects and mosquitos."

"I actually knew that, but I didn't see the plant, either," he replied, remembering he'd seen that reference on an internet search and picked it a few times on his journey already. He always found it growing alone and never would have recognized it in a cluster of differing vegetation the way Javier did.

At the end of the field, they reached what looked like any other part of the green, homogeneous, jungle. Javier walked around a copse of palms sticking a bit further out from the line of demarcation between the grass and jungle and pointed to a two-meter wide path, completely closed in under the canopy of the jungle. Though it was still light in the field the path was almost shrouded in darkness, vegetation making it look like a tunnel with deep green walls.

"This runs about 3 kilometers to the biggest man-made canal, which flows 43 kilometers in a straight line to Tortugero in the south. The path has no turns or branches off it. Just walk to the end until you hit water and the canal flows very slowly in the direction you want to go. There are very few open fields on the canal banks and they are all small. You should take advantage of them when you see them. Also, the rainy season is about to start in earnest. Virtually this entire region turns into a swampy marsh in a couple days and it lasts for a week or two at a time. Whenever you can take advantage of any high ground to rest, do so. You will find precious little of that between here and Tortugero once it starts pouring. When you first come on to higher, dry ground you must straight away check for snakes, crocodiles and other predators. With so little dry space, all the animals will be vying for it. You get it?"

"I do. Perfect. Thank you."

"Your animals are enormous, so the bull will likely lead and maybe you can get the cows to walk in pairs behind him, but it might be single file. I know nothing about water buffalo so that's up to you. I can't stress enough that once the flood waters come up you need to ride your bull constantly. Crocodiles almost always attack underwater and they will be on this path once it is submerged. They have a valve in the back of their throats to keep water out when they open their jaws under water. If you are sloshing through thirty-centimeter deep water next to the bull on what was dry path the day before, the crocodiles lying flat on the bottom will grab your legs under water and kill you. You're sure they won't make a try at your buffalo? They have attacked numerous cattle around here. You may have noticed we keep most of our animals on the islands in the river. The water and the predators create a natural corral and our animals rarely approach the water. The crocodiles reciprocate by rarely going on land where the cattle could injure them."

"I'm pretty sure. They'll be fine. Do you know if the path is cleared and roughly this wide all the way to the canal? That's important because I don't want to have to turn around and come back."

"So you say. We guides are starting to think you may seem crazy, but you are also far more shrewd and savvy than we originally gave you credit for. At night it is important that you stay on the path so you don't get lost. Once the path floods I repeat, you must ride the bull for your own safety. The jungle is dense and the path is the only clear area, so that should not be a problem. Unlike the other people you've talked to, I grew up without cell phones and internet and any of those things. I don't carry one even now. I spent my entire childhood in this jungle. It really is my home. I do not agree with what you're doing. Even with those beasts you have, it seems far too dangerous for someone like you whose eyes don't yet see everything they should. However, the way you are doing it appears to work. Just don't ask me to join you. To answer your question, the path is clear. I walked it a week ago to meet my nephew at the canal and go to Tortugero in his boat."

"That's a reasonable request. I won't ask you to join me." They walked back down to the river to wait for the other guides to return with the guests. Elias vainly tried to spot wildlife all the way back.

"Were there any snakes on the way back? Did I miss those, too?" he asked as they approached the dock.

"Of course not, we walked the same track back as we used to get out there. Didn't you notice we went over the same trampled grass? Anything that was there got disturbed and has since moved. Over time, if you survive and stick with this plan of yours, you'll learn. I had the luxury of a father to teach me. You seem to learn from trial and error. Errors out here can be costly." They both stood, watching the river and waiting for the guides and guests.

"What can I do about the sun? I'm getting burned up."

"Don't pretend to be stupid. Wear some clothes other than your shorts, young man. You need to observe the people around you. Don't you see all of us guides wearing long sleeve shirts, hats, and sunglasses? You need to get some clothes and a pair of heavily tinted glasses. I'll see if the guests who are visiting here tonight will give me a couple shirts to bring to you tomorrow."

"Thank you," Elias said appreciatively.

"Look out there," Javier said, pointing out at the river. "See that iguana moving, being swept along by the current and trying to get to shore?"

It took a few seconds, but Elias spotted the lizard, its head bobbing along, fighting desperately and futilely to get to shore against the current.

"I do."

"That iguana swims extremely well. If the current were the same as it was two days ago it would get to shore in a minute, but the current here fluctuates wildly. The ocean is less than two miles away and the shore is only a hundred meters away for that lizard. It will not make it to shore before it is taken out to sea, where something will eat it. The same will happen to you and your buffalo. That's why I happily showed you the path. Please use that method to get to the canal, regardless of what your buffalo think, especially since you have decided to leave when the heaviest rains start."

"I see your reasoning and I will. That's why I asked you to show me."

"Thank you."

XVIII. DINNER AND A DIAGNOSIS

"So you're the drifter, literally, that the guides and staff have been telling us about while we fish? You are a local legend. I'm Jerry." He and two friends had arrived in the Barra five days ago on an eight-day fishing excursion.

They watched as Elias pulled his fish off his grilling rock and ate it from the machete blade while he squatted near the fire. His beard now completely obscured his jaw and face as he sat.

"They haven't said that directly to me, but I am drifting predominantly. Hey, do any of you have a cell phone I can check my email on? It'll only take a minute."

"Sure," Jerry said and handed him his phone. Elias logged in and had only one short email from his father. "We know you saw your mother's last message because it had a read receipt – much like this one will. I'm answering because she is too heartbroken from your failure to reply. Please come home before you force me send people after you to get you with, or against, your will. If you don't think I'll go to that extreme, try me. Dad." Elias deleted the email and his browser history and handed the phone back.

"Much appreciated."

"No problem. We brought you some food from the lodge if you'd like it."

"Let's see what you have," Elias said somewhat skeptically, almost suspiciously. Jerry handed him a cellophane covered plate of grilled fish and vegetables. He uncovered it and looked to see what the options were and immediately smelled cooking oil.

"I'm sorry guys. Please don't be offended, but I can't eat this. I don't eat unnatural oils and try to stay away from genetically enhanced foods. I can smell that the fish was fried in one of those spray oils and these carrots and these squashes look like hybrid forms due the brightness of their color so I'd rather stick with what I have. Anyway, the locals gave me a bunch of crocodile meat from the animals my bull killed and I ate that this morning and afternoon. I never knew how delicious crocodile meat could be."

"No problem and no offense taken," Jerry said, happily extending his hands to take the plate back. "I always have room for more and don't share the same dietary restrictions you have." He noted Elias' vocabulary was quite strong and figured he had gone to at least undergraduate college.

"The guides said you told them you are living a nomadic lifestyle with the waterways as your travel routes. You must see some amazing sights that most people don't get to witness in their lifetimes. Anything stick out in your mind?"

"One late afternoon, several days ago, a mother jaguar and her cubs swam across a very narrow channel in front of us, moving from the east to the west. They were utterly silent, almost like watching an eerie dream. As I watched I actually had to convince myself it wasn't a dream. Even the cubs moved like apparitions. People who say they are alert have no idea how soundlessly these animals can move. They could sit next to you in the grass and you would not know they were there.

A day or two later before I entered what the guides call the bananas on the Colorado river, I saw a massive dark shape almost as big as one of the cows passing under the water in front of my bull while he stood shoulder deep in a lagoon and eating water vegetation. I had no idea what it was but the herd didn't care at all, so I assumed all was well. A few moments later a manatee and its calf surfaced for air, so close to me that I could see its whiskers dripping water. It stared at us for a brief second and went back to eating. I think it was sharing the same vegetation as the herd. I found that to be an extraordinarily communal experience."

"This week the confluence where the river meets the ocean has been too rough to traverse to get out a few times, so we fished upriver in the narrowest part of the bananas two days ago," Trent said. "With the water low, the channel probably only spanned fifty feet. Mateo anchored upstream and we drifted flies and lures into the river where it was deepest and narrowest, but even then it was only a few feet to the bottom. We caught a bunch of tarpon but Mateo had to release the anchor and drift with the fish on the line so the crocodiles didn't tear them off the hook. The tarpon had nowhere to go but up in that water because it's so shallow so the resulting acrobatics and aerials were awesome. We don't like gaffing the fish and we prefer if they unhook them in the water and release them. That said, in that stretch of water the guides have to lip gaff them to protect themselves from the crocodiles that follow the fish to the boat. Did you drift right through there?"

"I'm not sure if I went through that one of the three bananas, but I drifted through one of them at night with no moon so I never saw any of the crocodiles until the next morning. You guys seem to have traveled a lot. Where else in the world have you fished and hunted?"

"I forgot about the moon phase," Trent said. "We always plan these trips on or around the new moon because if it's a full moon and a cloudless sky the tarpon can look up through the water column and eat the sardines and ribbonfish they see above them. Then, when we go out in the morning the fish are stuffed and the bite won't start until the afternoon, if it starts at all."

"In the last 20 years we've been all over the world sport fishing and hunting," he continued. "We've been to Africa on safari many times and to New Zealand, Iceland and Alaska for salmon fishing. We also hunt and fish regularly all through Central and South America – dove hunting in Argentina, trout fishing in Patagonia, and peacock bass in Panama. We do two trips annually to Costa Rica – one for marlin on the Pacific and one for tarpon over here. Last year we went to the Congo in the summer to catch giant tiger fish. The hippos in the Zambesi river were three times the size of your bull and they literally attacked the crocodiles when they got too close to the calves. The hierarchy in the water there clearly put the hippos at the top of the heap unless an elephant came along. Never saw or heard of anything like that until we met you today. The crocodiles here aren't as big and haven't seen water buffalo so I assume that's why they unsuccessfully went after them."

"Maybe. I don't know. We've had very little physical interaction with them given how much time we're in the river. One of the cows responded to an attack a while ago and Nitro fought off a couple the other day like you said, but usually they stay away."

"Predators don't like to risk getting hurt unless the reward is great," Jerry said, while Elias pulled open a bag of granola and began munching.

The third guy in the group, Raymond, sat, listening and sipping his bourbon from an ornate, silver, pocket flask.

"I did a lot of moving around after high school and a stint in the Army," he said. "I never knew what direction I needed to go in. I kept sticking my thumb out on the road and going to the next town until I worked as a sheet metal guy and then decided to start my own HVAC company. Through a lot of hard work and some incredible good luck, now I just travel around and hunt and fish with these guys. I suspect I never lost that deep-rooted wanderlust. What has you doing this?"

"I was living with my girlfriend in San Jose after we moved here from New York. She dumped me right after I lost my job as a pilot. I bought these guys and some equipment then followed them into the river right after that."

Jerry had just finished eating the dinner they had brought for Elias.

"She must have been some girl to drive you to this!"

"Actually, I said that wrong. Our separation occurred mutually at the same time, but that isn't why I'm doing this. Until recently, against my will, I had been taking some antipsychotic medications. I forgot to take them one morning and felt so much better that I never took them again. They obscured my view of the world and made me operate in a near anesthetized haze. I'm thinking much more clearly since I got off them. In fact, I'm doing better every day."

"A lot of people might think what you're doing is anything but the act of a well-adjusted person," Jerry said.

"You know," Trent said, "sometimes they prescribe those things for a reason. Do you mind if I ask you what you were taking?" Trent, a practicing psychologist, suspected something was wrong but hadn't been able to figure it out.

"Symbycerol," Elias replied.

"That's pretty strong stuff," Trent replied, not betraying his profession. I had a friend on that. Don't they usually start you on lesser drugs and move you on to symbycerol if the others don't work?"

"Yeah. They gave me all kinds of stuff before they got to this one. It's all poison. They say they can analyze and change you but all they want to do is restrain you from what you want to do."

"What is it you want to do?"

"I want to live off the land in the same tradition of pastoral nomadism as my ancestors. I grew up in the modern world and I don't like it or the things it does to people. Earlier, I went to the store and the kid at the counter said he grew up here and didn't even know how to fish! He did, however, appear to have extremely flexible thumbs and a very high score on a video game he played constantly on his phone. These waterways and the jungle provide everything I need and I can trade with people for anything else that comes up. I live a simplistic life. I don't own or carry a phone. I have no daily schedule other than what the herd dictates. I eat when I'm hungry and sleep when I'm tired. I don't have a watch, either. I figure if it's dark it's night and if it's light it's daytime. I care for the herd and they look after me and none of us have an agenda."

"You seem to have a lot of modern advantages that your ancestral nomad cultural ancestors did not have," Trent continued. "I see you have a flint striker, granola, machetes, and some of the finest leather saddles and dry bags I've ever seen. These nomads also did not have water buffalo. They had sheep and cows and goats. You may be trying to emulate the nomads, but you have every advantage, particularly in that your animals are almost without threat here. They are, for all intents and purposes, the apex animal. Is that seeming contradiction by intent? It's like you want people to think you live on the edge but you know how to judiciously hedge your bets with these incredible beasts. I sincerely mean this. I applaud your planning."

"Thank you," Elias said.

"You said you were a pilot," Trent said. "How did you lose that job? If you can navigate out here I'd think you'd be invaluable on the amount of manual flying I've seen done here by all of the small plane pilots."

"That's what I thought, too," he replied, for the first time starting to get a bit agitated at the mention of his prior job. "When they found out that I took symbycerol they fired me on the spot. They probably thought I was too incapacitated to fly while I took it, but I stopped it long before I got that job. I would never put people at risk. I might have been the best pilot they had."

"Elias, I want to thank you for having us over," Trent said, doing what he could to immediately get off the job topic. "Whether you want to believe it or not, I think what you're doing is incredible. If it's your path, so be it. Please keep safe to the degree you can. It's getting pretty dark and we don't want to walk through the grass to the boat with no light in the sky. I can't read the newspaper without my glasses, never mind see my feet!" He extended his hand and Elias shook his and the other men's hands.

Javier and Mateo hung back for a few minutes as the other guides escorted the fishermen back to the dock.

"Elias," Javier said. "The weather the next few days is going to be really bad in terms of rain. If you leave during the storms you can call me and I'll get you out to the start of the path."

"Much appreciated, Javier. I think the herd is about ready to get going. Tomorrow I'll go out there and scout the start one more time carefully so I should be fine."

"I made you some hard cheese that will last a few days if you keep it wrapped," Mateo said. "I will drop it to you at lunch or after work tomorrow. I have a bit of crocodile meat left so I'll give you that for breakfast when I go to work. Your buffalo cheese sold in the village for top dollar so I think that's fair."

"Very kind of you," Elias said. "I'm going to the herd now. Nitro is already laying down and I want him to know I'm there before he goes to sleep." He left them and wandered into the dark away from the fire.

"My first impression was that the guy is pretty much completely unhinged," Trent said on the bow of the lodge pontoon boat as it chugged upstream to the lodge dock. "Symbycerol is used to treat schizophrenic, suicidal people who don't respond to conventional treatments. Did you notice how he only seemed to get excited when we asked about his motivations and the loss of his job? The attacks from the animals and floating in the middle of the river with predators everywhere was just a normal part of the day for him."

"Unlike you pretty boys with college educations, I served six years in the Army," Raymond said. "You guys know the acronym PACE?" Trent and Jerry shook their heads in a negative fashion. "It stands for Primary, Alternate, Contingent and Emergency plans. Any time you run a maneuver in the military you need to adhere to PACE principles. My take here is that Elias' primary plan was to live in New York with his family and have a good life. His alternate plan was to be medicated and live at home in New York. His contingent plan involved moving to Costa Rica and starting a new life without his parents, who seem unwilling to let him live at all without keeping him under their thumbs. When all three of those plans abjectly failed, he went to the emergency plan of abandoning everyone and everything and getting on the river. No one tells him what to do out here, though I dare say he'll be lucky to survive," Raymond said. "Until something bad happens, he's finally as free as a person can be – the master of his own destiny."

"Very astute, Raymond," said Trent. "His chances of survival remain the fascinating part of this for me. If he's truly suicidal, and I am not convinced that he is, he wouldn't have animals that can potentially protect him. He'd push the existential envelope in some other way. Don't get me wrong, medically speaking, the guy is soft as a sneaker full of puppy shit. I wouldn't do what he's doing on a bet. But he is definitely mitigating his risk the way he is operating. Did you hear him speak? He's educated and likely well off. Merely getting into a program with symbycerol is extremely expensive. Most patients on that drug are rich people who private pay since, as a general rule, insurance does not cover this type of treatment. If I had to guess, this whole nomad business is a cover story to keep him far away from anyone trying to get him medicated again. It's all a construct to rationalize his behavior and justify it. He likely isn't religious at all despite having his bible by his side. He's not suicidal, but he appears to be fatalistic about getting to live life on his own terms. He'd rather die than be controlled again.

In the US I could have the police pick him up as a threat to himself or others and have him involuntarily committed if I felt the need to do so. Here, he appears to be a free man."

"Sounds like you're both fascinated and disturbed by him," Raymond replied.

"That guy is the case study of a life time. I can't believe I came here to fish for tarpon in the jungle and found the potential holy grail of psychosis sitting next to a runway under a tarp. Like you said, he is not in Costa Rica by coincidence. He planned, perhaps subliminally, to come here and do something extreme so that he could run away from the people he perceives are chasing him. Patients like him with paranoia often think an undefined "they" are out to get them. Again, think about his gear and the quality. He didn't just up and go. He planned this. Guaranteed, his girlfriend and the people around him likely had no idea what he was formulating in his head because he acted normal as a defense mechanism until it came time to disappear. No doubt he knew the airline would find out about his medication and he had alternate plan bravo well in place before that happened. Jerry, if you have your tablet charged, look up this guy on social media when we get back. Guaranteed, you'll find bits and pieces of a back story. No way he found those animals on a street corner. Someone sold them to him and trained him on how to work in partnership with them. He did not get up in the morning and do this unprepared."

While Elias slept in a gentle rain with the herd, Jerry, Raymond and Trent reclined in cushioned chairs in the lodge bar, each with a scotch and a $75 Cuban cigar, and researched "water buffalo guy in the Colorado river" on the search engine of Jerry's tablet. Hundreds of hits emerged including pictures, observations of people who had seen him, and more than a few videos.

"Click on that one with the rancher," Raymond said as he pointed at the screen. "It says in the description that he claims he sold him the herd and that Elias' parents made the video."

Given the low bandwidth at the lodge, it took a few interminable minutes for the video to load, but soon they saw Leonardo on screen, shifting from side to side in his rubber boots and talking uncomfortably to the camera about Elias. An inset screen had an interpreter providing a simultaneous English interpretation.

"The guy showed up here and said he wanted to buy some buffalo. I laughed at first and then gave him a ridiculous price. He looked like a bum and I figured it would make him go away, but my father taught me to take every opportunity, regardless of how outlandish it might seem, seriously. My thought was that $30,000.00 US would do that, but he showed up the next day with the money, in cash no less. He paid thousands more for saddles and rented a pasture where only his herd could graze. I try to be an honest businessman so I gave him the absolute best animals I had and the best products I could to make amends for the obscenely high price. Then, over a month or two, he started sleeping out there in the field with them a few nights a week. I should have known something was amiss then, but that much money has a tendency to blind you."

Leonardo paused while he stared forward and listened to a question from an unseen interviewer.

"Well, I taught him to ride and how to call them and get them to rely on him for food and grazing. I showed him how to hitch them to harnesses for carts or pulling. Not in a million years did I ever know what he planned to do. How could anyone ever guess he'd go into the river with the herd? One afternoon he showed up with a bunch of gear and a ranch hand helped him bring his saddle and bags out to their field. One of my employees made the saddle and saddle bags. Like I said, he spent the night with them in the field often, so no one suspected he had a different objective that night. We figured he wanted to put all the saddles and bags on them and see how they all looked. When we went out to check him the next morning, his bull, five cows, him and all his stuff were nowhere to be found. The only place he could have gone was the river, which we told him time and time again was too dangerous to even stand near." He looked away from the camera for a second. "He never did take us seriously about that, looking back in retrospect."

After another pause and presumably, a further question, Leonardo spoke again through the interpreter.

"Look, water buffalo are the strongest thing in this country and they are not indigenous to Costa Rica. It's not like Africa where there are possibly things bigger or stronger than them hunting them down as food. Even there, lions won't go after an adult male. The African version of the water buffalo is the Cape Buffalo, which isn't as big but is much nastier. The biggest jaguar or a giant crocodile from here might have a distant chance against the water buffalo one on one, but head to head, if the buffalo is not injured, old or sick it will likely win and kill or cripple its attacker in the process.

They possess great stamina and can swim all day and the bull might weigh 1400 kilos all grown up. His horns will spread 1.7 meters or more and they are rock-solid and sharp at the point. Nothing here in Costa Rica would willingly attack six of them together unless starvation sets in. The greatest challenge an adult buffalo bull faces here occurs when I forget to close the gates and two males fight for dominance and the right to breed with the cows in the herd. I've seen them casually trample crocodiles or gore them to death at the river's edge and effortlessly pull themselves out of mud up to their necks that any other bovine would sink and drown in. They practically play in quicksand to cool off.

Despite everything that I've related about their abilities, no way would I go in the river and ride those animals thinking I was safe. That's not saying I wouldn't be safe as much as it is that I was brought up from childhood to respect, and have a healthy dread of, the river. For a dairy farmer like me, the river serves simultaneously as a lifeline and a liability. I made huge money selling him those buffalo, but I wish I never did it because sooner or later there is a chance he could die because of me. I have to live with that."

"This is unbelievable," Jerry said. "Even I can see he isn't living like the nomads he referred to. He has topographical maps, man-made canals to travel, bags of granola if he runs out of food and dry bags to protect gear. Hell, he used my cell phone to check his mail tonight. That book he put down when we arrived was a chumash, the first five books, also called the Pentateuch, of the Bible, in bound form rather than a scroll. From the cover his appears to be printed in Aramaic. I was raised Jewish and I try to follow the rules, but even I know that reptile meat is not kosher under any circumstance. He makes concession after concession to stay out here but must be able to justify them through some construct or rationalization in his head. You're right, Trent. This is almost surely an escape route. If he has enough money, he should have just bought an island in the Caribbean rather than go through this escapade."

"I know," Jerry. "Sometimes what he exhibited to us back at his camp is called "faulty perception." I told you he had money and he had this whole thing planned," Trent said. "This guy thinks people persecute him via treating him for his condition and he has to escape from them in any way he can. Maybe he thinks a conventional escape strategy would never work for some reason. I don't think anyone ever saw someone take it to this extreme, though. Scroll down through the videos and look for something posted by his family, most likely his parents."

"You must be a psychologist or something," Raymond said as he watched the screen over Jerry's shoulder. "That one has his parents. It says in the description they are making a plea for information about their son. Play it."

Jerry clicked on the frozen image and, after another pause to upload, a middle age couple appeared, looking into the camera.

"Hi, I'm Robert Ross and this is my wife Delena. We are making this video in the hope that anyone who sees our son, Elias, can get in touch with us." A phone number and email address appeared, superimposed on the bottom of the screen. "Here is a picture of our son the last time I saw him several days ago." The screen split and the couple re-appeared on the left and a photo of Elias came into focus on the right. He wore only his shorts, looked extremely gaunt and his facial hair had grown out extensively.

"Elias suffers from several psychotic disorders and has recently rejected and refused his treatments, treatments that are designed to help stabilize his thoughts, emotions and actions. As a result, according to his doctors, he is now more than likely acting out in a delusional state." Delena covered her face in her hands and began sobbing at his side.

"I saw him most recently in a village in Costa Rica, doing

something so dangerous I shudder every time I think about it. His doctors say this may be suicidal behavior, or simply the rashest and most impetuous attempt he can conceive of to get away from anyone he perceives may be chasing him." The screen paused while more of the video buffered.

"What did I tell you guys?" Trent said. "The reason this scenario is so unusual is that the course of action, though impulsive and foolhardy to the vast majority of people, retains a quality of foresight and planning that gives him a chance at achieving his goal of separation. He knows that no one in their right mind will do what he's doing, so he has created a buffer or barrier from anyone chasing him down. I think there is far more to his condition than a conventional diagnosis, though I, for better or worse, am actually seeing manifestations of behavior that other clinicians didn't have the luxury of witnessing. I suspect if they saw him operating in this environment, they would change treatment recommendations. I do not have access to his whole file and history, but I think symbycerol would likely be contraindicated."

"You were doing fine until that last diatribe, Trent. Now, you're talking like a damn doctor again. You know we hate that and you promised you wouldn't do that when we fish or hunt," Jerry said, somewhat sarcastically, chastising his friend without turning around. "To be frank, it remains the one immutable condition of you being invited to join us at all, although your suitcase that serves as our traveling apothecary goes a long way towards justifying your continued presence. I think I've taken every anti-diarrheal and jungle fever medication you stock at least twice!"

"Sorry, I offer you my most heartfelt and profound apologies," Trent replied even more sardonically as he took a prolonged sip of his bourbon. "Far be it from me to talk down at you semi-derelict simpletons whom I call friends. Please allow me the opportunity to restate my medical opinions in lay terms so you sensitive, caring, sons of bitches can follow me. The guy is fucked up and needs help, but he's likely not fucked up in a way that requires the symbycerol – definitely something else, but not symbycerol. That's generally for people who exhibit suicidal tendencies. If that were the case he could just drip chicken blood on himself, jump in the river and he'd already have made the transition to a smoking heap of crocodile shit drifting into the ocean by now - if that were the case," he reiterated with an emphatic wave of his glass. "The fact is that as much of a freaking nutcase as he is, he has taken extensive precautions to try to guarantee his survival, as opposed to making certain he dies. Write down the email and the phone number and I'll call his parents – and I won't talk like a fucking doctor. I'll use speaker mode so you guys can hear but shut the hell up when I call. Remember, I'm the alleged professional here, though Raymond was dead on with that PACE thing, too," and took another pull from his glass. "Before I call, anyone want to bet $100 that Elias is cursed with helicopter, tiger parents?"

"Nah," Raymond said. "We'll take your word on it."

"Smart move."

The video finished buffering and resumed.

"If you see him or know his whereabouts, please call us or let us know. We are doing everything we can to get him to return to the United States and get him back on his treatments before something terrible happens. I will send people to get him and pay a handsome reward to anyone who helps bring him back where he should be." The video ended with an image of the couple frozen on the screen, the father unrelentingly stone-faced and the mother pleading through her eyes for her son to return.

"Elias' dad is a piece of work," Trent said, and dialed the number on his phone, pressed the speaker button, and put the phone on the table.

"Hello," said a stressed female voice.

"Hi, you must be Delena. I'm Trent. I had dinner with your son a bit earlier tonight. He's a very nice young man."

Her tone went from stressed to hysterical. "Is he ok? Where is he? What is doing and is he off that hellacious river?

Tell me everything you know!"

"Well, he's perfectly fine as far as I could see. He arrived in the Barra Colorado a couple days ago. I didn't see him get here but I heard he rode on the back of a water buffalo bull with a herd of five cows. I know you don't want to hear it, but he was in the river."

"Oh God! He's still doing that. He's going to die. We raised him so carefully. We helped him with his homework. Bob coached all of his sports teams and was his Scoutmaster until he earned his Eagle Scout. We were always with him and did everything we could to make sure he turned out well. Our reward for that effort is that he's trying to kill himself in the most horrific way possible. I don't want to hear any more. Bob, take the phone."

"I told her to let me take the call," came the male voice. "She's so devastated and expects every call to be the one she doesn't want to hear. She really doesn't want to hear any of them."

"I can appreciate your concern," Trent replied, doing his best to stay out of his clinician's tone of interview.

"He really is perfectly fine, though. I would never do what he's doing, not on a bet and not for a million dollars, but there is a strange and compelling logic to his journey, not matter how crazy it may seem."

"How the hell could any of this be logical? Are you as crazy as him?"

"Look, I just said there's no way I'd do what he's doing. Those animals he has are enormous. I've seen them multiple times. Their horns are like spears and their bodies are massive. He told me that their hooves were designed for swimming. I am fishing at a lodge next to the ocean and our guide said this guy was camping next to the airstrip runway. I had to meet him."

"Why do you say there's logic to this?"

"Look, I don't want to upset you more than you already are but you asked for information. His buffalo, even the small female, have killed or wounded several crocodiles that attacked the herd or got too close. They, and your son, are wholly unscathed and he has traveled over one hundred and fifty kilometers in this river rife with crocodiles. Demented as it may sound, I think he might be relatively safe. It's as if his buffalo are the dominant river dwellers now. Your son has incredible gear and quite a skill set, likely from the Scouts from what your wife said, for surviving on his own. He follows the buffalo so that snakes either move as they approach or the buffalo stop and let Elias kill them with a machete, at least that's what my guide told me. He fishes and collects local fruit and trades milk for everything else that he needs. His actions, though downright and altogether mystifying, are taken in a shrewdly calculated manner. It feels like almost an escape route that no one will chase him down on."

"You're right about him thinking that," Bob said angrily, "but wrong to think I won't chase him down for his own good. Can't you pay a few locals to tie him down and strap him on the plane and get him back here? I'll reimburse you five times what it costs to do it. He is killing his mother and I'm not doing so well either."

"You know I can't do that. I saw your son and looked him up on the internet and found your video. I thought you'd appreciate knowing he seems healthy and happy, though a bit subdued whenever you ask him about his plans and how he ended up out here."

"He's insane and as unstable as a plutonium isotope. He was strapped to a bed and medicated for suicidal behavior. Then, he was given a successful course of treatment so he could function in society. If we had known this would happen when he said he was leaving for Central America we'd have stopped him, but he was adamant about going. What are his plans?"

Trent couldn't imagine where Elias inherited the adamant gene from. "He said he's going to live as a nomad with his herd and travel the waterways here trading for what he needs. He had a series of topographical maps and the guides helped him make a circular route around Costa Rica. He says he plans to circumnavigate the country a couple times a year."

"Jesus Christ! I'm going to hire some people myself, maybe some real-life mercenaries, to go get him and drag him out of there, kicking and screaming like he did the last time if need be, then throw him on a private jet and have it land as close as possible to the psych ward he was originally treated at."

"How old is he?"

"26."

"You can't just stop him at your whim. Whether or not you agree with it, he's an adult with a mind of his own. Don't kid yourself. No self-respecting mercenary would have the balls to go in the river to get him and you know it. They do not have a death wish."

"He's an insane adult then. You are, too, because you seem to tacitly agree with what he's doing. I can well afford the jet and pay the kind of people required to save his life. I'm sure I could find the right folks to get him wherever he is, no matter how far he goes in that jungle."

"Maybe you could. He, on the other hand, might believe you are trying to end his life by trying to medicate him. I think he came here with the notion of breaking free from people hovering around him and trying to make him conform. He assuredly took it to a crazy extreme, but subsequent history seems to show he knows what he's doing, at least to this point. You might want to try talking to him about what he wants and how to achieve it, as opposed to what you think is wrong with him and how you can fix him. Maybe that could lead you on a path to get him back to the States."

"You are as big a whack-job as our son. You don't debate with a nut, you complete asshole. You do what it takes to take control of the situation and remedy it. Thank you for telling us where he is and that he's alive. I'll take it from here. Good bye." The phone clicked and Trent made sure the connection was broken before he looked at his companions.

"You heard me tell his father I'd never do what his son is doing, but if I were Elias, I'd more than likely be strongly considering floating down that river, too. He hasn't had a bit of freedom since he was born. Earlier, I said sometimes people flee from an unquantified "they" chasing them. Elias knows exactly who is chasing him. It's his own mother and father. If I interviewed them I'd find out that everything they did was designed to make him safe and successful without much happiness or fun mixed in." He swished his bourbon around and slugged the rest back in a gulp. "Fill me up again, Yvonne," he called to the bartender. "I hope that guy doesn't find out I'm a psychologist," he said to the rest of the group. "I think he'd give me a really shitty on-line review and pay other people who never met me to do the same."

XIX. KINDNESS GIVEN IS RETURNED

"My grandfather said you like to fish, so I made this for you last night," said the boy. He looked to be about 10 years old and was standing in the early morning semi-darkness next to Elias' tarp. He held an empty two-liter plastic soda bottle that had been modified by adding a funnel made from another bottle on the top. The boy had punched a bunch of tiny holes in the bottom of the bottle and tied a five-meter piece of string to the neck of the bottle where it met the jury-rigged funnel.

"Who is your grandfather and what is that for? Why are you waiting for me here?" Elias said, not sure he wanted the contraption or the company.

"My grandfather told me to tell you his name is Mateo. My name is Hugo. This," the boy said as he proudly held up the altered bottle, "is a freshwater shrimp trap. You can set this in the water wherever you land and you can catch your own bait really quickly. My father and grandfather said to wait for you at your camp because you don't want people near your animals. Can I show you how it works?"

"That's very considerate of you. I'm always trading for bait. Of course you can, Hugo," Elias said, suddenly intrigued by the politeness and ingenuity of this child. "What do we have to do?"

"You speak really good Spanish," the boy said. "Most of the people who come to the lodge don't speak Spanish at all. Grampy is teaching me English."

"Well, if he's teaching you we can try to speak a little English here and there to help you if you want."

"Thank you. Let's go to the river bank. My father said it was OK as long as you go with me. He says it may be bizarre, but you seem to know what you're doing. He said not to follow you if you go to the edge of the water."

"That's nice of him." Elias checked to make sure the herd was ok and then they walked to the river while the boy explained the gadget he had contrived from the bottle.

"So, freshwater shrimp are the best bait in this river for all the small fish like jaguar bass and machaka and catfish and guapote. Those fish are the right size for you to catch and eat all at once. The big fish like gar don't usually feed on them, so most of the time you'll catch a fish that's just the right size for dinner. Also, if you aren't catching gar or some of the other fish with teeth, you won't have to worry as much about using your steel leaders all the time to avoid losing hooks. Some fish are spooked by those leaders and won't bite a hook that's connected to wire."

"I like what I'm hearing so far," Elias said.

He noted the boy automatically stopped about 5 meters from the river, unconsciously aware of the proximity of the water at all times.

"OK, so my dad brings these bottles to me if he sees them floating on the river. The holes I punched in the bottom help it sink and the funnel at the top acts like a guide and lets shrimp swim in but they never figure out how to escape."

"Cool. What do you use for bait for these shrimp?"

"That's the best part. Shrimp will eat anything, including coconut. You just drop in a few pieces of old fish or meat or a couple chunks of coconut meat and leave this in the water for half a day and you'll almost always have 10 or more shrimp when you check it. You can even eat the shrimp if you want to and you catch enough of them to make a meal. You need to bait the trap and toss it in the river and tie it off and wait. If you can set the trap so the funnel is facing upstream then the shrimp have an even harder time escaping against the current. That's why the string is tied to the neck of the bottle. Toss it in on the downstream side of the dock and let the current make it straight. Then you tie the string to the post closest to the shore."

"Well, let me get some bait and we'll try it."

"I brought some," Hugo said. He reached in his pocket and pulled a few slivers of coconut trimmed so they'd fit in the bottle neck.

"You certainly came prepared, kid. Thank you. Wait here and I'll bait this and go tie it off on the dock piling." He dropped the coconut in the opening and then walked out on the dock to the first piling. He dropped the trap into the brown water and it immediately disappeared in the silt-stained murk. He tied it off with a taut line hitch knot – another remnant of Scouts - and returned to the boy.

"You're sure this will work?"

"It always has for me. When you catch them, thread them on an anzuelo – a hook – the way you would a worm. Start at the base of the tail. Drop it in without a weight and the fish should bite almost immediately."

"I can't wait to see if it works. I'll catch my lunch that way if it does. Do you have school today?" he asked the child.

"Yes. Why?"

Tell your friends if they would like to meet my bull, Nitro, after school, they can come over and I'll let you pet him as long as I'm there. You have to check with your parents first. They can come but only the kids can touch the animals. How's that?"

"Is the bull the one that killed the big crocodiles? That's the one I want to see."

"Yes."

"For sure. We'll be here. Everyone wants to get close to him and see how big he really is. I'll make sure everyone asks their parents or brings them." He paused. "He's not dangerous, is he?"

"Good. See you then. No, he's only dangerous to things that threaten him or the cows or another bull trying to take his cows. Other than that you'll find out he's a big baby." Hugo smiled and went off to get ready for school and Elias went back to check on the herd until Mateo walked past on his way to the lodge.

"You see my grandson this morning?"

"Great kid, yes. He taught me how to make and use those improvised shrimp traps. Those are a very clever and resourceful use of old soda bottles. I wish the kids didn't drink the soda though. From the number of children I saw getting on the hospital boat to see the dentist, that much sugar isn't helping anybody out here."

"You're right. I'm sure he told you I pull them out of the water for him when I see them. His parents don't buy him soda. I admit I do sneak him one a couple times a year from the lodge."

"He did. Hey, thank you for sending him by. That trap will make my life a whole lot easier when I'm away from civilization."

"De nada, my friend. What are you doing today?"

"I think the herd will want to leave this evening or tomorrow night, so I plan to pack everything up after lunch and be ready if that is the case."

"Sounds good. I hear it is supposed to rain really hard later tonight and tomorrow, maybe around 5-8 pm, so make sure you know where the path to the canals starts so you don't get off track."

"I plan to walk out there again this morning."

"Perfecto. Here is some more cheese and I will bring you some wrapped up for your journey. It will last a couple days if you keep it wrapped well."

"Much appreciated. Oh, I told Hugo to bring his friends by to pet the bull if they wanted to after school. I told him anyone who comes has to get an ok from their parents."

"I thought you didn't want anyone but you touching them."

"I don't. He did me a big favor showing me how to catch bait so I want to repay him. It's the least I can do."

"That's very kind of you. I'm sure they will appreciate it. I see Javier walking ahead of me so I need to get to the dock to catch the launch to the lodge. We'll stop by after we drop the guests again at the end of the day. Perhaps we will see you before you leave."

"I'll ask the herd to wait until nightfall to go so that should work."

Mateo began walking away, a somewhat bemused expression on his face. "I hope they listen," he called back over his shoulder.

"OK." He said to himself as Mateo left. "I need to repack all of the saddle bags and make sure there's nothing else I need from the store. Then, I'll milk the cows for the people that have already left buckets. I told them to come at 10. Then, I'll check the bait trap for shrimp and make lunch if I can catch something."

With his routines now modified and streamlined by repetition and constantly adjusting to the whims of the herd, he retrieved the saddle bags from Luis' porch and filled them, equalizing the weight as much as possible so no one animal, however unlikely, became overburdened. He kept Nitro's bags as light as he could, only giving him essentials that he would, or could, need. "After all, ladies," he said to the cows, "he carries me all day. I will freely admit that I remain unconvinced that he even knows I'm there when I ride him."

The sun rose hot and the temperature progressively increased until it hovered in the low nineties. The temperature did not keep the women in the village from coming to talk with him.

"Elias, did you really say the kids could come out here and pet your bull?" one of the regular milk recipients asked.

"I did."

"Are you sure it's safe?"

"Yes. I worry about him looking at someone else as his

keeper, which would make controlling him very difficult, so I usually try to keep him only with me. He's safe enough, just really big. I'll call him over. You'll see." He clicked his tongue and Nitro, always watching over his cows, stepped forward towards Elias' milking area where he had almost finished with Bessie.

"Ladies, come on over and meet him with me," he invited them as he stood from his knees.

"He's so big he doesn't even look real when you stand next to him," one woman said. "His shoulders are taller than you are."

"They are. I'm about 175 centimeters and the top of Nitro's shoulders are around 190 centimeters. Come on, step up and pet him on the snout. He won't do anything other than lean forward to make it easier for you and, honestly, you shouldn't have your kids pet him if you don't want to. If you scratch firmly with your nails he'll snort a bit because he likes that."

Elias stood next to Nitro's head with his right arm stretched as far as he could around his neck while each of the women, tentatively at first and then more confidently, petted his snout and touched his massive horns.

"We thought he'd be so much more aggressive, but he's very gentle – and surprisingly handsome," a different woman said as she rubbed his nose. The bull comically snorted and slowly stretched his head forward so she could press down more vigorously with her fingertips. "His horns look as wide as I am tall," said another. "I can see why the crocodiles should avoid him."

"So you'll let your kids come and see him later?" he queried them.

"After this display, of course they can come meet him," another mother said. He heard a bit of acquiescent chitter chatter among them.

"Can we come back with them and take a few pictures?" the first woman asked. "We may never see an animal like this again."

"Absolutely."

"We'll all be back around 2:30 with the kids."

"See you then."

"Nice job," he whispered to Nitro as they left. "That's how an outwardly tough guy like you wins friends and influences people. You schmooze with the mothers and then everyone is your pal. You go back to your post with the cows. I'm going to bring a fishing rod down to the dock and see if the shrimp trap worked. If it did, I'll try to catch some lunch." The bull gave a little huff and wandered back to his herd.

"Now this is a revelation!" he exclaimed when he pulled the trap out of the turbid water. "Hugo told the straight truth on this one," he said as he counted out nine freshwater shrimp in the trap. The delicate crustaceans appeared nearly transparent other than their dark eyes and the reddish vein in their tails. He poured one out in his hand, using his fingers as a sieve, and lowered the trap back in the water so the rest would stay alive. He put the unlucky one in his hand on the hook as the boy instructed. With its claws still wriggling, acting like a wounded beacon to the predatory fish, he dropped it straight down in the water and waited about ten seconds for the tell-tale tug. He set the hook and pulled out a fat machaka without even having to reel.

"Teach a man to fish and you feed him for a lifetime," he said, quoting Lao Tzu. "That boy just made my life a heck of a lot easier." Not wanting to needlessly kill bait he would not use, he let the rest of the shrimp go and went to make lunch. With everything except last minute items already stowed, he sat under the tarp and read his chumash, keeping up his Aramaic language skills while he nibbled some granola from a bag.

"I didn't know the school had this many kids," he said when twenty or so children showed up with their mothers and a few curious fathers in tow.

"Should we have brought fewer kids?"

"Not at all. Because it's hot let's go to him. He's over in the shade by the river with his cows. I used to think he led them, but now I think they boss him around and tell him what to do and when."

They walked over and Elias went to the bull and started rubbing his nose and gave him a bite of granola from his bag. "OK." He said to the bull. "We're going to let all these kids pet you and sit on you if that's alright. They're all little so it'll be no problem. Sound good to you?" Nitro impassively chuffed at Elias' hand to see if there was more granola coming his way. "I'll give you the rest of the bag when we're done."

"Who's first? Actually, let's start with the youngest." A girl of seven or so years of age stepped forward with her mother and he brought her right up to his head. The bull lowered his massive head and horns slowly so that she could pet him. She squealed a bit when she touched his ears. "He feels like cuero de terciopelo," she said, using Spanish for the one word she hadn't learned in English.

"You're right. The English word for that is velvet. Get ready to take a picture, mom," he said to the girl's mother. "I'm going to put her up on his back. If I put his saddle on he'd assume we're leaving now so I'll help her stay in place on him while you take a picture with your phone. Is it OK if I do that?" She nodded affirmatively and he swung the girl up on the bull's back and held her hand while she posed and then hugged the bovine's shoulders, lying flat against him. One by one they all came up and he repeated the process until everyone had their visit with the docile animal that killed two crocodiles three days earlier.

"Well, all of you know him now and he may think of you as part of his herd. I'm not sure but it wouldn't surprise me if he remembers you all when we come back next year. Don't be caught off guard if he walks up to see if you want to pet him from now on. Before I let him go back to the herd, why don't we all feed him? I can assure you he'll always think of you as a friend if you feed him. He associates food with his friends. You're the first people to feed him other than me since I bought him." He poured a bit of granola into everyone's hand and then held each of their hands as Nitro delicately licked the sweetened grain out of their hands, not even coming close to nibbling on a finger.

"That's it," Elias said to the group. "Thank you for stopping by. He needs to go eat and drink because we'll likely be moving on tonight."

"We'll miss you," Hugo said.

"Don't worry. I'll be back in a few months." After they all left he turned to Dolly. "For the first time, no one said we'd all be dead before we got back here. That's a positive change from the usual morbidity."

XX. TIME TO GO

"Good afternoon, Elias. Those guests that visited you last night said Javier asked if I would give you these for them," Mateo said as he walked home for lunch, handing him a pair of sunglasses, three long sleeve pull-over shirts and several buffs.

"These are all 100 SPF sun shirts. They must have cost a lot. Do they want me to pay them back?"

"Not at all. When the lodge owner found out they were for you he sold them at cost and gave you an extra one. These are so lightweight you won't even feel it in the water when it gets soaked. The buffs," he said, holding up one of the ten inch tubular pieces of cloth open at both ends, "cover your neck and you can pull it up over your ears and right up to your eyes. Some people call them gaiters." He demonstrated by donning one, slipping it over his head and then stretching it to cover his face. "It protects everything except the top of your head and your forehead, so the guests also gave you these two hats." He pulled a baseball cap with one large flap sewn on the sides and back to cover his neck and the sides and top of his head and also shade his forehead. "So now you have sunglasses, three shirts, three buffs and two hats, all SPF protected. You can rinse them in the river and use them during the day."

"Please tell them I can't express my thanks enough," Elias said, trying on all three items without checking the labels to see what the fabrics were. The polyester didn't seem to affect him as it had in the past. "I never grasped how important sun protection was until I got out here. These are great. I'm going to leave them on. I can already tell it'll get even brighter and hotter later this afternoon before the clouds come in."

"You look like one of our guests now," Mateo laughed. "I told them you'd be leaving tonight so they may stop by to see you briefly before they return to the lodge. Remember, it's going to pour tonight. Thunder storms may come in as well."

"Buffalo don't worry about thunder so that's OK. There goes Javier. You better catch up and if the buffalo don't decide to leave early, I'll see you at dinner time."

"OK. I told you I had some cheese I'd bring to you at lunch. The lodge cook, Adelia, let me leave them in the refrigerator this morning." He gave Elias two kinds of cheese, one wrapped in paper and a softer block balanced on top of the paper. "Eat the soft cheese today and save the hard cheese in the paper for the next three days or so. Keep what you don't eat wrapped so it lasts. Next time you come through I will teach you how to make both kinds and you will be able to trade that as well. Everything I know from living here tells me you should not do this, but everything I've seen from you and your beasts so far makes it seem like it will work for you and I'll actually get to teach you how to make cheese in a few months."

"I can't figure out why you guys are so generous to me," he said.

"You get what you give, my friend. When you got here a few days ago, you seemed suspicious of us. Now that you know us, you give goodness, and that is what you get in return. Thank you for letting my grandson pet your bull. Enjoy the afternoon, amigo," he said as he walked away towards his house.

A few minutes later, a few women returned because he had not finished milking in the morning. "Why don't you ladies go visit with the herd again while I milk the rest of them one at a time? No need to hover over me while I do this." He gave the group a bag of granola to divvy up amongst themselves and went to work filling their bowls and buckets. "Make sure they all get an equal amount and feed the bull last so he knows he's not in charge when he's with my friends."

"Do you think he really knows the difference? You know, you act much differently than when you first arrived," one said.

"He definitely knows where he stands on the pecking order. I am the alpha – at least he was taught to think that. He fully gets that people are not to be touched unless they hurt him. As far as me, well, sometimes change is good and you ladies have treated my animals with great respect and kindness. I can't keep them away from everyone forever so it seems best that you folks are the first to mingle with them. When you first go over, the bull will want his treat before the cows. One of you put your hand on the side of his muzzle and push his head to the side and walk to the cows. He will pout a bit and then begrudgingly accept that his treat comes last when you do that."

They spent enough time with the bull and four cows for Elias to finish milking Bessie before they came back.

"You trained them so well. The bull did exactly what you said. He expected to get food before the cows and grudgingly went to the back of the herd when I pushed on the side of his face. If I didn't know better, I'd say he sulked like a little kid until we gave him his food."

"Age-wise, he's still only a teenager so he can sometimes exhibit a bit of petulance like that. I told one of the children that he's a big baby, but he's also well-mannered. OK, here's the last of the milk. We'll be traveling on a bit later so I'll see you again in a couple months."

"It's going to be a total deluge tonight," he said to the herd in midafternoon. "Look over there at those black clouds rolling in. Why don't we all take a walk to the start of the path without saddles and check it out together." He clicked his tongue and, in a change from his usual pattern, led the way himself, watching carefully for snakes. "You guys OK with this?" he asked the herd when they reached the cave-like opening into the jungle. In his estimation, Nitro's horns would extend within a foot or so of either side of the path. "We're going to walk this footway to the canals and then swim and forage our way to Tortugero down south. It'll take several days depending on how often you guys want to stop. Everyone said the Barra is the end of the road, but this path into the dimness of the jungle and the following forty kilometers is really the start of our journey alone. I feel like we've come so far already. You guys up for the trip?" None of the animals complained so he took it as a mute agreement and brought them back to the airstrip near his camp, all of which was packed into the saddle bags except for the tarp, which he left up for protection against the sun. Shortly, when the rain started, and that would be long before sunset, he knew he would not need that refuge and would stow that as well.

The fishing boats arrived at the dock sometime in the late afternoon while the buffalo wallowed in the mud nearby and the clouds continued to thicken and darken with each passing minute. Mateo, Jerry, Trent and Raymond found Elias sitting cross-legged on the wooden decking, watching the herd.

"So you're on your way south tonight?" Trent said. "We wanted to swing by and wish you luck."

"Thank you. I also owe you a thank you for the glasses, shirts, hats and buffs."

"I see you're sporting all but the shades," Raymond said. "You look like one of us old guys trying to pretend we're young enough to handle the tarpon. Without Mateo chasing them in the boat while we try to reel, all of them would get away!"

"Hey, take my name and number and email address, Elias," Trent said. I put them on this slip of paper. Maybe you can put it in one of your dry bags. Keep in touch if and when you feel like it. I'd love to know how your journey progresses not only geographically, but also out of curiosity for your desire to try this nomadic existence and for you personally. You now have almost unhampered freedom to do what you want out here. Not many people ever get, or make, a chance at that in life. They don't possess the nerve or the motivation you seem to enjoy. You took the bull by the horns in that regard, both literally and figuratively, so take advantage and learn as much about yourself as you can during the trek."

"I never thought about it that way, but I will."

"I suspect you thought of it exactly that way without specifically formulating that notion," Trent said. "I only met you a day or two ago, but it's clear you need freedom of mind and movement. Look at us. We're a little similar to you in that we travel all over the world to hunt and fish, but really we're just getting away from day to day stressors. We have to get back to the lodge before the downpour starts so you take care. You maybe thought we came here to talk you out of going, but we aren't going to try to convince you not to go. We're going to ask you to stay as safe as you can."

"Yeah," Jerry said. "Raymond and I don't possess flowery language like that silver-tongued bastard," he said pointing at Trent, "and I don't need a thousand words to make a point, either, so I'll keep it short. Don't step on a snake or a tarantula or fall off the bull into a crocodile's mouth. I want to see you back here next year so keep Trent posted as to when your rotation will bring you back."

"After I make the first loop I'll be able to give you a good idea." He shook their hands. "Thank you for coming to visit me." He watched them all walk back to the fishing boat at the dock.

"OK." He clicked his tongue and the herd came to him. "Let's get the saddles on and get going." Keeping the hat on, he took off his shirt and buff and put them away in a dry bag with Trent's contact information. As he cinched the bag and tightened the strap, the skies opened up and instantly soaked everything except his gear stowed in the dry bags. The torrential rain significantly obscured his view, but he peered towards the jungle where he thought the path originated and began moving there with the herd. The ground, solid only an hour or two earlier, already felt spongy from the rain's intensity. The naturally high water table made it impossible for the earth to absorb and disperse such liquid volume so quickly.

By good fortune and the prior practice excursions both with Javier and on his own, he got to the opening on the first try. He paused at the small, semi-circular break in the otherwise impenetrable jungle and peered inside. The trail within was in near total, ebon, darkness. Rainwater cascaded through the canopy like mini waterfalls from the broad leaf jungle plants onto the footpath. He climbed onto Nitro's saddle and looked back at the cows through the water flowing copiously off the visor of his hat. Lightning bolts started illuminating the sky and thunderclaps followed closely on their heels. Given the claustrophobically close quarters of the path, he held his machete in his right hand so he could cut any branches or growth that otherwise could, or might, brush up against him.

From a distance Mateo, looking through one of the few windows in his home, watched Elias and the buffalo through the blur of the torrential downpour. The limited visibility made the hat he wore and the machete he wielded give him the look of a bare-chested field general leading a charge of rider-less bovine cavalry against a hidden foe at the edge of the wilderness.

"We have to keep moving to live the way we want," he said to the buffalo after a particularly bright and loud flash bang of lightning and thunder. He clicked his tongue and the herd, led by him perched on the bull, disappeared one by one into the jungle, the ground already so saturated that their hoof prints immediately filled with water, leaving no trace of their passing.

Made in the USA
Middletown, DE
29 May 2021